MAFIA BOSS

Dark Mafia Romance

VI CARTER

Contents

ALSO BY

Other Books by VI CARTER

THE CELLS OF KALASHOV
THE COLLECTOR #1
THE SIXTH #2
THE HANDLER #3
THE BOSS #4

MURPHY'S MAFIA MADE MEN
SINNER'S VOW #1
SAVAGE MARRIAGE #2
SCANDALOUS PLEDGE #3

SONS OF THE MAFIA
SINS OF THE MAFIA #0.5

YOUNG IRISH REBELS SERIES
MAFIA PRINCE #1
MAFIA KING #2
MAFIA GAMES #3

MAFIA BOSS #4

<u>WILD IRISH SERIES</u>
FATHER (PREQUEL)
VICIOUS #1
RECKLESS #2
RUTHLESS #3
FEARLESS #4
HEARTLESS #5

<u>THE BOYNE CLUB</u>
DARK #1
DARKER # 2
DARKEST #3
PITCH BLACK #4

<u>THE OBSESSED DUET</u>
A DEADLY OBSESSION #1
A CRUEL CONFESSION #2

<u>BROKEN PEOPLE DUET</u>
BREAK ME #1
SAVE ME #2

WARNING

WARNING

This book is a dark romance. This book contains scenes that may be triggering to some readers and should be read by those only 18 or older.

JOIN MY NEWSLETTER

J OIN MY NEWSLETTER AND NEVER MISS A NEW RELEASE OR GIVEAWAY.
HERE

PROLOGUE

DANA

ICE COLD WATER HITS my face. The sting wakes me up, sending sharp pain across my naked body. Everything inside me trembles as I become more alert. My wet hair weighs my head down. I focus on my fingers, which shake in small pools of water that surround me. My naked flesh is screaming for warmth. Large feet appear in front of me, and my shoulders hunch closer to my ears as a second bucket of water is splashed across my frame. A short, broken scream is dragged from my lips before the sound of my chattering teeth takes over. The chains on my wrists rattle as I manage to raise my head through the pain and dizziness.

"Are you ready to talk?" The large Russian man drops the steel bucket, and the sound bounces around the wide space. The empty outhouse has been my cage for days now. I keep waiting for someone to come and find me, someone like Cillian. His name has me wincing, and I push the image of his face away. His memory is too painful.

A roar rolls from me. My fingers rebel and try to wriggle under the weight of the boot that is slowly crushing them. I continue to scream in pain, even as the Russian steps away—air stalls in my lungs as I stare at my hand, not daring to move a finger. The pain intensifies, and I'm burning up inside. Bile claws up my throat as I rock my body like I can extract the pain from my broken fingers.

"Just tell us about your father and all this goes away."

My breaths are shallow and fast as I continue to stare at my crushed fingers. My vision blinks in and out.

The Russian's footsteps come closer, and I quickly look up at him. I swallow the dryness in my mouth. I swallow the scream. I swallow the pain. "I never knew," I say when I see the disbelief in the man's blue eyes. "I swear." I cry out as he kneels down with a smile that sends waves of dread coursing through me.

"You are naked, beaten, and chained to the floor. He will not expect this level of loyalty."

His large hand touches my face, and I shrivel away from him, sending fresh pain into my fingers. "You have been strong." The man's smile remains.

I sob. The truth is, if I knew anything, I would have given up the information the moment they chained me to the floor. The moment they stripped me of my dignity. The moment they put their hands on me. The moment they took me. But I didn't know anything about my father's dealings.

"I swear, I don't know."

His smile leaves his face, and he rises on a long exhale.

I try to brace myself, but it doesn't matter; nothing could prepare me for the pain. His foot connects with my naked torso, which is already covered in bruises. Something snaps inside me, and I'm lifted off the concrete floor before I'm slammed back down onto the ground. The chains restrict me, and the heavy metal burns my wrists. The pain's forgotten as a large hand tightens around my hair and yanks my head back. I'm staring up into his face, begging him to stop this. I already know the answer before he hits me hard across the face. My head swings back, my mouth fills with blood, and I hit the concrete floor again, the small pools of water splashing up across my damaged flesh.

I can't see through the pain and fear. I curl up and cry, waiting for the next kick or hit, but his footsteps move away from me, and I start to cry some more. My body trembles as I lie there on the cold floor.

I try to tell myself that I'll be fine, but the truth is, I'm hurting. The pain is so deep, and I'm close to giving in to the demands of my body. My body wants me to let go. It would be so easy to just let go and slip away from all the pain.

Another sob sends ripples across the small pool of water that I lie in. Seeing my dark tendrils brings me back. Back to a moment when I was sailing through the air, my hair whipping in my face. I was so young—maybe ten—and I was with my best friend, Maeve, as she pushed me on my swing in my backyard. The day was hot, my mother was smiling, and I felt happy.

I'd laugh if I had anything in me. I'd laugh that Maeve's secret led me to this dark place.

My body shakes and my tears stop, and all I feel is pain. So much pain.

I return to the memory of that day on the swing. I had been free, just like Maeve always appeared. She had a freedom in her life that my parents never allowed me to have. I always felt suffocated, so I spent most of my teens traveling, trying to escape their smothering tendencies. They allowed me to travel, but something deep in the back of my mind told me I was never truly free or alone. I shook it off as paranoia at the time, but now I see that my father had men watch over me my whole life.

I can't stop the sob that rocks my body, sending fresh waves of pain down my side. Coldness seeps deeper into my bones, and I don't believe the cold will ever leave me. I don't think any form of heat could banish this level of coldness or pain. Time moves in shadows across the floor. My fingers reach out to the last stream of light like I can hold it hostage here with me, but like everything else, the light disappears, and I'm plunged deep into the shadows and the terror of what will happen next.

I don't sleep, but I'm not fully alert either. The tremors and agony keep me in a half-awake state. That is, until the door opens. I look up, unable to move as the Russian man enters the room again. The bucket in his hand swings, and I close my eyes and brace myself, but no water hits me. I look back up and notice something lumpy under his arm. He takes the material out from under his arm, and a blanket is spread across my body. I cry with relief.

It's a trick, my mind whispers, and I hush the pessimism inside me.

The large Russian man kneels and brushes long strands of hair off my face. His finger grazes a cut, and my body curls in on itself.

"You are resilient." He sounds impressed. "But that has no value here." His smile drips off his face, and unease skitters across my skin.

"If I knew anything, I would tell you." My chains rattle, and the blanket slips as I try to rise. His fingers press against my lips.

"Shh. It will be okay."

My vision blurs, and I know it won't be okay. I'm going to die.

My heart takes on a new beat. The pounding jumps to the point that I think my heart is ready to come out of my chest; the sensation feels like my heart is in my throat, choking me, cutting off the air from my lungs, and without the Russian lifting a finger, I can't breathe.

I crane my neck back and gasp in quick short breaths that do nothing to fill my lungs, and they aren't enough. The blanket slips completely from my battered body as I continue to gasp. I'm staring into blue eyes that laugh at me, but I can't look away. My body is shutting down, and I'm dying.

Loving life has me clinging to the man before me. I sway on my knees, and I know I won't recover if I hit the ground.

His eyes are blue. His hair is brown. I keep repeating this in my mind as tears cascade down my face. Another wave of dizziness hits me, and my body trembles violently.

I have no regrets. I wouldn't have lived my life any other way.

With this knowledge, I want to scream, because I don't want this to be my end.

Not like this.

Not like this.

CHAPTER ONE

CILLIAN

I'D LIKE TO SAY I'm broken as I stand in front of my father's grave. I'm pretty sure that's how I should feel—broken. A sense of loss should choke me, a pain that should take me to my knees. The priest looks up from his bible; he gives me a nod like I'm a soldier that has every right to rest or shed a tear.

But I don't. I'm not even close to any of those emotions. I feel nothing.

"Ashes to Ashes." The priest walks around my father's coffin, dipping a golden stick into a pot of holy water and sprinkling the contents over the coffin as he continues his prayer. We had to have a closed casket. My father's bones were charred black from the fire that burnt his home to the ground.

My mother stands tall beside me. She isn't broken either. She isn't a grieving widow. She is simply here to give her once-upon-a-time husband his final goodbye. I'm here as a mark of respect and as support to my mother.

I still lean in and wrap an arm around her, even though she doesn't need my support. The world is watching at our backs, so I will play my part. My mother turns her head, and I'm actually surprised at the level of sadness I see in her green eyes. It's unexpected, and I'm wondering who the sadness is for. It surely can't be for the man who's being lowered into the ground as we stare at each other. He wasn't a good husband or father. I never connected with him, though he tried. His belt was his favorite tool for making me hear his words, but all the beatings did was make me want to be a different kind of man.

One not like him.

"May he rest in peace." The priest draws my attention, and I release my mother as she steps forward and drops a red rose on top of my father's coffin. Her hands are clad in small black leather gloves that she joins in front of her. I do the same, and a line of mourners follows suit until the coffin is coated with red petals.

As they release their roses, they turn to my mother and me and shake our hands. "I'm sorry for your loss" is repeated. The words bounce off me, and a sea of faces morph into one another.

"I'm sorry for your loss." Robert's large hand grips mine tightly. "Thank you."

Robert is unnaturally tall. He towers over everyone else. He's a giant of a man with too much facial hair and not much composure. I'm not sure how he gained his position so high in the ranks of the

Jaguars. They controlled parts of the east of Ireland that weren't under the O'Reagans' control.

"We are all here." He pulls me slightly toward him before looking over my head. I follow his line of sight, and there they are—all the members of the Jaguars nod at me. My gut twists. I knew they would arrive. My father was a member, but as I look across from them and meet Liam O' Reagan's intelligent stare, I know everything is about to get very fucking complicated.

Robert addresses me while glaring at Liam O'Reagan. "We aren't afraid of no ghosts."

My mother clears her throat. "There is a time and place for that kind of talk." She speaks out of the corner of her mouth while keeping her voice low.

Robert releases my hand.

"They aren't ghosts," I warn him before he steps up to my mother and takes her hand. Robert isn't foolish enough to believe that the O'Reagans are to be underestimated. I haven't had a chance to tell the Jaguars that I'm now a king with the Irish Mafia. So much has happened in a short space of time.

I continue to shake hands, and when the line starts to dwindle, I'm looking from one side of the mourners to the other. Walking to the O'Reagans first would give a message to the Jaguars that I didn't want delivered. So, I leave my mother talking to the priest and walk over to Robert and the men.

Five of the front runners shake my hand. I grew up with them around our home, but I never joined them. I wasn't a member.

"Davy's death will not be in vain, son." Razor grips my shoulder. "We will have justice for his death."

I nod. "I can take care of it." The moment I say the words, I know they're the wrong ones.

Razor grins, dragging the jagged scar on his cheek higher. "Davy was a brother to me. We don't leave one man to take care of another man's death. We work together. We are strong as a unit."

Razor grips my shoulder tighter. "You are now a member, Cillian. It's your legacy."

"I need to take care of my mother." Movement to the side has me glancing in that direction.

Shit.

Liam, Jack, and Richard are approaching me, and everyone watches them. They have an air about them that demands everyone's attention. They piss me off to no end, but I keep that buried. Razor releases me and glances at them; a snarl twists his face.

"Only ghosts," Robert whispers to Razor.

I turn as Liam steps up to me with either son flanking his sides. He's the godfather, the center of the Irish Mafia, and he's to be feared.

Liam holds out his hand. "Sorry for your loss." I take it, and we shake, but he doesn't release my hand instantly. Instead, he looks at the Jaguars. "Robert, how nice to see you." Liam releases my hand as Jack and Richard give their condolences. Richard glares at me, and I try to ignore him.

"Have you any idea what happened to Davy?" Robert fires out, and I curse him. He's not very tactful.

"A discussion for another day," I interrupt. But Liam isn't taking my subtle interruption kindly.

"I actually do know what happened to Davy." Liam steps up closer to Robert, and I swear Razor snarls.

"We're all listening." Robert's smugness doesn't go unnoticed.

"That information is for Cillian since he is a king with us." Liam is ready to walk away after dropping his bomb. He should have given me time. Razor zeroes in on me, and there's no point denying that I'm now a king. I nod my head.

"Cillian is also a Jaguar, so that knowledge will be shared with us, Liam."

Liam's lip moves slightly. He doesn't look at me for confirmation. "Like I said, the information will be given to Cillian. After that, it is up to him."

Liam gives me his full attention. "Always use knowledge wisely."

A large black limo pulls up close to the road, and the slick vehicle garners a lot of attention. Robert smirks when he glances at the limo. The smirk remains on his face as his gaze dances between Liam and me.

"Skinner wants a word." Robert is too fucking joyful.

Any other time, meeting Skinner would be a privilege, but not right now.

"We will talk later." Liam makes it sound like a promise, and he starts to walk off with Jack and Richard flanking him. In the distance, I can see Shane O'Reagan as well. He gives me a nod when our eyes meet.

Razor drags me away from the O'Reagans. "Skinner doesn't like to be kept waiting."

I take a final look at my mother, who's still in deep conversation with the priest, and walk away from the Jaguars to the limo.

This felt like a coin toss. Skinner arriving here could be to give his condolences in person or to warn me away from the Jaguars. He never liked me, but he was very fond of my father.

The door opens, and all I see is his hand. The ruby-red ring on his forefinger gleams off the afternoon light. I take a final glance over my shoulder, my gaze drawn to the last place I saw the O'Reagans, but they're no longer there.

I climb in and close the door behind me. Skinner looks the part in his black suit and black shirt, and he even sports a pair of black sunglasses. The dividing window is in the process of rolling up, giving us more privacy.

"Davy was a good man," Skinner starts, but I can't agree.

My silence has Skinner sitting forward. "He was hard on you, Cillian, to make you a better man."

He didn't. He just made me hate the man he was. Once again, I don't voice this.

"Your mother looks broken." His words carry no truth.

"Yeah. She's hurting," I lie.

Skinner removes his sunglasses. It doesn't matter how many times I see his face. The scars and the missing eye still make me want to look away. I hold his stare.

"Your father saved me. When we were young, I nearly died. A group of men decided they wanted my blood spilled across the streets of Cavan. They got as far as removing an eye." He points at the eye as if I haven't noticed it missing. "Your father arrived. They laughed at him." Skinner's smirk twists his grotesque face.

My father was small and thin; he looked non-threatening. So Skinner's story rings true.

"You should have seen their stupid fucking faces when he removed his glasses and pulled off his top." Skinner's deep laugh rumbles as he shuffles closer to the edge of the seat.

"Blood was pissing out of my eye. I started to laugh at them. I remember telling them they were all going down. They turned their back on your father. Big mistake." Skinner sits back, the memory dancing on his lips, tugging them up into a smile.

"He was like a ghost, taking them down one after another. I had a front-row seat."

I'm smiling too, wishing I had seen it. My father was a skilled fighter. His hands were deemed weapons. My own skills, I owed to him.

"You know how you really know you have a good friend?" he asks.

"They give you money," I throw out.

Skinner laughs. "Close. They help you bury a body. He and I, well, we dug lots of holes." Skinner sits back and slips on his glasses. "I hear you are working with the O'Reagans."

There's no point in hiding the fact. "Yes, Liam has offered me a place on his board as a king."

Skinner nods. "Take it."

Irritation claws at me. Like I need his fucking permission. "I already have."

"Good. You know what they say—keep your friends close but your enemies closer."

"Liam O'Reagan is not my enemy," I say plainly.

Skinner smirks like he knows something I don't. "Liam is an enemy of the state. Don't ever forget that. He's everyone's enemy."

Politics and more politics. That's all I grew up listening to. "Thank you for coming to my father's funeral. I'm sure he would have wanted that."

Skinner sneers. "Take care, Cillian."

The door opens, and Skinner faces away from the sunlight as I step out of the limo. Crowds are still gathered around the grave, and I meet my mother's gaze.

The door closes as I step onto the grass, and the limo pulls away.

The O'Reagans, the Jaguars, and even Sheahan, who rules over parts of the north, will pull at me, each having their own agenda. But to me, there is only one: finding my sister.

That's all that matters to me, and If I have to play everyone to get my sister back, I will.

CHAPTER TWO

DANA

THE RED CARPET UNDER my bare feet changes as I enter an open living space. I'm surrounded by lush furniture and a cold interior that has me wrapping my arms around my waist. My heart hasn't slowed since I woke up this morning. I march across the floor, then pull on the round pearl handle and try to yank the door open. This is my morning ritual, and each morning, I waste energy. I can't get out of the suite that takes up half the top floor of Cabra Castle. There is a small door in one of the main bedrooms, and I remember loving the hidden passageway as a kid. The small winding stairs lead up onto the roof. I've tried to pry the door open with no luck. If I could get someone's attention, I might get out of here. Once they know that Liam O'Reagan's daughter is trapped in this suite, they will make sure my father knows.

There is that noise in the back of my mind, rolling down into my chest and tightening around my heart. Why did Cillian bring me to my father's castle? Does my father know?

That knowledge has me stepping away from the door as angry tears burn my eyes. I start my search through the suite all over again. I know pulling out drawers and turning the room upside down will turn out fruitless. I know I've been placed here because there is no escape.

I release a half strangled scream before running back to the room I've claimed as my own. I sink to the floor between the wardrobe and the wall and drag my bare knees up to my chest. I don't cry. My mother taught me better than that, and honestly, I think I'm all cried out.

Right now, I feel nothing but confusion. I keep going over the moment of contacting Richard, thinking he would know what to do, and how everything spiraled out of control. My family is Mafia. Does that mean my mother is too? I don't have many answers, and the only person I see daily won't speak to me. He pretends I'm not here, but today, I won't stop. Today, I will get the answers I seek.

I want to speak to my father. He'll fix all this; I just know he will. The niggling returns, and I drop my head onto my knees. The old castle makes a lot of funny noises I've never noticed before. I never stayed still as a kid, or even in my teenage years, to really listen. I found myself always running. I never knew from what, but now I think I knew something wasn't right about my family. They raised me under a protective canopy that became so weighed down with lies and secrets that it collapsed, leaving me the casualty in a war I knew nothing about.

My family is Mafia.

No matter how many times I acknowledge those words, they don't fully sink in. I'm picturing *The Godfather*. I'm picturing lots of money and old machine guns. I'm picturing a movie, a different era. I'm picturing everything besides my family.

Does Maeve know? Maeve is going to marry my brother Jack. My gut tells me she knows. But for how long? She's my best friend, and yet she never told me. I remind myself that I don't know that for sure. Maybe she has no idea.

The sound of the main door opening has me standing up while dragging my long black hair over my shoulder. I tuck the long strands behind my ears as I race into the living room. I pause. My frozen state is only for a beat, but Cillian has that initial effect on me. Even more so today. He's in a black suit, and I'd be a liar if I said I wasn't a little struck by his fierce good looks.

He closes the door, his broad back to me. He pockets the key before he turns, and his eyes meet mine. His eyes always catch me off guard. The green is a depth I never knew existed, but beyond the color is an emptiness that would make you believe there's no soul in this vessel. He takes a confident step into the living room, and he has the ability to make me question if I'm even in the room. I'm dismissed like I'm a fucking lamp or some random and insignificant object.

"I want to speak to my father." The words hitch. I haven't made this demand yet. Maybe it was fear stopping me; maybe it was hope. A hope my father doesn't know that I'm here, and I fear that he does.

I get a reaction out of Cillian. It's subtle, but his hard jaw gets a little harder, like he's been carved from granite. He's all angles and emptiness.

Cold as stone.

He moves through the living room, and when he passes me, something in my chest tightens. It's been days, and I've had enough of his silence.

"I'm speaking to you. You will answer me." My false bravado has Cillian turning to me. A half smile doesn't soften his features. No, it hardens them. The smile is fake, controlled, and a clear warning not to proceed any further.

"Will I now?" He tilts his head slightly, like he's given me enough of his attention, and I see in how his shoulders shift that he's ready to walk away from me again.

"Yes, you will," I demand and race up to him. His smile widens, and my heart cracks a little more. I'm sick of everything, but Cillian is infuriating to the point that my hand connects with his face. Flesh meets flesh, and the slap makes a louder noise than I expected. My hand stings from the contact, and his cheek starts to turn red.

"No, I won't." The words are growled at me.

"I want to speak to my father." My voice breaks and cracks. He walks away again, and my skin burns as my temperature soars. A half scream climbs up my throat.

"You can't do this!" I shout as he leaves the living room. His silence has me marching after him. "I demand to know what's going to happen to me." He doesn't stop walking, and once again, I'm on his heels. We move under the arch that warns me that we are entering the private bedrooms. It's darker under the arch, and when Cillian suddenly stops and turns to me, I feel like I'm down a dark alleyway with a possible serial killer. All my bravery fades and turns to liquid at my feet. I swallow.

"I just buried my father, so if you could fuck off and give me space, that would be great."

I don't know what shocks me more, that he just buried his father or that he told me to fuck off.

"No, I won't." I fold my arms across my chest.

His jaw clenches even further, and he grinds his molars before taking a step toward me. The space under the arch is small, but with him so close, it grows almost claustrophobic. My back hits a door, and I'm staring at his chest.

"Do you know what I see?"

I crane my neck back to look up into his eyes. My stomach tenses. I want to breathe in the smell of his cologne but manage to have some control over my body. My control is loose, and sadly, it wouldn't take much for my meagre restraint to slip. "I don't care what you see. Your words don't mean shit to me. All I care about..."

That pushed him too far. He leans in, his chest crushing my breasts; the heat and smell of his cologne rolls off him, and my body is too aware of how close we are. When my brain finally catches up, I'm standing in the bathroom and moving backward.

That practiced smile graces his striking face.

"You're a spoiled, privileged brat who I ended up babysitting. Right now, I just want you to shut the fuck up."

His chest still brushes mine, and the air is tinged with his cologne and my anger.

"No." Defiance grows, and I hold my head high.

I'm moving again, and I don't have time to process what's happening until I'm standing in the large open shower. His hand tightens around my wrist. Ice cold water pours down on top of me, and I scream and try to run. His iron grip keeps me under the stream of water.

"Are you done mouthing off?"

I blink away the cold water and try to calm down long enough to look at Cillian. He's in the shower, too, his suit soaking wet while water drips down his dark hair and onto his sculpted face.

"Fuck you!" I bark.

His laughter is different. It's not as soulless as his eyes or fake smile. His laugh is angry, but it's real.

I don't know what I expect, but when his mouth crashes down on mine, and his hand tightens on my wrist, I freeze under his demanding lips. I'm frozen, and yet he doesn't stop the kiss. His warm tongue runs along my lips, and I gasp at the heat compared to the cold water that beats down over us. His tongue enters my mouth, and he drags our bodies closer. His erection presses against me. His lips are soft and warm, which I wasn't expecting either. I don't respond to the kiss, and when Cillian breaks it, we are both a bit breathless—me more so than him. I feel like I'm spinning, and not in a good way.

"Is that what I need to do to get you to shut up?"

The question should infuriate me, but I'm shocked, and I have no idea how to respond.

The gleam in his eyes suggests he knows the effect he's having on me.

"Good." He releases my wrist and steps out of the shower. I'm left under the water as he vacates the bathroom.

I turn the knob with a shaking hand, and once again, it's like a fog starts to lift when he's not close to me. My tongue runs along my lips, and all I taste is him.

My heart jumps around in my chest. Water continues to drip from my pink summer dress that's clinging to my flesh. I leave the shower and stop at a large round mirror that has the same mosaic tiles decorating it as the shower floor. I should change; my dress is see-through. It's like a second skin against my breasts. I push my wet hair behind my ears, and I erase the trepidation and leave the bathroom. My feet pad on the wooden flooring. My heart is dancing a fast beat that my feet aren't matching, but I don't stop until I reach the room that Cillian sleeps in. He has removed his suit jacket, and his shirt is half off, his back a map of scars.

He glances at me over his shoulder, and a warning flashes in his eyes.

"I want to speak to my father." I keep my chin high. I'm waiting, but the man in the bathroom moments ago is gone. This one ignores me, and I'm all caught up as he peels the white shirt off his body. I can't stop tracking the scars that crisscross his back. He turns to me with a brazen look in his eyes and lets the shirt drop to the ground. Everything in me quivers, and I try not to let his tanned torso that's covered in art affect me. Under the art, I can see ridges of agony poke out from behind black flames and a lion's head. Ridges that look similar to the scars on his back. I tighten my legs closer together. The movement should go unnoticed, but it doesn't with Cillian.

"You want round two?" He touches his belt but pauses. Something holds him back. His jaw clenches, and a phone starts to ring somewhere.

A phone. My mind sings.

I'm sprinting out of the room. Cillian tears after me, and I'm waiting for him to tackle me as I race into the living room. My mind grows frantic as the ringing phone escalates my panic.

I need to find it, I want to scream. I don't see a phone—I already searched this place and never found one. If I had, I would have rung the Gardai.

I spin as Cillian enters the living room, water still dripping from his hair and onto his torso. I appreciate him for a second before the ringing phone has me going to a side table. I pull open the drawer; it's empty. Yet the phone continues to ring. I push a panel to the left—where the sound is coming from—and a box pops out. I pull the hidden compartment open, and a slick black phone sits inside the drawer. I reach for it, when a large body crushes into my back, and a strong arm reaches around me and picks it up.

"Cillian," he answers. His breath is close to my ear, and I can't help the shiver that comes from having him this close.

My reaction is really from the cold, I lie to myself.

"No problem." He hangs up the phone, and I try to snatch it from his hand, but he holds it above his head.

"You got your wish, princess. Daddy is on his way," Cillian whispers with pure hatred.

He steps away from me, and a tremble consumes my body. My lip drags down, and I feel physically sick.

My father knows I'm here.

CHAPTER THREE

CILLIAN

S HE DOESN'T FOLLOW ME this time. I suppose it's because she got what she wanted—daddy's attention. She's a privileged brat. One I wouldn't mind fucking, with her tight body and that fucking temper of hers. It hasn't been easy ignoring her for the last few days. I've spent most nights with a raging hard-on she'll never relieve.

Dana O'Reagan, the Princess of the Irish Mafia, is off-limits. Her father had cameras installed in every room of this suite. I know the arch that connects one side of the suite to the other is the only dark spot, and the bathroom has no cameras. Otherwise, we are being watched constantly, and Liam, ringing when she was demanding to speak to him, told me he had watched the whole show.

I enter my room knowing eyes are still on me and get changed into a fresh pair of black slacks and a white shirt.

My mind returns to my father's burial and all that transpired from the graveyard. Everyone is adamant about helping me find out what happened to my father, but I don't trust any of them. What can I say? I have serious fucking trust issues.

I check my phone for messages before sliding it into my trouser pocket. Liam arriving here isn't planned, but him coming here is perfect timing. I've organized to meet Shay for the first time since he handed me Dana. I can imagine all the questions he has for me.

I could use the excuse of Liam coming here as my reason for leaving. I'm just giving them some father and daughter space. I leave the bedroom, and I don't expect her to be in the living room. She's changed into a turquoise dress with large brown buttons up the front. Her hair is still wet and pours across her shoulders. She hugs a white beaded cushion to her chest.

"I can't imagine he will keep you waiting long." I have no idea why I'm interacting with her.

Her gaze snaps to mine; her eyes are rimmed red from tears she must have shed earlier. She has her father's ways, and I'm already wondering what her cunning mind is coming up with. The O'Reagans—all they do is use and abuse. Dana might be more dangerous than any other O'Reagan, with her beauty and large doe eyes.

She juts out her chin. "You should be terrified."

I let a smile grow slowly across my face.

Her eyes widen slightly before they narrow. "My father is Mafia."

A genuine smile takes over my face. The word sounds funny coming from her pretty little mouth. I should leave. "Is he now? How terrifying."

She throws the cushion to the side, and she's standing. Anger and fury tighten her cute face. "You think you can just keep me captive here, and there will be no consequences." She takes a step toward me, and as much as I love looking at her, I don't enjoy listening to her, so I walk away. She usually follows like a dog barking and biting at my heels, but today, she doesn't.

I take one last look at the Mafia princess. Blue eyes sparkle with pain, and she fucking confuses me. One minute she wears a look of pure devastation, and the next, she wears the mask of a spoiled brat.

I lock the door behind me and make my way through the winding servant passageways of Cabra Castle. Leaving through the front doors wasn't necessary or wise. I keep moving deeper under the castle and step into the old cellars. It's a maze down here, but Liam gave me a map of how to get out of the castle with Dana if anything ever went wrong. My gut told me Liam wouldn't share these escape routes with anyone. His daughter is far more valuable than he would ever admit. She wasn't someone who was flaunted or spoken about. We all know who Richard and Jack O'Reagan are—Liam made sure of that—but Dana was kept in the dark.

Now I wonder why.

I leave the cellars and climb up the stairs, coming out to the back of the castle where my car is parked. I don't have far to go to meet Shay. We agreed we would meet in Dun Na Ri park, which is across the road from the entrance to Cabra Castle.

I drive deeper into the back entrance of the park and leave my car among the trees before getting out. Taking out my phone—I have only one bar of reception here—I lock the car and walk deeper into the park. This part is covered in trees, and wooden steps that rise and fall are intertwined between the masses of greenery. As a kid, I loved it here.

This place holds good memories of my mother and sister. I swallow the pain, and a bitter aftertaste has the memories fading fast and hard. They have no place here.

I keep walking and don't stop, even as I hear footsteps behind me.

"I'm sorry about your father." Shay's voice is directly behind me, but I keep walking.

I hear the click of a lighter and the heavy inhale as he smokes. "You want one?" he asks.

I don't smoke. I stop walking and turn to Shay, reaching for a cigarette from him.

He pulls back the packet before I get the cigarette out. "You better have a good fucking reason for handing Dana back." Shay holds my gaze, and I know he won't take any of this kindly.

"I do," I answer, and he lets me take the cigarette. I lean in toward him so he can light it for me.

I inhale, and the smoke cuts the back of my throat. "Liam was helping my father find my sister, and when I found out my father was dead, I knew he wouldn't keep looking for her. And honestly, Liam was the closest we ever got to her. Not even Sheahan helped much, or the Jaguars." I take another pull of the cigarette. "So in order for him to keep helping me, I offered him his daughter back."

Shay throws his cigarette on the ground and crushes it under his boot. "Fuck any loyalty to me. Fuck our friendship." His angry words, I expect.

I take a deep inhale and swallow the cough. "My sister was taken, and the last time anyone saw her, she was with a Russian guy. They left the pub called The Swan's Neck, and no one saw her again." I throw the cigarette on the ground, and Shay stomps on it. Maybe he's trying to get rid of some unspent anger.

"She's in a trafficking ring, Shay."

He stops crushing the cigarette. "All you had to do was tell me."

"I didn't know at the time that the Russians would murder my father," I bite out.

Shay scratches his beard before looking away into the bushes. "You really think the Russians killed your da?"

I don't answer and wait for him to elaborate. He does. "I'd bet my fucking left ball that Liam, the fucking cunt, killed your da."

"I thought you were more attached to your balls, Shay?"

He doesn't smile at my sarcasm. "You have no fucking idea what Liam is capable of." A flash of what looks like pain leaves his face quickly, and I'm staring at Shay, who always looks ready for a fight. I'm normally not the one on the receiving end.

"He made me a king."

This time Shay smiles, but it's filled with madness and tinged with disbelief. "What a cunt he is."

I look around us. I'm looking for trouble. It's a habit, I suppose. "I took the place as a king. I want my sister back." I hope he can hear what I'm saying. I have no intentions of staying with the O'Reagans. Once I find out who killed my father and where my sister is, I'm gone.

Silence trickles in, and with it comes a sprinkling of rain. Shay looks up at the sky before ramming his hands into the pockets of his black jacket.

"You need a place to crash. I know some people," I offer. The Jaguars would keep him safe; they would do it for me.

"Nah, I have my people." Bitterness coats his words, and I don't want to part like this with him.

"The help is there if you need it, Shay. I'm your people too."

"I know. How's your ma?" Shay takes out his cigarettes and lights one up. I decline another one.

"She's grand, to be honest. She wants her daughter," I say.

Shay nods and blows smoke into the air. "I get that. If I hear anything about your sister, I'll let you know. But you're right; stay close to Liam. He will have contacts with the Russians. He dabbled in all that years ago. So he'd know the heavy hitters. You gotta be careful, Cillian."

I grip his forearm. "I will. You too."

"How's Dana?" Shay asks.

"With her daddy now."

"I'd love to be a fly on the fucking wall," Shay says.

I wouldn't. I'm sure it's lots of complaints and wanting her freedom back. Dana, the princess, sure is living up to my expectations of her. A brat who stomped her feet, and Daddy came running.

"I better get back. Are we good?" I ask.

Shay takes a long drag of his cigarette. He holds my stare for longer than I like. "Yeah. But the next time you decide to screw me over, a heads-up would be nice."

I smile. I can't help it. I've serious respect for Shay and don't like not being on good terms with him. So him forgiving me means a lot.

"I'll keep you in the loop."

"Now fuck off." Shay grins before walking away. His way of saying goodbye.

CHAPTER FOUR

DANA

I'M SITTING ON THE high-back red chair, waiting. Cillian said my father would be here soon. I'm still questioning if all this is true. Each time I think of seeing my father's face, my vision wavers like he's the end to some bad dream.

A fist hardens in my belly, and a cold finger runs along my neck, drawing my shoulders higher as the door opens. Dread tightens my jaw; I'm not sure why terror has hijacked my body.

Everything falls from me like a second skin and puddles at my feet as I meet his eyes.

"Daddy." One word that nearly snaps me in two. He closes the door behind him. I don't allow my brain to register that he locks it. That he has a key. That I'm still a captive. I don't let my brain register that he isn't panicked about this situation. Instead, I'm tearing up the floor under my feet; the moment he turns to me, I'm a child again as I launch myself into my father's arms. My sobs grow heavier as he wraps his arms around me like a security blanket I've recognized all my life.

My father doesn't say anything. He just holds me as I rattle and cling to him. Everything has hit me so violently, starting from the moment I rang Richard to help me—only he turned my world upside down.

I want to scream that Maeve killed Cian. That Jack and Richard know. That Shay kidnapped me and that Cillian has been keeping me prisoner, and he's so mean to me.

"I want my mother," I sob into his suit jacket, and my father's arms stiffen around me before he starts to peel me from his chest. I'm shaky as I look up at him.

"I want Mother." I'm nodding my head, trying to reinforce my words with a need that has me glancing at the door.

"Sit down with me."

His words are gentle, and he gives me one of his rare smiles, which makes my lip wobble.

"I need you to be brave, Dana."

My teeth sink into my lip, cutting off the tremble. I swallow the hysteria as my father leads me to one of the couches. He allows me to sit down first, and I tighten my hands in my lap so I won't reach out and cling to his leg like a five-year-old.

I try to get a grip on reality and push the feverish fear aside.

"How are you?" My father unbuttons his suit jacket before sitting down beside me.

The couch dips, and I keep still and stop myself from curling into his side like a wounded dog.

"Deep breaths." He smiles again.

It's funny that it doesn't calm me but only escalates the anxiety that clogs my arteries, making my limbs feel heavy.

"What's happening?" I ask. My voice reaches my ears, and I sound calm.

He nods. The smile is gone. "I need you to stay here for a while with Cillian."

I'm ready to protest, but he holds up his hand.

"I understand that Maeve told you she killed Cian."

Words fail me.

My father's hands take my tightened fingers. He uncurls them, and when his warm ones cover mine, my body sighs like this just might be over soon. He can fix all of this.

"Maeve is sick."

Alarm shoots through me, pulling at my spine. "What happened?"

His hands tighten on mine. "Nothing happened, Dana. She has a sickness like her mother."

"A drinking problem?" I didn't think so. Maeve grew up with an alcoholic mother and a brother who battled drug addiction. If anything, she never drank, even when I pleaded with her to have just one drink.

"No, far worse. It's her mind. She's unstable."

I want to pull my hands away, but I see the truth in his eyes.

"I've always seen her illness, but you favored her. So I allowed the friendship."

Allowed. That word spins too fast in my head.

My father leans in like he's about to share a secret with just me. My body craves this moment with him, and I lean closer. "A mistake that has cost me so much."

My stomach sours, and I have this overwhelming sensation to apologize to my father. Yet, I don't fully understand why this need is growing and manifesting until it feels like a giant black shadow is hovering over me.

"She has always been so jealous of you. I've said it a million times. She would always watch you."

This doesn't make sense to me—Maeve has been a friend. Yet my father means every word.

"So, she didn't kill Cian?" Confusion spins fast and hard, and I cling to my father's hands to keep me grounded.

"Cian had too much to drink and fell from the balcony at Jack's home. Maeve was there, but she was drinking too."

"She said Shay shot Cian in the head." The words are low, but the reaction on my father's face is like someone blasted the volume.

"I'm sorry, Dana. She's very sick."

He releases my hands, and I try to let that sink in. Maeve is sick, so sick that she couldn't see what was happening with Cian. Did he fall? Did she think that she pushed him?

Jesus.

"Jack and Richard confirmed it?" I fire back.

My father nods. "Jack loves her. She has poisoned your brother."

An uncomfortable sensation crawls up my back, and I tighten my hands around my waist. *Poisoned* makes it seem like she is lethal.

I sink back into the couch, the energy zapped from me. He doesn't speak, but he's still seated beside me, and that gives me comfort.

"Are you Mafia?" My mind takes another turn, and I'm grateful for it. Maeve being sick doesn't bode well for my fragile system. There is relief that no one killed Cian, that it was just an accident.

"Yes."

The confirmation has my body growing stiff. I glance at my father, who speaks so well, dresses so well, and who wouldn't hurt a fly. He isn't violent or wicked.

"You don't look like the Mafia." I chew the inside of my jaw.

He smiles again, and I wonder for the first time if maybe he's joking. He doesn't joke, and that takes the air from my lungs. He's Mafia. So what does that make me?

"Do you hurt people?" Fear tightens its bony fingers around my throat.

"Dana, I want you to breathe."

Breathe? I am breathing. I analyze my body and he's right; I need to allow air into my deprived lungs. I take quick breaths. The air is sharp.

"Slow down." My father touches my back, and it's as effective as a brown paper bag to my over-oxygenated body. My breaths grow more controlled.

"Think of what you know." He continues to rub my back. "I run hotels."

I nod. Yes, that's what my father does.

"Jack runs a nightclub."

I nod again as I focus on my breathing.

"We are just businessmen that have been labeled Mafia. A label I accept."

There is no pride in my father's voice; it's just fact.

"You may hear that I am a king."

I'm thinking of kings and queens, princes and princesses. Cillian calling me a princess starts to make sense, but is it true? Does this make me a princess?

"What am I?" I ask instead.

My father leans in, still rubbing my back. "My beautiful daughter."

My lip trembles and wobbles into a small smile. *Daddy.* My body sighs.

"You look so much like your mother." He touches my face, and I sink into it as my body relaxes further. I'm ready to go home. I want my bed. I want my mother. I want to see Maeve and find out what I can do to help my friend.

"I'm sure Mother is beside herself." I half laugh.

My father withdraws his hand. I don't like that he doesn't answer me.

Something inside me quivers, and the security blanket his presence has covered me with starts to feel too hot, almost suffocating.

"I'm ready to go." The words are strangled.

"Soon." My father rises and starts to button his suit jacket.

I rise too. "I don't want to stay here."

"I hate the mess we are in, but I want you to stay here for me, Dana."

"Things have gotten complicated. You and Maeve haven't made things easy."

Heat scorches my cheeks, and the overwhelming feeling to apologize again nearly chokes me.

"So in a few days at best, I should have things restored."

I'm shaking my head. "I understand now that she is sick. I get that what Maeve said isn't true. Please, Daddy, I just want to go home."

My father releases me. "It's not that simple, Dana. Words are powerful things, and in this case, they have been welded into a weapon I am trying to control."

I have no idea what he's talking about.

"We are Mafia, and it weakens us to other people that we would kill each other so easily. Maeve is considered one of us since Jack insists on marrying her."

"Jack's still getting married." I need to sit down. It's all too much. "Dana."

My father's sharp tone has my body growing stiff again.

"I need you to be brave. Cillian will watch over you for the next few days."

I'm ready to protest again.

"Do this for your father. A few days, that's all I ask."

I swallow the sob and pain.

"Can I go outside for walks?" I try to bargain.

My father is past that stage. "No, Dana."

"Daddy, it's a prison," I grit, feeling like the princess that Cillian accused me of being.

My father leans in, and I get that feeling again, like he's about to share a secret.

"We have lots of enemies, and right now, tensions are high. I can't risk you getting hurt."

Dread dulls any light inside me. "Am I a target? Of who and why?"

"Yes, you are a target. But I will deal with it."

"How?" Is this the part where he hurts people? My vision blurs, and it's like holding back a wave that's ready to crash down and smash everything in its path.

"Do you trust me?"

I'm nodding my head, but a worm of anger wriggles in the pit of my belly.

"Just a few days." My father doesn't give me a final hug or a kiss.

I'm staring at his back. I want to run after him and beg him not to leave me.

Be brave.

His words whisper against my skull, and I stay rooted to the spot. The door closes, the lock turns back into place, and I finally collapse onto the couch behind me.

CHAPTER FIVE

CILLIAN

AFTER LEAVING SHAY, I call my mother.

"You left early?"

I run my hand through my hair, which is damp from the drizzling rain. "Yeah, I had some people to meet." I feel bad leaving her, but my mother is strong. She's a pillar that has held up our family my entire life.

"I saw Edward talking to you."

Turning the key in the ignition, the car comes to life. My mother is talking about Skinner. She always uses his first name. She never gave into nicknames. My mother calling them by their first names always made the men seem like boys when she was around. That thought makes me smile.

"He was giving his condolences. He asked about you," I say.

I can hear her tut. "He could have just asked me himself. It doesn't matter," she adds, but clearly, him not asking her how she is does matter. My mother doesn't use words unnecessarily. It makes me question her friendship with Skinner; is their relationship more than I had thought?

"Will you be back later?" she questions.

"Yeah, I'll drop by the house tonight," I promise. Her being close to Skinner is none of my business.

"Okay. I love you."

I start to reverse out of the forest. "Love you, too." I hang up and drive back to Cabra Castle. I check my appearance in the mirror. My shirt is showcasing the earlier rain, turning the white to a light gray. I always keep a spare jacket in the trunk. Once I park, I get out and remove the black jacket and cover up my shirt. Running my hands through my hair one more time, I enter the cellars under the castle.

My footsteps bounce around the space. The cellars remind me of a setting for some bad thriller on a low budget. I'm always on high alert, always waiting for a threat. So I notice the slight movement telling me I'm not alone.

"These tunnels were used during times of wars." I pause my steps at Liam's voice. "When the castle was overrun, the family of the castle would use these tunnels to get out safely. In the history of the castle, that only happened once. But the family never actually got out of the cellar."

He materializes from one of the dark corners, looking like the villain he likes to portray. I haven't made up my mind completely about Liam O'Reagan. The jury is still out on just how bad he is. Dana doesn't look like her father; she must have her mother's beauty.

"They were killed?" I ask, like I give two fucks about what happened to the family from—how many eras ago?

"No. They got trapped down here by the invaders, who closed off both exits, and they starved to death."

"Seems cruel." They could have shot them.

"Some say cruel. I think the invaders were marking their territory. Sometimes it takes one harsh act to save us doing lots more."

I don't answer. Liam removes his hands from his pockets and trails one along an arch. "History can teach us so much. But today is not the day for a history lesson."

"I never was a good student," I respond.

Liam smiles. "You just never had a good teacher."

I smile too, but it's not filled with happiness and warmth. It's stuffed to the snapping point with memories of beatings and harsh words and of digging a small grave.

Liam clears his throat; he has my full attention. "Dana is very upset."

Fuck.

She must have told him about me forcing her into the shower.

"She doesn't like being cooped up or being told what to do." Liam smiles fondly at the mention of his daughter. "So, she's angry right now and needs to remain here."

So I still have to fucking babysit her. If that's what it takes to get my sister back, then that's what I will do.

The smile melts off Liam's face as he extracts a cream piece of paper from his pocket. He holds it out toward me.

"This will get you started on your search for your sister."

Surprise filters through me as I take the paper; it's thick, almost like cardboard. I open it, and a name is scrawled across the page in Liam's handwriting.

"But be warned—this is the road your father went down. The road that got him killed."

I stuff the paper into my pocket. "I'll be careful." Nothing would stop me in my search for my sister.

Liam watches me for a moment. "We are convinced your father's death was at the hands of the same people who have your sister, so I would tread *very* carefully. Don't go alone. I'll send one of my men with you."

I nod. "Thanks, but the fact my father died because of these bastards makes getting my sister out even more important." I won't be taking one of his men with me, and I refuse to allow my mind to conjure all the horrific images of my sister being tortured, beaten, or even raped.

All I want to do right now is track this fucker down so I can find my sister. My feet are eager to move, but Liam isn't finished.

"Dana is off-limits, Cillian."

I'm ready to tell him no problem, but he holds up a finger.

"She can be very persuasive. She is my daughter, after all." The smile returns as he speaks of her. "Some might even say she is manipulative. But don't tell her I said that."

Liam's humor doesn't quite land.

"I'll remember that."

Liam steps closer. "Good." He gives a curt nod before turning his back on me. "Good luck on your hunt." He disappears into the shadows, and I reach into my pocket and touch the paper. I don't need luck. I'll find my sister.

I won't fail where my father did. He was a bad father to me, but not to my sister. Aoibhe was his Achilles' heel. I knew he would have died for her, and funny enough, he had.

I'm still on high alert as I leave the cellar. The thought of my sister has rattled me. Leaving here and charging headfirst into danger will only get me killed, just like my father.

I need to be smarter. I need to fight. The want in me needs someone's blood. Now!

I enter the bar. A fire burns under a black plasma screen that looks out of place in the castle. A set of high-back chairs clad in green suede line the bar. A bartender polishes glasses and immediately stops, gives me a smile, and steps closer, ready to take my order.

"A whiskey."

He moves quickly, and I dip under the arch that leads me to a more private part of the bar. I sit down in a large cream-colored round chair that's placed beside a second fire.

I don't have to wait long before the bartender arrives with a mat and places the whiskey down.

"Can I get you anything else, sir?"

"You can put that on Liam O'Reagan's tab."

The bartender doesn't question me but nods and takes his leave.

I drink the whiskey, and the alcohol burns a path before settling heavily in my gut. I don't want to return to the top floor of the castle. I finish the glass of whiskey, knowing I'm prolonging the inevitable.

Dana is off-limits; I need to keep that in mind. Liam said she was manipulative, and that, I just might agree with. My attraction to her isn't something I have experienced before. Ladies come and go, but already she has gotten under my skin, and I hate how much of my time is consumed with the thoughts of fucking her. I should be focused on my sister.

Anger has me standing—anger at Dana, who I need to get out of my system one way or another.

CHAPTER SIX

DANA

The longer I sit here, the more confused I feel. It's like my father took with him a haze that was slowly lifting, and the conversation I had with him keeps replaying over and over in my head. One minute I allow his words about Maeve to sink in, but the next, they don't make sense.

Maeve would never lie to me. Richard and Jack confirmed what Maeve said was true, yet my father said Maeve wasn't well. She has a sickness like her mother. I keep going back to the conversation with Richard. Did he actually confirm that Maeve killed Cian? My frantic mind can't pinpoint Richard saying that she had.

Fresh tears well up. Maeve had a hard upbringing, but why didn't I see how damaged she truly is? I wipe the tears away. Maeve has never been jealous of me, but my father said she is. That when we were younger, he saw how she watched me.

I get up off the chair. I want to speak to Maeve. I want to hug Maeve. I want to slap Maeve, too.

My vision blurs with a fresh wave of pain that punches me hard in the stomach. Really, he only confirmed one thing. He is Mafia.

Mafia.

My mind continues to spin and reel until my stomach tightens and loosens, threatening to bring up its meagre contents.

The door rattles, and I'm standing as Cillian enters. My system crashes and my core tightens at the sight of him. His hair is slightly damp, and it looks like he's been running his hands through it several times. He gives me a glance over his shoulder as he locks the door.

He's here to keep me safe. That's what my father said. I just wish Cillian had explained that to me instead of constantly ignoring me. Hitting him was wrong.

"I want to say I'm sorry for slapping you."

Cillian takes off his suit jacket, not even glancing my way.

I take a step toward him. "I know you're here to watch over me, so we don't have to ignore each other."

I swallow when he glares at me. He removes his phone from his pocket. A slip of cream paper floats to the floor. I'm about to tell him that he dropped it, when he speaks.

"I'd much prefer it if you stayed out of my way." He glances at his phone before stuffing it into his trousers pocket. His dark eyes land on me.

"I'm trying to apologize here," I grit out, not understanding why he's being so hostile.

"Apology accepted," he growls and walks away.

"You don't have to be such an asshole."

He stops walking, and his shoulders rise and fall. My heart rate heightens as I wait, but he walks away and disappears from the living room.

I tighten my fists and push down the loneliness that threatens to swallow me up. My gaze snags on the cream piece of paper on the ground. I take one final look at the arch Cillian disappeared under before picking up the paper and opening it.

Bednar Novak.

I keep looking from the name on the paper to the arch. Why did Cillian have this name? I know the last name. Not sure if I've met Bednar, but the last name is from my mother's side in the Czech Republic. She doesn't talk too much about her past, but I traveled to her hometown and stayed in our summer home there. It was a summer of freedom, or so I had thought.

The second thing that tells me these are my mother's people is that the name is in my father's handwriting.

I curl my fingers around the paper and follow Cillian to his room. His door is open; he never closes it. He's dragging on a fresh black shirt. He gives me a half glance over his shoulder but doesn't say anything. His body speaks of irritation at my appearance in his doorway. I usually don't have this effect on people.

"Bednar Novak. Why do you have his name?"

Cillian freezes, and slowly, his hand slides into his trousers pocket and comes up empty. He turns to me with his shirt open. His bare feet somehow make him look more threatening as he steps toward me, his jaw like steel, his eyes burning with anger.

I hold the paper up between two fingers. "You dropped this."

He snaps the paper out of my hand and leans in. His cologne and natural smell circle me, and I want to inhale deeply.

He moves even closer while my heart rate triples in speed. His mouth is close to my ear, and I'm tempted to reach up and touch his chest. This close, the heat of his body comes off him in waves, and I want to lean into him.

His warm breath fans out along my neck. I'm hoping he's shedding some of his anger.

"I had a conversation with your father before I came up here today." His low words send a shiver down my spine. Cillian moves back, and I miss his warmth instantly until he walks around me. I don't move but close my eyes as he leans in and whispers in my other ear.

"He told me how manipulative you can be."

My eyes snap open, and I try to turn, but Cillian's hand locks onto my shoulders, keeping me in place. "Don't touch my stuff again." He releases me, and a tremble takes over my body. "Get out of my room." Hate coats each word.

My father would never say those words. Me, manipulative?

"I know who Bednar Novak is."

That gets his attention. He buttons up his shirt, and all his tanned flesh disappears.

His smile is fake as he walks toward me. "You want something for the information?"

I didn't want anything, but now that he says that, maybe I should barter.

"Yes."

He sneers and shakes his head.

My stomach hollows out. I hate how he looks at me, like I'm some manipulative woman.

"Forget about it." I turn to leave.

"Tell me what you want," he growls.

I know asking to leave the suite isn't going to happen.

"There is a door that leads to the roof. I want it opened."

His laugh is more like a bark. He walks toward me and clenches his fist. "Get out." He grips the door. I have no idea why he's pissed.

"I want some fresh air."

He spins around when I don't leave. "I'm sure there is another way off that roof that you aren't telling me about."

"You think I'm lying? Fine." I march from his room but slow down as I pass the threshold. "He's a relation of my mother's."

"How do you know that?" Cillian's words sound like they've been dragged out of him, like he would rather have this conversation with anyone else but me.

I face him and don't speak.

"I'll check out the door and inspect the roof space. If—and I mean *if*—it's safe, I'll let you up."

My heart lifts, and I smile for the first time. "My mother is a Novak." I leave the room. Cillian doesn't stop me.

My throat closes, and the air grows thin as I return to my room. I have no idea what to do. Everything that has happened chokes me and demands the spotlight, but I'm exhausted after my father's visit. My body just wants to give in and sleep, so I give into the demand and lie down on my bed.

I hear Cillian moving around. I've left my bedroom door open, so I don't feel so locked up or lonely.

A fresh tear rolls down my face, and I feel like I'm five again. I want my mother. I want her to tell me this isn't real. I want her to just hold me and tell me this has all been one big misunderstanding.

My mind races through everything—from the kiss with Cillian that has burned itself into my mind all the way to demanding to speak to my father. The phone rang as I had demanded my father. I sit up on the bed. My heart starts to jump around in my chest.

No.

I get off the bed and walk around my room, looking for what I hope I won't find.

I find a small black camera in the corner of the room. My abdomen twists painfully and bile rises. I leave the room and step out into the darkened arch.

Cillian's bedroom is empty, but I spot the camera over his door. My heart continues to hammer as I enter the bathroom. Humiliation burns my face when I think of how Cillian put me in the shower. How he kissed me, and I did nothing. I swallow more bile. I can't find a camera in here. I leave and check three other rooms and find cameras in them, placed neatly in the corner.

When I enter the living room, the main room door closes as Cillian carries a tray to the table. My food has arrived just as it has every day that I've been a prisoner here. My gaze roams the room, and I spot two more cameras.

I wrap my arms around my waist as I try to understand why my father is watching me. What the fuck is all of this?

"Your food, princess." Hate and bitterness coat Cillian's words as he drops the tray and removes the silver lid, but I'm walking out of the room as my belly threatens to expel its earlier contents.

"There are children starving in Africa, Princess Dana." His mocking words stop me, but I don't turn around.

"Stop calling me that." My voice doesn't shake like my body does.

"Why? Does it annoy you, Princess Dana?" The taunting in Cillian's voice has me launching myself back into the room.

His anger is almost tangible around his high frame. Warning bells tell me I should run, hide, take cover. He releases the lid that hits the table with a loud bang.

"Yes, it fucking does!"

I'm ready to cross the room, and I'm ready to strike out, because I don't know what else to do. That is until Cillian starts to laugh.

It's short-lived, but the sound freezes me. His laughter is deep, almost a heavy growl. The sound stops quickly, but I see the amusement in his deep green eyes.

"Tut, tut, Princess Dana. A lady shouldn't curse."

I tighten my hands into fists. I want to lash out; I'm so close. I take a quick peek at the camera in the corner, and I look back at Cillian. He's no longer smiling. He's no longer angry. His face and eyes are devoid of any emotion.

He picks up the lid and re-covers my food. There's a deadness in his eyes that I don't want to see. I wrap my arms around my waist, wanting to curl in on myself.

He takes a step toward me, and again, something inside me tells me to run, but I stand my ground as a new wave of anger consumes him. Anger that's directed at me.

CHAPTER SEVEN

CILLIAN

S HE'S TRYING TO ACT the victim. She's looking at me from under a set of heavy dark lashes like a curse word wouldn't pass her ruby-red lips. I'd believe that, only I just heard her curse. Hearing a word like that coming from her mouth is delicious. She's still staring at me, and I'm waiting for her to either bolt or attack me. She's holding back since spotting the cameras in the room. I should take notice, too. I take another step toward her, with the camera at my back.

"Starve if you want to," I bark.

She flinches.

I move past her. Her mother is a Novak, and this man is a Novak. The connection is too easy to make, so that makes me distrust Liam straight away.

I'm too aware of Dana's movements in the living room. I hate how something inside me relaxes when I hear the noise of cutlery. I shouldn't give two actual fucks if she eats or not.

I enter my room and retrieve a penknife my father gifted to me on my eighteenth birthday. I flick it open and return to the living room. She's sitting at the table, moving her food around her plate. I want to say something smartass again. I want to rile her up. I want to see her snap. She's sexy when she's angry.

"Which room has the door that leads to the roof?" I ask.

She doesn't look at me, but her bare shoulders stiffen. Her skin is smooth, and my mind goes back to the shower. Seeing her clothes wet and clinging to her, all I wanted to do was fuck the beauty there and then.

"The bedroom next to mine." She peeks at me from under her lashes; her eyes widen like she's never seen a knife before.

Manipulative, I remind myself as I turn and make my way to the bedroom. She's Liam O'Reagan's daughter. No matter how innocent she appears, it's all a facade that I'm not stupid enough to fall for.

I find the room that Dana said had a doorway to the roof. I rattle the handle, and it's locked. The door is old. I slide the knife along the paneling beside the lock and force it away from the wall. It's old, as I thought it might be; layers of paint flakes fall to the floor. Pushing the frame toward the door will give the lock some wiggle room. My foot connects with the door, and it pops open and doesn't shatter. A trick my father taught me.

I have to hunch as I climb the stairs. The passageway only has light that filters in from the open door below me. I climb and stop at a door; my fingers glide over the handle. The door opens easily, and I step out onto the roof of Cabra Castle.

The wind has picked up, along with a light rain that starts to soak me quickly. I walk around the perimeter. A door toward the back of the castle roof is locked. There are two ladders, but each has a lock, so they can't be dropped down to the ground level.

When I take another sweep of the roof, I feel more content. I pride myself on being a man of my word, so I will allow Dana her freedom. I take a final look over the edge. The Irish flag beats wildly in the wind, and pride swells in my chest. Our country is the best country in the world, but only if you are standing amongst the right people. That is a small detail that I need to change.

I return to the suite, and Dana is in the hallway with her arms wrapped around her small waist. Anger and the desire to fuck her bleed together in my bloodstream. I tighten my jaw to keep from reaching out to her. To hurt her. To take her.

"I've opened the door for you to go up on the roof."

Surprise lights up her blue eyes, like she's spotted a rare find. "Really?" she stutters.

I want to hurt her.

"Yeah, really." A sneer accompanies my words. I turn away from her and go into my room to change my clothes again.

She still hasn't moved from the hall. I keep my back to my open door and take off my shirt before pulling on a fresh one.

"Thank you." Her voice is soft.

I face her as I button my shirt. She bites her lip.

I grin. "Take all the time you want, princess. I don't mind you checking me out."

Her cheeks pink, but she doesn't run from the room.

If she did run, I'd want to give chase.

She fills the space with lust and her own flavor of anger, and I'm sure if I kissed her, I'd taste it on her tongue.

She looks away, and her pretty lips form a thin line. She still hasn't left as I slide on a suit jacket.

"Are you going out?" Disappointment coats her words.

"None of your business." I don't have to answer her. She's still standing in the doorway, and I walk up to her and lean in. Her breath halts in her throat. "Move the fuck out of my way."

She stumbles back and steps into the hallway; I brush past her and ignore her alluring scent. Her presence is assaulting me with too many different beats that cause my cock to harden.

She doesn't follow, and I leave the suite. I lock the door and make my way to my vehicle.

***

I arrive at the address that Liam gave me. The building soars five stories into the air. The exterior is extravagant, like it's an ancestral home that has always had a keeper who loved it and breathed life into the property over the centuries. A red door is manned by two guys—each in a black suit with an earpiece attached to their left ear.

I get out of my car and make my way toward the building. Seven steps rise up, and I climb them.

"I'm here to see Bednar Novak."

Neither of the men look at me, but one presses the device on his ear and speaks in another language. I can't imagine my father taking this approach, knocking on the front door. I'm sure he staked the place out, made friends, and tried to get inside. Now he's dead.

"Any time soon would be great."

"Mr. Novak is busy. So, piss off." The security man's accent is as heavy as his thick blond eyebrows.

I step closer. We are close in height. No doubt he's packing, but I'm not leaving. "Liam O'Reagan sent me. So, if I don't get through this door, you'll have him to answer to." I'm playing a card that's not actually in the pack.

Both men glance at each other. One of them speaks again in his own language.

Apparently, using Liam's name is wise.

The red door creaks open, and I don't wait for a welcome party; I enter. The interior is as extravagant as the exterior—old money. When the British claimed parts of Ireland, they stamped everything with their own engineering and structures. This isn't Irish, but old British. I hate everything about the building.

I stretch my arms as I'm patted down. I'm two guns lighter after they check me.

"What is your business with Mr. Novak?"

"That's for Mr. Novak." I grin.

"Sit here." The security man points at a chair that sits in a row along a wall. The wall holds an obscene amount of artwork, all in gold frames. The red cushioned seat isn't comfortable, but I sit, and the security man leaves me. He disappears behind one of two pillars that soar into the ceiling, the focal point of which is a large golden chandelier adorned with small leaves and roses.

I'm left waiting for well over thirty minutes, so I get out of the chair. I'm sure I'm being watched by cameras. I move around the hall, looking up at all the artwork. Nameless faces stare down at me—white faces that are not part of this Russian mobster's history; he must have claimed this historical building as his own.

Money.

The click of the front door has me turning.

Smoke leaves the mouth of a blond-haired man in his late fifties. He grins at the security men who walk past me and approach him. He holds up his hands, and the red door closes behind him.

"You must be Cillian," he says while being patted down. They impressively confiscate three guns and a knife.

"And you are?" I ask, taking a step closer to him. He isn't Bednar Novak. He's too Irish-looking, and his accent is from the Northeast.

"Darragh O'Reagan." The security steps away with the weapons. "I want my guns back when I leave," he warns them as they disappear, not giving two fucks about what he says.

So this is who Liam sent to help me. His brother. How did he even know I was here? Unless he's watching me. Of course he's watching me.

"I don't recall asking for backup," I say.

He holds out his hand and I take it. His shake is strong, and his grin grows wider. Blue eyes dance with a touch of madness. "You don't have to ask, brother. You're part of the family now."

Bullshit.

"Good to know. But, I got this."

He releases my hand and glances around the space like I haven't spoken. "Nice crib."

My brain races through all the information I know about the O'Reagans. Darragh is a twin and the wild one. Drink, drugs, and women. He's no stranger to debauchery; maybe the word was created just for him.

He also isn't known for being subtle. My father hadn't been a fan.

"Some ugly motherfuckers up on these walls." He glances at me with a grin.

I won't be fooled by how relaxed he is.

"Do you know much about Bednar Novak?"

"He's a lovely guy. Gives to charities and runs a school full of nuns." His answer is fired over his shoulder. Darragh glances up at a camera over a large mirror that covers half the wall further down. He winks.

"Brownie points," he says as he turns to me.

"You can take a seat." One of the security men steps out from behind a pillar.

Darragh takes chewing gum out of his breast pocket and places it into his mouth. He sits down and drags one leg over the other like he's here for a hair appointment. He's too relaxed.

"I think I've waited long enough to speak to Mr. Novak."

"Take a seat." The security man points at one. They are wasting my time.

I don't move, and another security man moves from behind a second pillar. "You fuckers keep appearing."

A hand clamps on my shoulder, and I turn to Darragh and shrug his hand off me.

He grins at the security. "He means no harm. We will wait."

The security steps back. A sharp tang of violence tinges the air. It's coming from us all.

Darragh returns to the chairs, and I follow him.

I don't want to play by their rules, but I want to find my sister.

Darragh takes out his phone. I can't see what he's reading, so I keep my focus on the security men who are visible. I count six of them.

My foot taps against the chair when I think of my sister. I roll my neck and try to sit still. I'm being watched. Pushing the image of my sister aside, I focus on the ugly paintings. Specifically, one of a woman with a large nose that makes her unappealing and material draped across her body, just covering her folds of stomach fat.

"How is my niece?" Darragh asks.

I glance at him. "Fine."

"I'm sure she's freaking out." He puts his phone away.

"She's fine," I repeat. I don't want to talk about Dana, either; even her name has the ability to cause a chemical reaction inside me that isn't healthy.

I'm standing again. The security men move closer, and I'm so fucking sick of waiting. It's been an hour.

"Any time today," I speak up to the cameras.

"You haven't done this before, have you?" Darragh asks as he opens another stick of chewing gum and stuffs it into his mouth. He plays with the paper as he speaks. "You know, the more you act out, the longer you will wait."

"Can't you do something to speed up this process? You are an O'Reagan, after all."

Any humor that Darragh had flees, and it's a quick and sharp reminder of who he is. We both know he has far more power than what he's displaying. He's allowing himself to be left sitting in this hallway being treated like some fucking goon.

"I'm a patient man." He settles in.

I'm staring at the chair when the machine that my father buried deep inside me switches on. It roars to life, demanding I don't allow myself to be treated like a fucking monkey.

"Can I have that?" I ask Darragh. He holds up the small sheet of silver paper.

I nod.

"Sure." He hands it over.

"You wouldn't happen to have a pen?"

He grins as he pats his jacket and produces one. I take it and scrawl my full name and number on the small piece of paper. I walk over to a security man, who steps toward me, blocking me from going any further into the house.

"Here is my name and number. Tell Mr. Novak to call me." I slide the piece of paper into his chest pocket.

"Now get me my guns."

The security man leaves, and I turn on my heel. I throw Darragh his pen, which he catches.

"It's like that, is it?" Darragh asks, but I hear the amusement in his voice. I stand close to the red door.

"It's pointless," I say.

"I thought an O'Hara had a little more in him."

I glance at Darragh as the security man arrives with my weapons. I take them and put them back in the band of my trousers.

"See you around, Darragh O'Reagan."

The red door opens, and I leave. The light outside seems too bright for a moment as I jog down the steps and across the road.

I slide into my car and glance back at the building. Darragh still hasn't left. I'm tempted to sit here and see how long it takes for him to leave, but my patience has been rattled, and the monster inside me is waking from its slumber.

My father had a darkness in him, so did his, and now it flows richly in my veins. Controlling the darkness is an art form I don't feel I've mastered well.

I start the car and drive away. The last time I lost control of my darkness, I woke up wondering who I was and how deep my depravity really ran.

I leave Dublin city behind me and drive back toward Navan. Back toward my people. My real people who will help me. It's starting to become very clear that Liam O'Reagan isn't going to. Not truthfully. He would throw me scraps. I wonder if he did the same to my father. I can't imagine my father scrambling around like some starving idiot.

Bad habits start to rise, and I tighten my hands on the steering wheel. The want to reach for a release that our culture uses as a crutch squeezes me. An escape from what we can't cope with is what I crave. Most people take it in the form of drugs, drink, or sex. For me, it's the chase, and of course, the sex after.

Dana's dark eyes flash in my mind. I have a right to exercise my depravity on her. She might be an O'Reagan, but I don't have to build a fucking shrine or pedestal for her to stand on.

I could take her down a peg or two or three.

I allow the dark fantasy to play out as I continue past Navan and toward Kingscourt. The Jaguars will help me, and that's where I'm going. I will return to Mr. Novak's house—not alone, but with my own fucking army.

CHAPTER EIGHT

CILLIAN

I ENTER THE BELLY of the beast. Sin floats in the air, and I inhale it deeply. The club is full, and the music dictates the slow movements of the half-naked women. Behind the scenes, a dance can transform into anything you want—for the right price, of course.

This is where you can sin, and no one here will pass judgment. It's been a while since I've been here at one of the Jaguars' dance clubs. As I walk toward the back of the room, I pass a lot of new faces, but that's not the only thing. Each face has a smile of bliss, a far-off look that's not caused by the women dancing in front of them.

I stop at the bar and nod at Andrew. He takes quick steps over to me and leans in so I can speak in his ear.

"You do know there's a lot of drugs here tonight?" I ask.

He doesn't look over my shoulder to clarify. Andrew nods. "If I had to kick out anyone for doing drugs, you and I would be the only ones standing."

Drugs aren't something that the Jaguars allow, or that was once the case. I tap the bar. "Thanks, Andrew. Are they out back?"

"Yeah, I'll let them know you're here." He walks away and picks up a black phone.

I leave the bar and make my way to the back of the club. The double doors are guarded by new recruits. One looks to Andrew for confirmation that I'm cleared to be let through.

The door is opened, and I leave the heavy music and sinful ways behind, only to walk deeper into the beast.

The hallway bounces with sounds that slide under the doors—some sounds of pleasure, some pain, some just voices.

I reach the last set of guarded double doors.

"Cillian. I'm sorry about your dad." I take Richie's hand. He's close to my age and has hung out with the Jaguars since a young age.

"Thanks, Richie." I release his hand, and he pushes the door open for me.

The lush room has a cloud of cigar smoke hanging over the three men who turn to me.

"Cillian." Razor smiles, the scar on his cheek stretching, almost threatening to tear apart.

I sit down beside Robert, who leans across and taps my knee. "How are you holding up?"

"Fine," I answer quickly and look toward Big John, who's watching me behind a pair of sunglasses. Everyone is still in suits from the funeral.

"How's your mother?" Razor asks.

I don't want the small chit-chat. "She's strong."

"A cigar?" Robert leans forward and picks up a wooden box. He opens it and presents me with a selection of cigars.

I'm too hell-bent on getting Bednar Novak. I shake my head. "I got a lead on my father's killer."

No one really reacts. Robert closes the lid on the cigars and places it on the table. "Is that so?"

I focus on Razor. "I just ran into a problem."

"Tell me, Cillian…" Razor stamps his cigar out in the large ashtray that's been used all night and is almost overflowing. "Who gave you this lead?"

"Liam O'Reagan."

Laughter comes from Big John. "Well, let's all jump on that fucking train."

I clench my jaw. "It's a solid lead, Razor."

Razor sits back and drags a leg up. I sense the hostility of these men. I didn't expect that. I thought I would be among family.

I sit back and allow my body to breathe, even if it's just for a moment. "Don't worry about it. I'm sure I'll figure it out." I knock three times on the wooden table and stare at Razor. His jaw tightens. No one stops me as I get up and leave them.

Growing up, we heard so many myths and ghost stories. Some stayed with us; some embedded themselves so deeply that we took them and made them our own.

I reenter the club and stop at the bar, waving at Andrew.

A whiskey arrives in front of me, and I finish it in one gulp. When I was young, my mother told me that a ghost would come late at night and knock three times on your door when someone in the house was about to die. People claimed this story to be true. Claimed they had received three knocks before someone in their house died.

Mrs. McLaughlin claimed she heard three knocks, and her husband Dick died the next morning.

I've taken the three knocks and used it for my own foretelling. It's a warning that I just issued to Razor for blowing me off. A warning that won't go unnoticed.

I signal Andrew for one more just as my phone rings.

"Mr. O'Hara. It's Amanda from Cabra Castle."

"What's the problem?" I ask and down the whiskey before walking away from the bar.

"We do apologize, but someone broke into your suite."

My steps grow faster as I make my way out of the club.

"Have you caught the person?"

"No, she ran off across the fields. We have security giving chase."

Dana. What the fuck was she thinking?

"Which direction did she go?"

"I'll have to find out."

"Do that and ring me back straight away." I hang up and leave the club. I'm tempted to glance back as I jog across the road and jump into my car. No doubt I'm being watched, and my antics have made me a target.

I pull out as the phone rings.

"Well?" I bark.

"She was seen running toward the river." Amanda's voice shakes.

"Describe her."

"Long black hair. Five-foot-six, maybe. She was wearing a turquoise dress."

I don't need any more information. Dana escaped.

I push my foot down on the accelerator and hang up on Amanda. It's past one in the morning. I told my mother I would stop by the house tonight. That isn't likely to happen now.

It doesn't take long to reach Cabra Castle. I'm driving parallel to the fields and stop at a gate. My car won't thank me for this, but I need to catch her before anyone else does.

The car bounces roughly across the field as I tear toward the river with my lights on bright. The water rages, and my gut tightens. How stupid is she to run close to a river at night? I spin the car as I near the river and drive alongside the thrashing water.

Speeding, I see a flash disappear into the sparse forest ahead. The excitement that's lifted by depravity roars to life. My foot touches the floor as I push the car as hard as possible, and I pull up the handbrake and spin the steering wheel. The car turns and stops with a roaring screech. The grass is torn up under the wheels. I jump out and give chase. My beast pounds its fists against my chest. I pump my legs faster as I crash through the underbrush.

I hear a scream and shift in that direction. The only light is from the moon. This is a wet fucking dream.

I could shout at her to stop. I could threaten her. I could do a lot of things, but I stop, close my eyes, and listen.

Off to my left, I hear twigs break. I take off in the direction. My father took me hunting as a kid. Tracking and hunting are in my blood, a skill that never left me.

She's close. Her noise has increased, and I slow down, not wanting the chase to be over yet.

My cock turns to heavy steel in my trousers, and all I can think about is her mouth around my shaft.

She stops running; her breathing is loud, giving away her position. I creep up close to her. She's behind a tree.

Perfect. I approach the tree and reach around, gripping her throat easily.

She squeals, but I cut it off by tightening my hand as I walk around so she can see me.

A sheen of sweat on her chest shines under the moon's light.

"What the fuck do you think you're doing?" I lean in, pushing my body hard against hers. I tighten my hold on her fragile swan-like neck.

She stiffens against me, and I loosen my hold on her neck.

"Get your hands off me."

"There you go again, princess, telling me what to do." I grin and move my face into the light so she can see me. A new light shines in the distance. I'm not the only one looking for her. I don't want this to end.

"I should punish you." I let a hand trail down her side, stopping at her large breasts. She inhales sharply as I drag my thumb across the swollen lumps. She's not wearing a bra. Her nipples harden under my touch, and she gasps in pleasure. I tighten my hand on her throat.

"You're turned on?" I push my cock harder against her.

A tremble enters her body. "Let me go."

I release her, and she sinks a little before gripping the tree. "Run," I tell her.

"What?" Terror is etched into her perfect face. "Run, princess, or I'm going to fuck you hard against the tree."

She sprints past me, and my cock roars in pain. Flashlights move closer, and I take off after Dana. She's fast but easily tracked. I hunt her for another ten minutes, putting distance between us and the other men.

She's breathless when I stop her, and this time, she's trembling. She's easy to pin to a large tree. Her head rises as I grip her neck, and I see the excitement mixed with dread in her eyes.

"Don't move," I warn her. She hasn't tried to pull my hand away, but I release her neck as I slide to my knees. Her chest rises and falls rapidly, and her eyes widen as I push up her little turquoise dress. Her panties tear easily in my hand as I remove them.

She's soaking, and I bury my face into her sweet wet cunt. Her hands sink into my hair, and I run my tongue along her clit.

Gripping a leg, I hoist it up on my shoulder so I have full access to her pussy. I taste her again, sinking my tongue inside her before running it along her swollen clit.

I hear the noise growing closer before Dana tries to drag her leg back down, but I don't allow the movement.

"Cillian," she whispers, sounding disorientated, "someone is coming."

"Let them watch." I lick her again, and she gasps but tries to pull her leg away. I release her this time before getting off my knees. I don't give Dana a second before I harshly press my lips to hers, wetting her face with her juices.

She's startled when I grip her nipple and squeeze. "Run, Dana."

She's shaking her head. "You're fucking sick. I don't want to do this."

"Run, or you can suck my cock."

She darts again. I hear her whimper of fear, and it's the most delicious food to my beast. The men are close—a few more feet, and they'll see me. I take off after Dana, only I don't leave the gap as long as before but grip her by the neck and spin her so she's moving across the forest and away from the men.

"Run," I bark, and she does. I think she's starting to enjoy our little game.

Everything in me throbs. All I can think about is fucking her pussy. I should be worried about Liam, but right now, I'm the hunter, and Dana is my prey.

When the noise of the men disappears, I catch up with Dana. She's stopped behind a tree again, making this too easy. I walk around, and she lets out a scream that freezes me. The delay costs me, but I jump forward and slam my hand over her mouth. She sinks her teeth into my palm, and the pain she inflicts on me, I inflict right back, slamming her into the tree. She cries out, her teeth leaving my skin.

"What a fucking stupid thing to do," I whisper, done playing with my food.

I remove my damaged hand, not ready for her attack. She runs her nails down the left side of my face before sprinting away.

Fuck. Pain burns my face, and excitement mixes with pain as I give chase.

"You know what I like, princess," I mock, not keeping my voice down.

"Fuck you!" Her roar has me moving faster, only this time, not to silence her.

"You talk a lot about fucking."

I'm close when she dives to the right, and I don't stop. She's moving back toward the castle. Exactly where I need her to go.

"Is that what you want, princess?" I ask.

She stumbles, and it's all I need to reach her and grip the back of her neck.

Her lip trembles. "You're sick."

I tighten my hold and whisper in her ear. "You have no fucking idea."

The words have her growing rigid under me. Her breath grows shallow, and for a moment, there's nothing else but she and I, standing in the forest that's blanketed by darkness and filled with her growing terror.

I force her to walk, not letting her go until my mud-covered car comes into sight.

I release her neck. "You can either get in, or I'll put you in the trunk."

She stumbles and looks at me with the anger of a possessed woman.

I grin. "Which is it, princess?"

I'll give her five seconds before I make the decision for her.

CHAPTER NINE

DANA

"Pick, princess." Cillian takes a threatening step toward me.

Flashlight beams split the darkness with sharp rays that bleed into the trees. Cillian glances back at the tree line. I could run back; I could beg them to save me. But from whom? Cillian? My father?

My vision blurs as I walk around to the passenger side. I get in. Cillian slams his door, and the loud bang sends my heart pounding. It's so final, so frightening; I'm trapped. My fingers reach for the door handle, but Cillian has already started to drive. Mud splashes against the side of the car. The faster he goes, the higher the mud hits, and it soon covers my window. Cillian tears out onto the road. He doesn't even stop to see if any other traffic is coming. I cling to the seat before frantically reaching for my seat belt. We hit the road hard. I lose the seat belt as I'm lifted off the seat. I slam back down and grip the handle above the door. I glance at Cillian again. His knuckles have turned white from the death grip he has on the steering wheel.

"What were you running from?" The words are growled at me.

Is he fucking serious?

"You."

He glances at me, and surprise flitters in his eyes before they grow dark and hard again—laughter bursts from his perfect mouth. The sound sends my head and stomach into a spin.

"Oh, princess. You are a piece of fucking work."

Confusion and anger have me ignoring him as I get my seat belt finally latched into place.

We drive further away from the castle, and my gut tightens. Dread makes a slow and cold path along my spine. My summer dress feels light, and the air feels cold.

"Where are we going?"

No answer.

His phone rings, and he removes it from his pocket and glances at the screen before tightening his jaw. He appears as if he's debating about answering it.

He answers.

"Bednar Novak was a dead end."

I can't hear the voice on the other end, but I'm listening since he's speaking about the name my father wrote on the piece of paper.

Cillian glances at me, and I can't read the look that flashes in his eyes. More icy fingers grip the back of my neck.

"I want a meeting with Bednar Novak." The look that Cillian gives me should have me reaching for the door handle. He hangs up the phone and refocuses on the road.

"Where are we going?"

Cillian returns to driving like a lunatic.

"Where the fuck are we going?" I scream and garner his attention for a fleeting second. "I want my father," I demand.

"You won't be seeing your daddy for a long time."

My heart crashes frantically against my chest. What does that mean? Where is he taking me? What is going to happen to me?

My throat starts to close.

Cillian looks at me again, and he wears a disturbingly happy smile. "Your father fucked up."

I lash out. "Stop the car." My hand connects with his face, which already sports nail marks from earlier.

The car swerves. Cillian gets control, and I'm jerked forward as he jams on the brakes before I'm slammed back into the seat. The air is ripped from my lungs at the impact. I have no time to react before Cillian is in my personal space. His hand grips my throat.

"You listen to me."

Horror plunges so deep into my heart that it's like a sharp knife being dragged across my bare flesh. All the hairs rise on the back of my neck. I push myself deeper into the seat. My breathing returns in quick and shallow gasps that sound as frenzied as I am inside.

"You don't get to ask any fucking questions. You keep your mouth shut and do as I say." His fingers tighten like a vise around my throat.

A smile that's jarring sends my heartbeat roaring, forcing too much blood around my body. "Nod if you understand."

I blink and nod slowly. His hand loosens, but my breathing is erratic as hysteria crowds in around me.

Cillian doesn't move away but forces his fist into his mouth like he's trying to force some words back down his throat. Words he is clearly too angry to share.

I'm still nodding when he removes his fist.

Something red hot and scorching takes over—the need to know what's happening. The warning in Cillian's behavior tells me to keep my mouth shut. His angry gaze settles on my mouth. My understanding of what is going on is like a thin string of pearls that snaps and scatters across the car floor.

I'm ready to open my mouth, even against my instincts. Cillian's phone rings, and he releases me completely and gives me back some of my personal space. He's staring at the phone. He jabs the red button before he scrolls through his contacts and hits someone else's number.

My fingers tremble as I reach for the door handle. I'm so close.

"I need a safe house." Cillian speaks into the phone, and in his moment of distraction, I think I can escape.

The locks click noisily. The air is pulled from my lungs once again as I turn and face Cillian.

An explosion of rage erupts behind Cillian's eyes, and his fingers tighten around his phone. The hard plastic rebels, and I'm waiting for the phone to snap.

"Fine. Just get the address."

He hangs up and pulls back out onto the road. Bile rises up my throat as I stare at this dangerous stranger.

We drive in heavy silence. Every once in a while, Cillian flashes me an angry look. I have no idea what's going through his head, but I try to keep still and quiet.

Night turns to day. His phone rings several times, but each time he looks at the screen, he hangs up. I'm exhausted. My body trembles with a tiredness I've never felt before, but I don't dare close my eyes. I need to see where we're going. We leave the main roads and enter a maze of back roads. A new terror squeezes my heart; I have no idea how to get back.

The car slows down, and in the light of day, Cillian's eyes are a dark green lightless glass that has trepidation dripping slowly down my back.

The car stops outside a small white cottage with a green tin roof. "Get out."

My stiff fingers scramble to open the door, but I don't get far as the belt keeps me pinned to the seat. I reach to remove it, but the click of the seat belt opening has me looking up at Cillian. He's already vacating the car.

My legs feel heavy as I follow him to the cottage. It's like lead fills my shoes. Cillian's broad back looks bigger than before. His hands are larger, more dangerous. His gaze is more deadly than ever before.

I glance around at the forested area that surrounds the small cottage. My heart is pounding. It's almost painful but slowly rhythmic against my chest.

Cillian opens the red door that's been painted one too many times. He holds open the door for me, not to be a gentleman, but because he doesn't trust me.

I have to dip my head and walk under his arm. He's on my heels as we step into a small hallway. The stone floor under my feet has been polished recently. The door to my left has a latch with no handle. Cillian reaches over my head once again and presses down the latch. I step into a wide living space with a cold open fireplace. As I step in, I can see a small kitchen around the corner.

"Stay here." Cillian removes his suit jacket. The marks on his face are stark and red as he faces me fully before leaving the room.

An invisible fist punches me in the chest. The room grows smaller, and I spin, looking for an anchor to keep me from passing out. I walk to the sink and turn on the cold taps. Sticking my hands under them, the ice-cold water causes a sharp pain, taking the focus off my chest. For a moment, it's like a crack in a rock, and I'm oozing fear that manifests into an onslaught of tears I can't control. I keep my hands in the sink as I cry for every moment I felt freedom, only to have it ripped from me.

My father placed me here, but I wanted him now. I want my daddy.

The air is thin as I turn away from the sink and face the rest of the room. Water drips from my wet and numb fingers while I make my way back to the closed living room door that leads out into the hall. I don't open it. Cillian is in the hall, and he's not alone.

I recognize the voice: Shay.

He's my cousin. I should be banging on the door for him to help me. I should be opening the door so that he can see me.

My legs carry me away from the door as numbness spreads from my hands across my whole body.

CHAPTER TEN

CILLIAN

"What did you do?" Shay lights up a cigarette.

My face aches, but I try not to touch my cheek. I've been stabbed, shot at, had several broken bones, but the scratches on my face sting like a motherfucker and distract me.

Her scratches.

"He said he could help me find my sister. He lied."

Shay looks at me from under his lashes. "He's a fucking liar." Shay jerks his chin toward the living room door. "You alone?" He's reaching for the latch.

"No. I've Dana with me." I see the shift in his gaze as he steps back. "He fucked me over. I won't get my sister without a bargaining chip."

Shay throws the cigarette onto the tiled hall floor. "You dragged me into this." He turns his back on me before spinning around. "You're some cunt."

"I'm your friend who's asking for help."

"Listen to yourself. You took Liam's daughter. My cousin." Shay stares at me like I've lost my fucking mind.

Maybe I have.

"I want my sister back, and I don't care who the fuck I have to sacrifice to get her." Anger tightens my fists and closes the distance between Shay and me.

He grins dangerously. "I'm very fucking concerned right now, Cillian." Shay turns away from me again. Thinking. Analyzing.

"Does Liam know you took her?" He glances at me over his shoulder. When I don't answer, he shakes his head. "You're a fucking moron."

I'm shaking my head. "I had no other choice. She escaped. He fucked me over, so I took her." A split-second decision.

Shay laughs, but the sound dies quickly. He reaches for the latch and opens the living room door. Dana is sitting on the floor against the couch, and she looks like she's been chased through a forest and kidnapped.

Shay flashes me a warning before he steps into the room. Dana doesn't react. She has tracks of tears down her cheeks. Shay approaches slowly. He kneels down in front of her. "You okay, love?"

"Fuck you, Shay."

I smile at her feisty words. No matter the odds, she still holds on to her temper.

Shay laughs and takes out a pack of cigarettes. He offers her one. She shakes her head, and he lights his own.

"Listen, love. It's going to be okay."

She looks up at him. Her gaze flickers to me before returning to Shay. "I want my father."

Shay rises while nodding his head. He takes a pull of his cigarette. "We can arrange that."

I have no idea why the fuck he's lying to her.

Shay steps back into the hall and closes the door, cutting off my view of Dana.

"Frankie, my brother, was killed in a cage fight." Shay isn't looking at me as he speaks. He takes another pull of his cigarette, and smoke circles him.

"I'm sorry," I mumble.

"I did everything to find out what happened to him." He looks up at me. "I found his killer, Cillian. I know you want your sister back, but this"—he points to the door that Dana is behind—"isn't the way."

"I have no other choice," I say.

"Call Liam—"

I cut off Shay. "I tried to get help from the Jaguars, but they won't help me. I'm backed into a fucking corner. I'm not calling him."

I touch my cheek again. The pain is a bitch. Shay's gaze zeroes in on the nail marks. "I've no one else to turn to."

"I have your back. Always, Cillian. But this is a mistake. I won't have a hand in this."

I turn my back on Shay and run my hands through my hair.

"Listen to me, Cillian. Liam doesn't like being threatened. He'll kill your sister out of pure spite."

The image of my sister being hurt torments me. "She's my sister."

Shay moves quickly and grips the back of my neck, dragging me toward him. "I swear to God, Cillian. I get it." Pain like I've never seen before radiates loudly in Shay's eyes.

Energy slowly leaches out of my body.

"If you don't hand Dana over, everyone you love will die. Fuck, if he finds out I'm here, he'll hurt everyone I care about."

His words have the pain riding higher inside me. The cost of losing my family is too steep. My mother has lost enough, my sister... Quick flashes of memories dig into my flesh.

"Does he know you took Dana?"

I shake my head. "No. He knows I have her, but I didn't specify my intentions," I confirm.

Shay leans back and opens the front door; he flicks the cigarette outside before turning back to me.

"Tell Liam she tried to escape, so you aren't sure who saw. You took her to a safe house to keep her safe."

I'm already shaking my head.

"Don't be so fucking stubborn. You want your sister back? Stay in his graces. Make amends with the Jaguars. Pull your head out of your ass, and you will get your sister back."

Slowly, very slowly, Shay's words sink in.

"What were you going to do, Cillian? Threaten Dana?"

"Yes," I answer.

"You wouldn't just have Liam to deal with. You'd have Richard and Jack too."

I look at the door like I can still see Dana sitting on the floor. "And what about you, Shay? Would I still have you?"

Shay grins. The look on his face is familiar. "That doesn't matter, because you're going to use your fucking head. Tell him you were being followed. You panicked and got her to safety. He will reward you."

I can hear each word Shay is saying, but calling Liam O'Reagan after the fucking goose chase he sent me on has a lump of rage forming in my throat.

"I don't think I can, Shay," I admit.

"Then pick out your sister's coffin."

I can't answer as hot hate burns up my blood.

"And your mother's. And anyone else you love. Because that is what happens when you fuck with Liam."

The next words pain me. "I'll make the call."

Something close to relief flitters across Shay's face.

I take out my phone, but my fingers won't move across the screen. "Did you ever get the person who killed your brother?"

The relief flees Shay's features, and he's violent all of a sudden. Everything about him—his eyes, his jaw, even his fucking teeth—appears violent, dangerous, deadly.

"No, but I know who did it."

"Who?"

"You make that call, and I'll tell you."

Liam answers on the third ring. "This better be good." His voice is low, but the current is lethal.

"She escaped. The Castle rang me. When I tracked her down, she wasn't alone. I think someone knew she was there."

Silence. Uncomfortable silence. I glance at Shay, who's lit another cigarette.

"Where is my daughter?"

The temptation to tell him I have her and he'll never see her again has my lip tugging up.

Shay's ready to take a pull of his cigarette. He reads something on my face that makes him tilt his head and shift his body toward me.

"Cillian." The growl from Liam has me looking away from Shay.

"She's here at a safe house."

"Good."

Is that relief I hear in Liam's voice?

"I want to speak to my daughter," Liam asks.

It's an understandable request, but I don't move.

"What, you don't trust me?" I find myself questioning.

Shay shakes his head.

"Your sister," Shay mouths.

"I'll get her now," I tell Liam. The moment I click down the latch, Dana glances up at me from the floor. My gut tightens with something similar to guilt.

"Your father." I hold out the phone, and she jumps off the ground and snatches the device out of my hand. I'm waiting for her to start wailing that I manhandled her. I'd deny the accusations and say I was only trying to get her to safety.

She smiles through a sob. "Hi, Daddy."

I can't hear what Liam is saying.

"Yes. Yes." Dana looks at me with pure hate in her eyes. "No." She turns her back on me, her shoulders hunched.

"Remember two years ago when I stayed in Italy?"

I zone out as she talks about her travels. Maybe she wants to go traveling again. A real fucking Mafia princess.

Shay is watching me.

"Philip... He hit me." I pause at the threshold at Dana's words. I shouldn't care.

But I do.

Dana snivels. "I often wondered what happened to him."

"What did you do?" She's sobbing.

I look at Shay, who shrugs.

I leave the living space and pull the door slightly closed.

"You did the right thing." Shay slaps my shoulder. The relief he's showcasing isn't just for me.

A fist tightens in my gut. "So who killed Frankie?" I ask. The answer, I think I know.

Shay holds his head high. "Liam."

"Fuck, Shay. Does your dad know?"

Connor O'Reagan wouldn't take something like that lightly.

Shay shakes his head. "I never told my da. He needs his peace."

"And you?" I ask. Shay isn't a man at peace. He is at odds with the world, and now he is making more sense to me.

"Peace." He sneers. "Like a motherfucking unicorn."

What happens now? That's what I want to ask, but Dana is wailing in the other room. Her sobs cease, and I'm ready to go in when the door opens. She hands me the phone. I take the device from her, and she turns on her heel and sits on the couch, curling herself into a tiny ball. She wears a look of devastation. What the fuck did he say to her?

I raise the phone to my ear.

Liam speaks. "Cillian."

"Yes," I answer and pull the door closed.

"I gave you a meeting with Bednar Novak. But you disrespected that appointment."

"He kept me waiting over an hour."

"Did you not train with the special forces? Can I assume patience is something they drilled into you? Maybe you missed that part?"

Bastard.

"I did train with special forces and qualified. But the only life on the line was my own. My sister's life is on the line, so my patience is a bit frayed."

Shay's eyeballing me. I can almost read the waves that pour off him for me to tone my attitude down.

"She's close to Dana's age," I find myself saying.

"Don't bite the hand that feeds you, Cillian."

You don't fucking feed me.

"I'll be in touch." Liam hangs up, and I look up at Shay.

"I'll help you kill him."

CHAPTER ELEVEN

DANA

"WHAT DID YOU DO?"

"Dana, why are you asking me about this?" My father isn't fazed by my line of questioning.

I'm sniffing and trying to compose myself and control the hysteria that wants to save me from this new reality. My body wants to crash and leave here, even just for a while.

"You said you don't hurt people."

"I never said that."

I bite my lip.

"Did I ever say I don't hurt people?" he questions. My father is moving around.

"What did you do to Philip?" I ask again. My heartbeat has reached its maximum rate that throbs in my ears.

"He will never put his hands on you again."

My legs give out, and I'm burning up from the inside. Sobs consume me. "I hung posters up with his mother!"

"Put Cillian back on the phone."

"I want my mother!" My screams are dipped in wildness. "You took her son from her." I blink and tears spill. "How could you?"

"I know this is a lot for you, Dana. But I need you to be brave." His words don't calm me.

"I need my mother." I'm slowly pulling myself together. "I can't do this." My voice is low, a whisper of pain.

"Put Cillian on the phone."

I sob. "No."

"Dana."

The warning in his voice isn't one I've heard before. My feet carry me to the door, and I open it. Cillian and Shay stare at me. I hand the phone to Cillian, and he takes it. I want to tell him what my father has done.

"Yes." Cillian's voice has me closing the door and returning to the couch. I can't sit still for long; my mind hasn't stopped reeling. I'm on a fast track, and I'm not sure how to get off. I stand again and wrap my arms around my waist, walking up and down the room.

I'm startled when a set of arms wrap around my shoulders. I can smell smoke and know it's Shay. He's not my favorite person in the world right now, but I need someone, so I spin and cling to him. He hesitates, holding me, but finally, he hugs me and pulls my head into his chest.

"Get it out, love."

"Fuck you, Shay," I say through sobs. I'm sick of men telling me what to do. But my loneliness keeps me in my cousin's arms.

In that moment, I go back to Italy. I go back to the days of pinning up posters of Philip's handsome face. His mother's eyes held a devastation I tried to keep away from. I never told anyone that he put his hands on me. It was only once. He said he was sorry and that he loved me. The next day, Philip vanished. I finally know why.

Another sob breaks me. His younger sister helped hang up posters; she was five. Francessa shouldn't have had to face a loss at such a young age. Now I know why it happened. It was because of my father.

Through the memories and pain, time fizzles away, and I'm surprised that Shay hasn't run from me. Cillian has reentered the room and left on several occasions. The last two, he's let out heavy sighs. I want to lash out at him, tell him to just leave us alone.

"What's going to happen?" My voice cracks and breaks.

Shay releases me instantly, like my words are magic and have freed him from a crying female.

"You feel better, love?" He holds my shoulders. He's trying.

I nod. "Yeah." Did I feel better? No. All I feel is a crushing sensation I'm trying to keep at bay.

Shay releases me, but he doesn't run. I'm awkward as I stand in front of him. I wrap my arms around my waist. Cillian steps into the room again. A muscle twitches in his jaw before he leaves, and this time, he doesn't close the door behind him.

"You want to talk about it?" Shay asks.

I look at my cousin. "Do you really care?" I ask.

Shay lights up a cigarette, offers me one, and I decline.

"I was engaged."

Shay's brows rise as he takes a drag of his cigarette. "Congrats."

"My fiancé went missing."

Shay forces a smile. "There's plenty more fish in the sea."

I should end this conversation. Talking to him about feelings is like talking to a nun about sex.

Yet my mouth keeps moving.

"My father killed him." My vision blurs as I continue to let that knowledge sink in.

"What did he do?" Shay asks.

"Maybe he did nothing." The lie sounds feeble and stupid. "He put his hands on me."

"Your da was protecting you, Dana."

I nod. Cillian reenters the room, and I catch his eye. "So anyone who puts their hands on me without my permission will die," I say plainly.

Cillian meets my gaze fully, but no fear enters his features. I wonder if he is remembering chasing me through the forest.

"It doesn't work quite like that, love," Shay admits.

"Exactly. Because it wouldn't suit my father to kill, let's say, you, for argument's sake. I mean, you kidnapped me and handed me over to him." I point at Cillian, refusing to give him a name.

"I did it to protect you, and your brothers gave me their approval."

"What about my fucking approval?" I'm snapping, the seams of my sanity loosening. "What about Philip's mother? What about his sister? Did they give their approval to have Philip killed?"

"You need to calm down," Shay says, and it's the wrong thing.

"Calm down. Are you fucking kidding me?"

"Lock her in a room until she calms down." Cillian flicks a hand in my direction like I'm some pest.

"No one will lock you in a room," Shay says instantly.

I'm ready to launch myself at Cillian. "I need fresh air," I bark.

Cillian snorts. "So you can run away?" Something else enters his gaze.

My cheeks heat. "I can't breathe in here."

"Let her go," Shay says.

Cillian holds out his arms. "That's on you," he says to Shay.

"I'll take responsibility." Shay walks toward me. My cousin has always carried a menacing air about him, but knowing who he is makes that menacing air grow and rise in a way I can't fully calculate.

"Some fresh air, then back in, love."

I nod. I have no intention of running. I leave the small cottage and go outside. Morning has come again. In the light of day, things often feel better, but not for me.

I can't get Philip's weeping mother out of my head. They never found him. I cover my face with my hands to try to keep the trepidation that's rattling my bones at bay.

I don't know how much time has passed when the door opens.

I glance at Shay.

"Did Cillian put his hands on you? Is that why you were asking what your father would do?"

I'd laugh if I had any energy left. "If Cillian turns up dead, you'll get your answer. Won't you?" Anger bites into my words.

"That's not an answer, Dana." A warning enters Shay's voice.

I face my cousin fully. "What would you do, Shay?"

Shay takes a step toward me. I hold still. "Tell me."

It's a command.

I could say he did, but each time Cillian touched me, I had wanted it. I had craved his touch—my cheeks heat.

"No," I answer honestly. "I'm going to bed."

Shay doesn't stop me as I enter the small cottage. Cillian's presence in the living space draws my gaze, and I meet his eye. Was he listening to Shay's and my conversation? I look away and enter the small room that has a double bed facing the door. There's no lock on the door. I didn't think either Cillian or Shay would come in here. In fact, they will avoid me.

I climb into the bed, and I'm waiting for the tears to come, but my exhausted body falls into a deep slumber. I wake with the afternoon sun pouring into the room, some parts still covered in shadows that shift. My heart gallops as my vision adjusts. Green eyes stare at me from the corner of the room.

"Cillian?" I say his name, and confusion and awareness crash into me at once.

He doesn't speak as all the events smash into me at once. "Philip." Covering my mouth, I try to suppress the agony of knowing he's dead.

"Here are some fresh clothes." Cillian's words are tight, like he's fighting for control.

He places a bundle of dark clothes at the foot of the bed. Black isn't a color I wear.

"I hate black," I mumble.

Cillian snorts. "Of course you do, princess."

My gaze snaps to Cillian. The sneer on his face twists my stomach painfully.

"Get out of my room."

His gaze trails down to my chest. My face heats because I hate that if he came closer, if he reached out and touched me, I wouldn't stop him.

With a final sneer, he turns on his heel and leaves me. I don't lie back down; my heart is too heavy, and I need to get my mind off Philip. I pick up the clothes and leave the bedroom.

The tiny bathroom has no lock, either. I'm not feeling as settled about showering with an unlocked door, but I don't have a choice.

I don't delay but wash and change into a fresh pair of black sweatpants and a black T-shirt. They fit okay.

Opening up the mirrored cabinet above the sink, I find a toothbrush in a wrapper, along with some toothpaste. I brush my teeth and wash my face. I find a comb and spend some time combing my hair out.

I leave the bathroom, and the tiles in the hallway are cool under my feet. When I enter the living room, Shay is still there. That surprises me.

"How are you feeling, love?" Shay asks while sipping out of a piping hot mug of coffee.

"Better." It's the truth. I'm still shaky, but I do feel better.

I hadn't noticed Cillian until he stepped out of the small kitchen area. He looks larger in the light of day, and more handsome.

My abdomen aches, and I sit down on the couch beside Shay.

Cillian's gaze hardens. "I'm heading out for a while. Don't even try to leave." His anger is directed at me.

I'm feeling brave with my cousin beside me. "Or what?" I spit back.

I don't think he'll threaten me in front of Shay, but Cillian takes a step toward me. "Or I let you run." His smirk is cold and sends waves of fear, along with want, down my spine.

If I run, he'll chase. I take a peek at Shay, who continues to drink his coffee. He has no idea what happened in the forest, and I need to keep it that way.

I look away from Cillian.

"I'll check-in." This is directed to Shay.

The moment Cillian leaves, I don't feel relief like I should. I find I want to know where he is going. When will he be back?

"You hungry, love?" Shay asks.

"Yeah," I mumble, my mind still on Cillian. I get up and walk to the window. I can't see a vehicle, but I'm sure I see a flash of dark clothing move through the forest.

"I cook a mean sausage," Shay announces.

I turn and follow him into the small kitchen. There's no table or chairs, just a breakfast bar that I sit at. Cillian's empty plate and cup are stacked in front of me.

Shay puts the sausages in the pan. I pick up Cillian's fork and place it into my mouth. I have no idea what possessed me to want to taste it.

Heat scorches me, and I drop the fork. The noise has Shay glancing at me over his shoulder. A cigarette hangs out of his mouth as he cooks my food.

I want to tell him not to get ashes in my food, but instead, I gather up the plate and mug, carry them to the sink, and start washing them. My mind is still stuck on Cillian.

"Where did he go?" I ask the suds.

"Who? Cillian?"

I should drop this line of questioning. I shouldn't show that I care. "Yeah."

Shay takes his sweet time before answering. "I don't know, Dana."

I'm so used to him saying love that I turn to him. He's really looking at me.

"Cillian and I used to rob kegs when we were kids." Shay turns the sausages and puts out his cigarette.

"Always knew you were trouble." I dry my hands.

Shay grins. "I'm the innocent one."

I laugh. "I remember you always getting Jack into trouble."

Shay tuts and wags his finger. He wears a grin. "Dana, my love. You have no idea. Jack was such a little fucker."

He's right. They were thick as thieves. I want to know more about Cillian as a boy. "Did you and Cillian drink the kegs?"

Shay laughs. "No. We used them to build a fort."

"A fort. Such boys," I tease, and this moment is nice with Shay.

Shay plates up our food and brings it to the breakfast bar. I sit down beside him. "We finally got caught."

Shay cuts up his sausage and starts to eat.

"I suppose you boys got sent to your rooms?" I'm smiling at my food. When I look at Shay, my smile melts off my face.

"No. Cillian took the heat off me. His father dealt with him."

Shay returns to his food. "How?"

I'm thinking of the scars all over his body. No. No father would do that, but there is something in Shay's eyes that almost confirms it.

"How, Shay?" Why did this matter so much to me?

"Dana, Cillian is a good friend, and I'd trust him with my life. But most of us move through life and end up a bit fucked up in the head. There's fucked up, and then there's Cillian's level of fucked up."

"His father beat him?" I ask.

"Yes. Dana, Cillian isn't a place you want to go, love. You hear me?"

My cheeks burn. "Yeah. I hear you."

"I'm fucking serious, Dana."

My appetite plummets while my anger soars. I glare at Shay. "What's with you men telling me what I can and cannot do? I'm sick of it." I start to leave the kitchen, when Shay lets out a string of curses.

"I'm sorry. Come back." He's never this soft, and that scares me. Maybe his feeling badly will give me some answers. I stop walking but don't turn around.

"Come on, Dana. I just slaved over a stove making you breakfast."

I turn. "It was two sausages, Shay. Hardly slaving."

He's grinning. "I don't cook."

"How long do I have to stay here?"

Shay's humor flees. He returns to the kitchen, and I follow. "That is something I can't answer." He finishes his breakfast while I glare at him.

"Am I in danger?" I ask.

"I can't answer that either."

"My father said I was a target."

He picks up his plate. "Then you're a target." He makes it sound like it's not a big deal.

"I can't protect myself." It's whispered, but Shay hears it.

"Cillian will protect you."

I step fully into the kitchen. "What if Cillian isn't here?"

"I'm here. Or if I'm not here, I'm sure someone else will be," Shay answers before I can ask more questions.

"I want to know how to protect myself." I fold my arms over my chest. "I know your father is a boxer, and so are you. You can teach me."

Shay hides a grin, but I see it peeking through.

"I'm not joking, Shay. I'm not some fucking damsel. I want to know how to survive." Anger has me unfolding my arms.

"I'll think about it," Shay says.

I'm ready to have another go. "I said I'll think about it, Dana."

CHAPTER TWELVE

CILLIAN

I TRUST SHAY WITH my life. But placing all that control in Liam's hands doesn't feel right to me. I can't stay for one more second in the cottage with Dana crying.

I told Shay I had business, but I didn't. I decided to check in on my mother. Not showing up last night would have made her worry. But sitting in the house and drinking tea with her has been agony.

"What's troubling you?" my mother asks. She's wearing a long-sleeved black dress, and her blonde hair is pinned up high on top of her head.

Since we buried my father just yesterday, most people wouldn't ask such a question, but my mother knows me too well.

"Work stuff," I rumble.

"Is that what kept you away last night?"

"Yeah. I have a new assignment that's taken longer to wrap up than I thought it would."

My mother reaches out and touches my hand. "Are you sure that's all?"

My mother should have been a leader. She has the ability to make harsh decisions under the most strenuous situations, which would bring most men to their knees, but not her. She rose to her feet through adversity, and I love every inch of her for that. She's strong when she needs to be but kind when necessary—like now, touching my hand comforting me.

"I promise. Don't you worry." I remove my hand from hers and get up.

"Edward told me you joined the Jaguars."

I place my cup slowly in the sink. "When were you talking to Skinner?"

"He came by last night to give me his condolences." There is a tightness in her words.

I return to the table so I can look her in the eyes. "He had no right to tell you."

She forces a smile. "I already knew you would join one day. It flows in your blood." My mother holds my gaze, and there is so much more to that statement that I back away from.

"Yes, I am part of the Jaguars." I need to tell her about Liam. "Before someone else says this to you, Liam O'Reagan offered me a position with him."

"A king. I heard."

My mother's words hold a bitterness.

"Skinner," I bark, wondering what the fuck he's playing at.

"Yes." My mother reaches out and places her hand over mine. "Cillian, my son. I can't bury you too." She half smiles. "I don't think that is a loss I could bear."

"That won't happen," I reassure her.

She nods. "Good. Edward will help you in any way possible. He gave me his word."

"Don't go making bargains on my behalf. Jesus, Mother, what did you barter with?"

She waves me off but gets up from the table with her own mug. "We have been friends for a lifetime. Edward thinks a lot of you."

What utter bullshit. Edward doesn't like me. But I don't bring that up. The fact that I already went to the Jaguars for help and they turned me down tells me he was just entertaining my mother. So I do the same.

"Okay. Thanks, Mother."

My mother plants a kiss on the top of my head. She lingers, and I wonder what she is thinking.

"I'll be away for a few days. Will you be okay?" I ask.

My mother steps away from me. "Of course. Just check in."

I get up and push in the chair. "I will. I love you."

My mother walks me to the front door. "Love you too."

I place a kiss on her cheek before departing.

***

I take my time going back to the safe house. I stop by my home and get some fresh clothes and weapons. I also return to Cabra Castle.

No one is around as I enter the suite. Dana's bedroom is pristine. Opening the wardrobe, all I smell is her.

She's not good for my system. I pull down as many clothes as I can and stuff them into a suitcase that sits on top of the wardrobe. I empty her drawers. I stuff her undergarments in quickly as my cock starts to grow.

I return to my room and take out my spare phone, gun, and money. I leave, and by the time I return to the cottage, the sky has darkened. I'm surprised Shay hasn't rung me wondering where I went. I leave the bags in the car and return empty-handed.

The moment I enter, I pause in the hallway. I listen to her laughter. She sounds carefree—a side I've never seen. Shay is spinning some story, and she's eating it up. My fists tighten, and I talk myself out of barging in and gripping him by the throat.

He's my best friend and her fucking cousin, I remind myself.

I get a grip on my anger and enter the room. Her laughter stops, and that pisses me off further. She's sitting cross-legged on the couch. The black sweat pants and T-shirt look delicious on her. Her hair is dragged over one shoulder, her cheeks flushed with her previous happiness.

"Don't stop on my account." I close the door behind me.

"I was just telling Dana a few tales about her brothers."

"Riveting, I'm sure."

"God, you're an asshole." Dana gets up off the couch and storms from the room.

I feel like an asshole, but I don't let it show.

"Sorry I took so long," I say to Shay.

He doesn't respond, but he's watching me. I've known him long enough to know something is up.

"You don't have to stick around." I remove my suit jacket.

Shay gets up and moves behind the couch. He bends over and reappears with a bottle of Jack. "For emergencies."

"I'll get the glasses." I unbutton my shirt, get two glasses from the top cabinet, and return to the living room. Shay has the bottle open and is drinking from it.

I hold out the two glasses, and he fills them up.

When he's put the lid back on the bottle, I hand him his drink and sit down with mine. "What a fucking day." I clink my glass with his and drink it down.

"I keep thinking of all the ways I want to kill him." Shay empties his glass. He doesn't have to say who he is talking about. After what he did to Frankie, I know it's Liam. I don't blame Shay.

"Each time, it's not enough. It's not slow enough. It's not painful enough." Shay bends down, picks up the bottle, and refills his glass. I honestly never knew the effect his brother's death had on him. But I get it. My sister isn't dead, but some days it feels like it. Not knowing, I think, is worse. Hope is dangerous, and it's something I've clung to all this time. My biggest regret is allowing my father to take the lead, believing he would bring her home safely. I hold out my glass to Shay, and he refills it. "To taking him down." I clink my glass with Shay's. Whatever he needs me to do, I'll be there for him.

Speaking of killing Liam while his daughter is in the next room keeps my mind tied to Dana. She's a sinking ship, one I need to get off. In theory, ignoring her seems wise. But in reality, when she's in the same room, I'm drawn to her. It's her beauty; it's her spirit.

"Did she eat?" I ask.

"Earlier on. But I'm sure she's hungry." Shay speaks to his empty glass. When he glances at me, an uncertainty clouds his gaze.

"Say it, Shay." I empty my glass.

"She's been through so much."

I get off the couch, anger pushing me away from Shay. "Aoibhe's in a trafficking ring. Dana's holed up in a safe house, fed, warm, and unharmed." I shake my head to stop more bitter words from pouring out.

Shay nods. "Okay."

"She's still my responsibility, so I'll make her some food." I don't look at Shay in case he can hear the lie in my words.

The sad fact is, I don't like the idea of her being hungry.

"I'm heading out for some fresh air." Shay leaves, and I open several cupboards, looking to see what I can make for Dana. I'm aware I have no idea what she actually likes—we don't have the food here that was served to her in the castle.

I opt for a salad; it's easy to make, and I've seen her eat one before. I make a cup of tea and then carry them to her bedroom door. I'm tempted to knock, but I don't.

I push up the latch with my shoulder and step in. She's sitting cross-legged on the bed. Her mouth opens, no doubt ready to tell me to get the fuck out. Blue eyes swim with pain, and I find once again that I don't get her.

A small side table along the wall is empty, and I put the food and tea down without a word. I look back at Dana, and she's watching me. Her cheeks turn pink.

Glancing around the room buys me some time. I want to ask about Philip. The thought of anyone putting their hands on her doesn't sit well with me.

"Tell me about Philip." My voice is harsh, and I'm waiting for her to tell me to fuck off.

"You don't really care about Philip." Pain mixed with resentment lines her words.

She's right; I don't care about Philip. Another glass of whiskey sounds like what I need right now.

"He was my fiancé."

She tightens her hands in her lap. "He wasn't a bad person." She speaks to her fingers. "He had a younger sister, Francesca-Rose, but we called her Fran." Dana smiles, and a tear slips from the corner of her eye.

I regret asking. I don't give two fucks about Philip or his family.

"We had too many drinks one night. He was mad about my talking to the bartender." She shrugs. "When we got home, the fight escalated..." She lifts her dark lashes, and I'm staring into a pair of crystal blue eyes. "He hit me."

I shift my stance.

She shrugs again. "It was only once." Her voice is as small as her excuse.

"The next morning, I woke up, and he was gone."

Silence. She shrugs again. Her gaze slides away from mine and to the food.

I'm holding her up from eating. "Go ahead and eat."

She nods and watches me like she's waiting for me to leave. But I can't.

Dana eventually slides off the bed and over to the salad. She brings it back to the bed. I can gather that her awkward movements are due to me watching her.

"Then what happened?" I ask. I walk away from the door so she can relax and eat.

"What do you mean?"

I look out the small window that looks out onto a tense part of the forest.

"What happened to Philip?"

"I don't know. I never found him."

I have to look at Dana to gauge her reaction. Is she happy or sad about that fact?

"But you think your father killed him?" I ask.

She flinches. "Yes."

"He had no right to put his hands on you."

"You're right, he didn't. But he didn't deserve to die for it."

I hate the pain that bleeds out of her. It coats her in darkness, consuming her light.

"He might not be dead. Maybe your father warned him away."

"You really think so?" Hope blossoms in her blue eyes. She's nearly coming off the bed.

I didn't think so. Philip is most likely buried six feet under, maybe in parts. That should be a stark reminder to me of why I need to stay away from this beauty.

"I'll let you eat," I say.

Her eyes dim.

"I packed some of your clothes. I'll get them tomorrow." I grip the door handle, not looking at her.

"Thank you." Her words are low, but I hear them. I leave her and return to the living room, where Shay still drinks.

I get a fresh glass out of the kitchen and let Shay refill my drink. "How long can we stay here?" I ask.

"As long as you need."

"Jack and Richard want the address," Shay admits.

A slow grin burns my face. "Wouldn't that be fun? All of us in one room."

Shay snorts. "Yeah, a real knee slapper. Jack is sound. You know he's solid."

I'll take Shay's word for it. "What about Richard?"

"The verdict is still out on Richard. I like him."

"Do you trust him?" I ask.

Shay glances at me. "He's an O'Reagan. So trust isn't easily come by."

I finish my drink. "You're an O'Reagan too," I remind him while clinking my glass with his. Shay goes to refill my glass, but I hold my hand up. "I need some sleep."

A floral couch under the main window is calling to me.

"You take the first watch?" I ask, settling down on the couch.

"You got it." Shay slouches back and drinks from the bottle.

It takes me some time to fall asleep, but I finally do.

***

The room is dark when I wake, and I'm not sure at first what woke me. I sit up straight, listening. Shay's snores make it hard to hear anything else. The empty bottle is lying against his leg. I hear a click.

The front door.

I take a final look at a sleeping Shay and make my way to Dana's room. Her bed is empty. I leave the cottage in a panic, but she's standing with her back to me, her arms folded over her chest. I'm glad she can't see my face, that she can't see my panic at finding her bed empty.

"What are you doing?" I ask.

She doesn't turn around. "Getting some fresh air."

I take out my phone. "It's three in the morning." I have only one bar of reception. I slide the phone back into my pocket.

"I couldn't sleep."

I step closer to Dana, the fresh air waking me fully. "Which is it? You couldn't sleep, or you wanted fresh air?"

Dana glances at me over her shoulder. A soft smile is on her stunning face. She's like some mystical creature, standing under the moonlight on the edge of the forest. She wears a look that says nothing matters, that here and now is all there is.

"Me and my friend Maeve used to knick knack as kids. Have you ever knick knacked?"

I step closer to Dana. Anyone else and I would fuck off back to bed. But with Dana, I'm drawn to her. "No." I didn't play games as a kid. My childhood didn't exist. I've always had to be a man. A man whose hands were heavy with decision and tools.

"Okay, so you run up to someone's house—"

I cut her off. "I understand the concept. Knock on the door and run away."

"Yeah. We loved it. There was this field at the back of the estate that Maeve lived in. We would hide out in the long grass, hidden from sight but the darkness too." Dana's brows draw down. "It was such a rush. Would we get caught? I used to think I was so fast, running at night, not knowing if I would fall or where I was running too. The air was so cold and fresh."

I'm with Dana in the moment, running through long grass. Only I'm not the one running. I'm the one chasing.

Dana looks at me. Her nostrils flare, like she's made a decision. She turns away and dashes into the forest. It takes my brain a moment to catch up as she looks back at me. Her gaze holds not fear but excitement.

She disappears, and my cock instantly turns to steel. I strip off my suit jacket and drop it on the ground before chasing after her.

CHAPTER THIRTEEN

DANA

THE NIGHT AIR FEELS harsh against my skin, and I recognize the sensation. Just like I had last night with Cillian. Sitting in the cottage and thinking about Philip, my family, and the lie that is my life, small snippets of memories keep bursting through. Better days, days when things made sense. Just like when Maeve and I would run. The rush is hard to explain, but tonight, it's amplified.

I can't hear Cillian behind me, but I trust he gave chase. I stop. My body wants to keep going. That instinct that doesn't want to get caught urges me to keep running. I hold still. The bark of the tree is rough on my back.

My heart heightens to a level that's terrifying as a hand tightens around my neck. All my worries fade away as Cillian steps into view. His fingers loosen, but his hand stays in place.

"What do you think is going to happen, princess? You think I'm going to lick your pussy?"

My face burns, but excitement sends wetness between my legs. That's exactly what I want. I want the bliss he offered me before. Only this time, nothing can stop us.

His smile is sinister and makes me wonder if I made a serious error.

"You didn't hide. I don't like when my prey lies afraid. I don't do belly rubs." He releases my throat and steps back. His gaze travels across my flesh. "You're too easy."

My stomach squeezes, and all I see is disgust in his eyes. I read him so wrong. "Fuck you."

I step away from the tree, only to have Cillian block my path. "You can't start a game and not finish it." He grabs my hand and drags me closer to him.

His cock strains against my hand that he forces over the bulge. "Maybe it's my turn for pleasure."

I swallow the saliva that's building up in my mouth. He pushes me away.

Mortification burns my face and body.

"Go back to bed, Dana."

He makes me feel like a girl who wants to play with a man. Maybe he's used to women. I'm not a child.

I run again, but this time, I don't listen for him. I just run. I go full speed. Branches whip at my hair and tear my bare arms. Each bite of a thorn or the jagged end of a stick only propels me further.

I hear Cillian. He isn't quiet as he tears after me. A glance over my shoulder is a mistake. It costs me seconds, and his arm circles around my waist and I'm airborne. I land gently on a bed of leaves as he takes me to the ground.

I can't breathe when Cillian bends over me. He's a beast, and I'm his willing victim. Terror clogs some parts of my brain—doubt that he will want me—and anger makes another appearance.

Cillian's harsh breaths mix with mine before his lips crash down on me. His mouth is warm; the contrasts against the damp leaves under me and the cold air heightens everything about him. The taste of whiskey has me sliding my tongue into his mouth. He lowers his body down on mine. His cock presses heavily against me.

All I can think about is that moment when he licked me. My core tightens and flutters in anticipation.

The cold air coats my body as Cillian gets off me. The noise of his belt buckle is like a gunshot, and I'm starting to doubt what I'm doing.

"Get on your knees." The command is delivered as he pushes down his trousers and boxers. His huge cock springs free.

I'm not so sure.

Cillian takes his cock in his hand and gives it several long strokes. I can't seem to move.

"You want to lie there and watch me come?" he asks and he strokes himself faster.

My panties grow damper by the second. I've never seen anyone masturbate before, yet I want to touch him. My body doesn't obey, and I stay lying on the ground.

Cillian releases his cock and steps over me.

I want to look away. Watching him feels private.

"Watch me, princess." Cillian takes his cock again and starts to stroke it. He keeps eye contact, and there is no shame, only pure lust and anger that drive each strong stroke.

I reach up.

"Don't touch me."

I drop my hand.

"Take off your top," he says after releasing a slow growl. His strokes grow faster.

I sit forward and pull my top off. Goose bumps burst across my flesh from the cold air.

I want to lie here and watch him, but I also want to touch him.

"Ah, fuck." Cillian's strokes are almost violent. He's staring up into the night sky. His breaths are coming out in cold gusts.

I should be shivering lying on a damp ground, but I've never felt so hot. My body burns, waiting for Cillian to finish himself on top of me.

I've never done this before, never wanted to. But with him, I want every part.

His gaze swings down to me. Fire burns his eyes. "Are you ready, princess?" he growls.

I manage a nod before he comes all over my chest. I can't look away from Cillian as he continues to cover me with his cream. I can't look away from his face, scrunched up in concentration and ecstasy. He gives a few final strokes before letting out a satisfied sigh.

The wetness under me starts to soak into my flesh. I don't move as Cillian pulls his boxers and trousers back up. When he's fixed himself up, he kneels down. All the fire hasn't been doused from his eyes.

I have never wanted someone to touch me so much. My body aches, and right now, I'd do anything.

Cillian picks up my T-shirt and hands it to me. "You should clean yourself up."

He stands and walks away. The cold and darkness crash in around me.

Humiliation takes on a whole new meaning. As I start to rise, Cillian's cum shines on my chest. My body still hums for release. I run my finger through his cum and taste it. There is a moment of bliss from tasting him that escalates into disgust and anger.

I viciously wipe the rest of his cum off me. I'm snapping looks around me, expecting him to laugh or step out from some dark corner of the forest, but each step I take back to the cottage, my face burns hotter.

He just left me.

I must have run a good distance. It takes some time before the small white cottage comes into view through the trees. I turn the T-shirt inside out and slide it on. The wet substance rubs against my skin; I don't want Shay to see the stains or put anything together. He should be asleep, but just in case.

A hand clamps down on my mouth, and I'm ready to sink my teeth in when Cillian's breath roams across my cheek. "Don't bite, princess, or I won't let you come."

My body instantly forgets any embarrassment and comes alive. Cillian's chest is hard against my back.

He keeps his hand clamped over my mouth. I want to tell him to stop. What if Shay looks out the window? He might see us.

Cillian's hand sinks under the waistband of my sweatpants and dips into my panties easily. His fingers sink inside me, and I almost crumble in his hand. He extracts his fingers, and even through my thrashing heart rate, I hear my wetness before he sinks his fingers back inside me. Cillian slides his free hand up my body until his thumb is pressed against my lips. He forces it into my mouth, and I suck on his thumb. I taste the earth, but this is the hand he jerked off with. My nipples are pebbled; the slight movement of the material brushing against them is painful. His cream is sticky against my skin, and I suck his thumb harder as he pumps his fingers deeper into me.

Cillian pushes his growing erection into my back, and I've never wanted someone so badly. His fingers pump harder, his thumb pulls the side of my mouth painfully, and I can't hold back. My pants grow frantic as he pumps harder. My release is almost violent, and it takes me several moments to get my breathing under control. Wetness rolls down the inside of my leg. Cillian slowly extracts his fingers from my pants. He removes his thumb from my mouth, and I miss his warmth instantly. He steps around so I can see him.

His green eyes are the darkest I've ever seen them. His smile is wicked as he places two fingers into his mouth and tastes me.

I didn't think there was anything left in me, but even though my body might have released, it hasn't let go of Cillian. It's nowhere near done with him.

He turns away. I watch him bend down, pick up his suit jacket off the ground, and put it on. I step out of the tree line and toward the door that he holds open for me.

"I hope you can sleep better, princess."

His words should make me smile, only they hold a shitload of resentment.

I dip under his arm. The living room door is open, and Shay is staring right at me. My heart races and I can't let him see what happened. In the light of the hall, I notice my clothes have mud and leaves stuck to them. And I'm sure I wear the look of someone who just had a tumble in the forest.

I duck into my room and close the door, not sure how I'm ever going to face Shay or Cillian again.

CHAPTER FOURTEEN

CILLIAN

Dana avoids me over the next two days. She stays locked up in her room. Shay still hasn't left. He clearly isn't trusting me with Dana.

The night in the forest, Shay asked me why she was in such a state. I was semihonest, saying she had run, and I had brought her back.

Maybe that's why he was staying. Maybe he heard my half-truths.

Each night, I have waited with an excitement I haven't felt in a long time to catch Dana creeping out. That hasn't happened.

I thought maybe once I gave her the clothes I'd gotten her that she would sneak out, but not a fucking chance.

I enter her room without knocking; I like catching her off guard. She glares at me from the bed. The little purple dress is begging to be torn from her body. Fuck, I want her so badly that my cock hasn't stopped throbbing.

"Your breakfast." I place the tray on the table.

"No 'princess' today?"

She's aggravated. I have no fucking idea why.

"Enjoy your breakfast, *princess*." I grin, pissing her off further. "I'll be out all day. Be a good girl."

She sits up straighter. "Where are you going?"

I tut. "None of your business."

She bristles, looking sexy as hell. Roiling her up has become a joy.

"How much longer do I have to stay here?"

"Why don't you ask your daddy?" I fire back. I want answers, too. Maybe Dana asking Liam will get us the answers we both want. Having no word from Liam isn't sitting well with me.

"I need your phone." She's off the bed.

"I'm sure Shay will accommodate you." I give Dana one final look.

She's standing with her arms folded across her chest. Her feet are bare and she looks fucking stunning with her long dark hair pulled to one side.

I want to ask her why she's avoiding me, but her keeping her distance is smart. I should do the same.

***

Big John reached out to me, saying Robert and Razor wanted to meet. This situation is another thing I should be happy about, but I'm not. Too many unanswered questions don't sit right with me.

Razor and Robert made it clear they wouldn't work with me. Now all of a sudden, they want to talk, especially after my threat. Only one thing would make them do such a three-sixty: Skinner. He's the only person with the power to make the Jaguars change their mind. He is the boss, after all. My mother saying Skinner would help sinks in now.

What did it cost her to make such a deal?

We aren't meeting at the strip club today. Instead, I've been invited to Robert's home. I've never been here before. The large white mansion is set deep in fields of green grass. The gate is manually lifted, reminding me of a military base. It makes sense—most of the Jaguars served with special forces. I walked in the same footsteps as them. My training over two years was severe. Sixty-two of us started together; only three graduated.

I drive up toward the mansion. The front door is wide open. I don't see anyone near it. I park the car and am ready to get out when a tap sounds on my window.

I glance at the guy who waits while I roll it down.

"Mr. Jordan is waiting out back for you."

I'm ready to roll up the window.

When the guy clears his throat, he looks nervous. "On foot. No cars are permitted out back."

I roll up the window and get out.

The guy lingers behind me as I walk to the side of the house. He keeps clearing his throat, and I want to tell him to fucking clear it already.

I move to walk down the side of the house.

"Sorry, but you have to go past the stables."

Robert is having a fucking laugh. The stables are long and filled with horses. Once I reach the end, the fucker behind me starts to clear his throat again.

"Spit it out," I bark, getting fucking sick of all this trekking.

"It's through that gate, two fields over. He's down by the lake."

I'm staring at this guy, thinking he's playing with me. "You said out back?"

"That is out back, Mr. O'Hara."

The saying 'Don't shoot the messenger' comes to mind. I hop the gate and trek across the two fields. My shoes are worse for wear by the time I arrive. Robert is sitting beside a lake with an easel, painting the landscape before him.

"I didn't know you paint," I say as I join him. I keep any annoyance about the walk to myself.

"It settles me. Sorry about the long walk." Robert doesn't look at me but continues to paint. He's not sorry.

"I enjoy the fresh air."

He glances at me with a pity-filled smile on his face. He's pissed, and he can't hide it. No doubt about my threat during our meeting at the strip club.

"I'm going to be honest with you, Cillian."

I stuff my hands into my pockets. My father always said to never trust a man who hides his hands. Robert's gaze flickers to my pockets.

"This order came down from Skinner; otherwise, I wouldn't be doing it."

"What order?"

"To help you," Robert bites out.

"Glad to know I have friends in high places."

Robert's eyes flash with something I can't decipher, and he returns to his painting. "Well, tell us what you need."

"Bednar Novak. I tried to have a meeting with him, but it wasn't successful. I want to meet the man."

"We will try to do that." Robert stops painting and looks up at me. "You've been hiding?"

It's a statement and a question.

One I don't deny. "I've been guarding Liam O'Reagan's daughter. We are holed up in a safe house."

"I didn't know she was at risk."

"Neither did I," I say honestly. "But she's his daughter, so..."

Robert nods. "Your working for Liam does complicate things."

"When are things not complicated?" I ask.

Robert flashes a tight smile. "My son, Collin, trained with you in Cork."

"I remember him. He was strong." It's the truth. Collin had everything to make special forces—except a control on his temper. He lashed out at one of the sergeants and he was removed. Otherwise, I do believe he would have been one of the best.

"He was removed unfairly." Robert places the paintbrush down on a palette, picks up a white piece of material, and wipes his hands.

"I agree."

A nod from Robert shows his appreciation for my words. "At the time, I wasn't one of the top dogs with the Jaguars." Another tight smile vanishes. "So I went to Skinner. One word from him"—Robert snaps his fingers—"and my son would be back in the forces."

I can assume that he didn't agree to help Robert.

"You know what he told me." It's not a question. "He told me my boy made his own mistakes, and he wasn't cleaning them up."

Robert rubs at his wild beard aggressively. "By the time I climbed ranks, my son didn't want to go back to the special forces. The sergeant who dismissed him, well..." Darkness with a mix of evil flashes in Robert's brown eyes. I've seen that look in too many men's eyes recently.

"Who you are accounts for everything in this world. Not your intentions, not your morals, not your worth. But who you are; who you know."

I can see where Robert is going with this. "Skinner asking you to help me, is that what this is all about?"

"Skinner didn't ask, Cillian. He commanded." Robert gets up from the small stool. He towers over me. His seven-foot frame is large enough to block out the sun. "Aren't you asking yourself why?"

I have my theory. My mother and he must have gotten friendly lately. She must have called in a favor. I just have no idea of the cost.

"Yes, of course I am."

Robert walks closer to me. "Secrets never stay buried. That's something I've learned."

Robert faces the lake and pushes his hands into his pockets.

Irritation claws at my skin. "I'm getting the feeling you know why Skinner is helping me."

Robert glances at me. "I never agreed with how Davy treated you. I always said it was wrong."

I face him fully.

"He knew he wasn't your father," he says.

Inside, I take the hit, but on the outside, I think of my training. My control.

"Skinner is your dad," Robert finishes before facing the lake. He keeps his gaze on the water, waiting for my reaction.

"Is that all you wanted to tell me?"

His dark eyebrows drag down. "Yes."

"Just find a way for me to get close to Bednar Novak." I walk away.

"You didn't hear it from me," Robert calls after me.

"Hear what?" I fire back.

He snorts.

But I'm not fucking laughing. Each step restricts my lungs. I know he's still watching me. I can't show him how much his words are affecting me.

I loosen the top button of my shirt. I'm across the fields, and the stables appear before I see my car.

I'm driving. I can't remember starting the car. I can't remember leaving Robert's home. I'm driving on autopilot.

My mind is touching memories like dipping a toe into cold water. I want to dive in and get this done and over with, yet the knowledge hasn't fully sunk in. I want it to.

"Davy isn't my father. Edward is," I say out loud.

My body doesn't react to my words. To the truth. To the buried lies.

I'm close to the cottage when I finally pull over. A ball hardens my gut, and I get out of the car, taking my gun with me. I fire as I walk. I keep firing into the same tree until my gun is empty, but my finger keeps pulling the trigger.

Getting back into the car, I place my gun in the glove compartment and button my shirt. I'm near the cottage. Shay and Dana are outside. They must have heard the gunshots.

I grin as I stop the car and get out. Shay's looking at me expectantly.

"Sorry. Target practice," I say.

Shay doesn't believe me.

I don't meet Dana's gaze.

"Don't stop on my account," I fire over my shoulder. The idea of them training together has fury burning up inside me. I'm ready to go into the cottage.

"I have to go home for a day or two." Shay stops me from entering the cottage.

I face him.

"What happened?" he asks.

I take a look at Dana, whose back is to me. She's plaited her hair, and she boxes the air several times.

"She's taking her training seriously."

"Did you find a risk?" Shay drags my attention back to him.

"No. I just needed to release some anger, so the tree took the brunt of it."

Shay snorts. "Looks like you have a lot more to release."

I try to relax and calm the craving for violence that flows thickly through my veins. "I'm fine, Shay. Go. I can handle this."

He hasn't stepped away. "You could continue to train her."

Is he fucking serious?

"You think she's ever going to get that close to combat that she can fight hand to hand?"

"It's a release for her, Cillian. Might do you no harm." Shay slaps my shoulder before entering the cottage. Dana isn't very focused on her punches—she's aware I'm watching her. Even in a black T-shirt and sweatpants, she's still beautiful. Maybe even more so.

Shay comes back out of the house. "I'll be in touch."

"Take care."

He stops at Dana. They don't hug, but he pats her shoulder. She folds her arms across her chest and watches Shay as he disappears into the tree line.

"Where is he going?" She's still staring at the area that Shay disappeared through.

"I'm not his fucking mother."

Dana swings around, and she opens her mouth to say something but stops. I don't know why.

I peel off my suit jacket and roll up the sleeves of my shirt. "You want to train?" I ask.

"With you?"

I grin at her. "Are you afraid?" Right now, I need a distraction. Fucking her would be nice. Maybe our training together would lead to sex.

Her answer is to hold up her fists close to her face. I take a few quick jabs, tapping the side of her head. "Hold your hands higher."

Dana is a good student. She never questions the whys but does as I say. She also retains the information. After an hour, she's coated in sweat.

"Take a break."

"No. Let's keep going."

"Well, I'm taking a break. You have to know when to stop too, Dana." I return to the house and get two bottles of water out of the fridge.

When I come back outside, she's sitting on the ground. I rejoin her and hand her a bottle.

She drinks nearly half of the water. "The gunshots earlier. Was something wrong?"

I don't look at Dana as I speak. "You're safe."

"I know." She has my attention. She slowly puts the lid back on her water bottle.

"I got some news that didn't... please me." I can't look away from her lips. I want to kiss her.

"I'm sorry." She places the bottle to the right of her and pulls her knees up to her chest. "Sounds like we have a lot in common." She forces a smile.

We have nothing in common. "I doubt that, Dana. I think you and I are nothing alike." She's a reminder of my sister. A reminder, once again, of who you know in this world.

"We both got news we didn't like."

"The man I grew up believing is my father isn't," I say sharply. Dana reaches across to touch me, and I get up. "We have nothing in common," I reinforce.

Dana looks away from me, her cheeks burning up.

"Let's get back to training." Teaching her is a distraction I need. I'm waiting for her to stomp back into the house and ignore me again, but she stands up and gets into position.

Maybe we do have something in common.

CHAPTER FIFTEEN

DANA

AFTER TRAINING WITH CILLIAN, I shower and get dressed in yet another dress. Why did I have so many dresses? They aren't functional here. I slip on the red dress, and the long sleeves are soft against my skin. I opt for bare feet as I walk to the kitchen. I'm not much of a cook, so I rummage together a salad.

Cillian's still outside. His news about his father must have been devastating, and after hearing about his father beating him, my stomach sours. What kind of childhood did he have? Mine was good—built on lies, but while I was living my childhood, I never knew anything was amiss.

I set up the small breakfast bar with the salads and some tea. I keep rearranging the plates. Should I sit on the left or the right? Are the chairs too close?

I step away. I'm driving myself crazy.

"That looks good."

My heart leaps in my chest, and I step away from the breakfast bar like I've been caught red-handed.

Cillian isn't looking at the food; he's staring at me.

"It's only a salad." I clear my throat and sit down. The moment Cillian joins me, I know I've moved the chairs too close. Our arms brush each other. I shuffle my stool a bit away, but if Cillian notices, he doesn't say.

"Shay said you were best friends growing up." I kick off the conversation to try to banish the awkward silence.

"We still are," Cillian says. His salad is nearly gone.

I start to eat mine. I chew everything I put into my mouth, but with Cillian this close, I don't taste it.

"I spent most of my childhood up north. My dad—Davy—had to work up there, sometimes for weeks. So I got to meet Shay."

"Lucky you," I say.

Cillian gives me a sideways glance and a smile that skyrockets my heart. "He's one of the good guys."

I'm aware he started to say 'my dad' but switched it to Davy. "Did you get along with Davy?" I don't look at him. He grows stiff beside me. He doesn't know what Shay told me about Davy beating him, so the question should appear innocent.

"Not really. How about you? Do you get along with Liam?"

Everything grows heavy in my belly. "I mean, I did. I don't know." I'm not ready to talk about my dad. I know it's unfair to expect Cillian to talk about his. "I don't know," I repeat.

"Did he hurt you?" Cillian turns on his stool so he's facing me.

I shake my head and place my knife and fork on my plate. "Not in how you are asking, Cillian." I look up. "My father would never put his hands on any of us."

"Lucky you."

"Are you not one of the lucky ones?" I ask and turn my chair so I'm facing him fully, too. Our knees rub each other, and the contact sends my mind somewhere different.

"Davy liked his belt."

"I'm sorry." I want to reach out and touch him, but I can already see him withdrawing, and I'm not ready to let Cillian go.

"I don't want to be alone," I say as he gets up.

Cillian's jaw tightens. "You're not alone."

"There's an empty bed in the next room." I can feel my cheeks heat. But I can't get the thoughts of having Cillian out of my head. Out of my system. Maybe if I have him once, I'll stop obsessing about him.

Surprise lights up his green eyes. He scratches his brow before speaking. "I don't get personal, Dana."

My abdomen clenches. What the fuck did we do in the forest? If that wasn't personal, I have no idea what is.

"It's already personal." I stand and look up into his angry eyes.

A storm is revving up in them, turning the light green back into a mossy color. Shadows play out across his face. His jaw clenches.

"Not to me." Crushed. That's how I feel. It's a funny kind of pain. I gather the small amount of dignity I have left.

"Good to know." I force a smile. "Good to know," I repeat. I need to move. I want to run, but my legs won't obey. He's standing there staring at me like he didn't just crush me.

"Are we good?" he asks.

"Great." My jaw aches as I continue to push my smile forward so he can't see the cracks behind it.

"It's easier this way," he tries to explain.

I can't hold the smile any longer. "Stop." I pick up the plates. The tremble in my hand is humiliating. I carry them to the sink, and when I hear his footsteps disappear out of the space, I almost sag against the sink.

Don't cry.

Be brave.

I refuse to break down. I wash the plates and tidy up. When I enter the living space, he isn't there.

CHAPTER SIXTEEN

CILLIAN

I DON'T GET PERSONAL with women. I bang them and leave. That's it. I've honestly never had the time or the interest to get to know any.

But Dana not speaking to me for the last two days is making me antsy. I want to ask her how long she's going to keep this up, but each time I even look at her, she cuts me with a stare.

She's pissed.

She's avoiding me at all costs. Each time I move through the hall, I hear her movements behind her door. When I leave for a while for a jog, I come back and the evidence that she's been in the kitchen is clear. In the mornings, the shower is steamy. I have no fucking idea what time she's getting up and to what lengths she's going to avoid me.

I get ready for a jog and leave the cottage. This time, I wait only minutes before arriving back in the kitchen. My suspicions are confirmed. There she is, ready to cut a sandwich in half. She's glaring at me, but color slowly seeps into her cheeks. I pass her and get a bottle of water from the fridge.

"I was starting to think you were avoiding me," I say and drink slowly.

She resumes cutting her sandwich. "Nope. Why would I do something like that?"

I move up behind her. I can smell the strawberry shampoo on her hair.

"Maybe I hurt your feelings?"

She stalls for a moment. "Nope." She turns, but there's nowhere to go.

"Well then, maybe you want to do some training today?"

She cranes her neck back. She wants to say no.

I don't want her to say no.

"Unless I hurt your feelings." I step back and let her slide into the chair beside her.

"I'll be ready in ten minutes." She bites into her sandwich.

"I wouldn't eat too much. Wouldn't want you to get a cramp while running."

She coughs on her sandwich, and I feel satisfied. I reach back into the fridge and slide her the bottle of water I remove. She unscrews the lid and takes a deep gulp.

"I'll be outside."

It's a fresh day, and I'm hoping that going for a jog will help me to clear my mind a bit. Knowing Davy isn't my father pisses me off. The idea he isn't my father isn't devastating—it makes sense. He hated me from the get-go. Each time he looked at me, I saw the hate there, and now it makes sense who my father is. Knowledge I hope to leverage.

I do some warm-ups. Dana arrives out front, ready for training. She's fuckable in her training clothes.

"You took your time."

She glares at me before doing some warm-ups too. She bends over and touches her toes, giving me a full view of her rear. My cock wakes up.

"I thought a jog would do some good."

She straightens and nods. I grin as she jogs past me. I don't mind going second—the view is fucking delicious.

We jog along the outskirts of the forest. She's very careful not to enter.

"I'm pissed." Dana's breathless when she stops and spins around toward me.

I jog past her. "No time for talking, princess."

I hear her small growl before she catches up to me.

"What are you pissed about?" I ask, knowing full well what's bothering her. It's been bothering me, too. I said it wasn't personal, but it is. With Dana, it is.

She stops jogging again, and I turn but keep jogging on the spot. "You aren't going to get fit this way, princess."

"I'm serious, Cillian."

Dana saying my name twists something inside me. I stop jogging.

"It is personal," I say.

Her eyes widen. She opens her mouth and closes it.

She nods. "I'm glad we cleared that up." She's fighting a smile as she jogs past me again.

I thought that would be a lot harder—her asking me to explain why I said it wasn't personal or start talking about feelings. All that bullshit.

I jog after her. "That wasn't hard," I find myself saying.

I'm waiting for her to respond, but she darts off to her left and into the forest. She doesn't pause or look back, and I wait for a few beats before giving chase.

She's quick. She swerves in between trees and jumps over fallen logs. The forest seems to sway and creak, and I power after her.

She doesn't glance back. My footfalls aren't quiet. She knows I'm close. I can smell the strawberry shampoo from her hair; I'm that close to her.

She's easy to lift off the ground as I wrap my arm around her waist. I don't expect her to react. She kicks out—the force and surprise have me loosening my hold on her—and she darts off again.

She glances at me and grins. My cock turns to steel, and I chase after her. A squeal erupts from her mouth as I close in. This time, I'm ready for her attack. When I grab her, I keep her tight against my body. She kicks, but I widen my legs and drag her back to a tree. I spin her, and I'm not gentle as I push her against the bark.

"You want to play rough, princess?"

She's excited. I can see the swirls of glee in her eyes, but behind it are sparks of anger. Anger that prompts her to lash out. Her hand connects with my face, forcing me back away from her.

She doesn't dart away like I expect; she grabs my T-shirt and pulls me to her. Her lips are heavy on mine, and she moves with an urgency I match. I grab her ass and squeeze, causing her pain. She hisses but doesn't stop me. Instead, her tongue sinks into my mouth and I taste all of her. She's almost feverish while kissing me.

I grip the hem of her T-shirt and drag it up. She breaks the kiss and slowly raises her hands into the air. I drop her top and allow her to take mine off. She stands back, and I know in the light of day my scars are stark. Her eyes widen when I step closer, gripping her face.

"You run from me, and I'll chase you," I warn.

"Why would I run?" She pulls her face out of my hands. I box her in against the tree.

"Do I frighten you"—I lean in and press a kiss just below her eye lobe—"princess?"

"Yes."

I smile before looking her in the eyes. I grip her face again. "Good." I want to tell her to run. This isn't healthy, but neither is my want for her.

She looks so innocent as she stares up at me. I shouldn't care. I should take what she's offering, but I pause. "I'm not good for you."

"I'm not good for you," she fires back.

She's right.

I make a bad decision and kiss her. Her mouth is warm as I sink my tongue inside. My lips trail along her cheek and to her neck before I spin her. She gasps as I push her against the tree before pressing myself against her.

Brushing her hair aside, I press a kiss to her neck that causes her to shiver. Her ass is arched out. My cock groans against my sweatpants. I pull hers down slowly, until they are around her ankles. She looks down at me as I press kisses up her leg before stopping at her ass. Then I bite.

She squeals and tries to move, but I push her back into the tree. All I want to do now is pull her panties off her and bury my cock deep inside her.

Reaching around, I run my hands under her bra and feel her large breasts. She groans. Puffs of fresh air leave her mouth. I don't feel the cold. All my body wants is Dana. Leaving her breasts, I grip her panties and tear them off.

She hisses, and I kiss the red marks that are already appearing. Dipping lower, I spread her legs as far as her bottoms will allow. I take in her ass and long legs—she's fucking perfect. Just as perfect as her sweet pussy that I taste. She's soaking, and I lick up her juices.

Her groans have me sinking my tongue deeper. My cock aches and I stand, pushing down my own sweatpants and boxers. My cock is hard as I stroke it a few times. Dana tries to look around, but I push the small of her back, forcing her face against the tree. Moving closer, I press a wet kiss to her face.

"You taste so good," I whisper as I reach down and insert a finger inside her. Bringing it back up, I place my fingers in her mouth. She sucks them, and it's my turn to groan. With my other hand, I stroke my cock a few painful times before removing my fingers from her mouth. Pulling off her sweatpants completely, I lift one of her legs with her still facing the tree and position my cock at her wet opening.

I slam into her violently and fast. She squeals, and it pushes me harder as I stretch her leg out further, letting myself bury my cock deep inside her. Her groans grow frantic, and my balls slap against her as I pound harder and faster. I want all her juices on my cock. Reaching around, I pinch one of her sensitive nipples hard. She screams and I keep squeezing it. She tries to push my hand away, but I don't stop as I keep pounding into her. I stop once I get what I want, and she cries out as she comes all over my cock. I withdraw before I can come inside her.

"Get on your knees."

She appears disorientated, but like a good girl, she falls to her knees. Her chest is marked from being pressed against the tree.

I stroke my cock, knowing it won't take much. She's staring up at me, and I'm so close. I don't expect her to move forward and place her warm lips at the tip of my cock. When she does, I sigh and pump harder. Her tongue brushes against the head of my cock. When her fingers start to play with my balls, I pump even faster, so close to release.

I take one final look at Dana, naked on her knees, and empty my load into her mouth. She looks up at me as she drinks it down, gulp after gulp.

It's the sexiest thing I've ever seen. When she's swallowed it all, I stop pumping, and she gives a final lick to my cock.

My breaths are harsh as I help her up off the ground.

"I think jogging is a new favorite sport of mine," I say.

She smiles, and she's fucking beautiful. I pull her to me and press a kiss to her lips. I taste the salt before pulling away.

Dana picks up her clothes and starts to get dressed. I'm watching her as I get dressed. I can't see one flaw on her body. She's perfect.

Dangerous, I remind myself. She is Liam O'Reagan's daughter, but not by choice. She was born into that family. She must feel my eyes on her as she looks at me while pulling on her top. She's fully dressed when I pull on mine. I'm ready to continue our jog—maybe play a few more games—when a voice to my left freezes me.

I've never felt so fucked in all my life.

"We aren't alone. The Russians are here." Shay walks to me, but I notice how he point blank refuses to look at Dana. I take the gun he hands me. Automatically, my hand reaches out and takes Dana's.

"You need to stay behind me at all times."

She nods, but her face is paling by the second. Her gaze flickers from the gun in my hand to the gun in Shay's.

Shay isn't helping with his stone face.

"How many?" I ask.

"Six. Seven, maybe."

Our odds aren't good.

"Take Dana back to the cott—"

Shay cuts me off. "They're at the cottage."

"How did they know?"

Shay tilts his head. "I don't fucking know."

I hear the snap of a twig. It's like a gunshot in the forest. Dana's hand fists my T-shirt behind me. I turn around and detangle her from me.

"I need you to stay here." I slowly guide her back to the large tree I just fucked her against. She's shaking her head. "Dana. It's going to get ugly. I want you to stay here until either Shay or I come back for you."

She bites her lip but walks back to the tree.

I want to say something more meaningful, or do... something. But Shay is busting my balls, so I turn away from Dana and jut my chin out to the left.

Shay nods and moves right. We need to create a circle. Push them out. If it were nighttime, this location would be a dream. I duck as a gun is fired.

Fuck.

I rise and try to see where the shooter is. Another shot is fired and Dana screams. I take a quick look to confirm she's still at the tree. She's crouched down and is covering her head with her hands. I return my attention to ahead of me. A flash of black near dense trees freezes me. I aim my gun, close one eye, and the world falls silent around me. The click as I cock the gun back is loud in my ear. I pull the trigger. I don't have to wait; I start to move as the body hits the ground.

I reach him and check his pockets for a phone or some device that he might have to communicate with the other men. But he's clean. I take his rifle and push my own gun in the back of my trousers. Balancing the gun on the dead man's back, I look through the telescope. I see another man. He's doing what I'm doing: scooping the area. I have the gun ready and wait until he's looking directly at me. The rush has me pulling the trigger, and I roll as he pulls his too. A tree behind me splinters as the bullet embeds itself in it.

I retrieve the rifle and find the location of the shooter. He's dead. I hear shots fired off in the distance and hope Shay is holding up as well as I am. I fall back into position and scope the area. The gunfire in the distance stops. The forest sighs; a bird takes flight. I keep looking, but I don't see any movement.

Dana's scream has me off the ground. I sling the rifle over my shoulder and extract my gun as I run, then I come to a halting stop.

She's been dragged out from behind a tree. The dark-haired man has a gun to her head. His arm is tight around her throat as he moves her to the left.

His gaze is steady; the gun in his hand is steady, and the safety is off.

"You know who she is?" I ask. He has to. What other reason would they be here for?

He nods. "Drop your gun."

Dana's staring at me, and the horror in her eyes is wrong.

"I can't do that." I hold my own gun steady. I have to call his bluff. They didn't come this whole way just to kill her.

"You're Cillian." His accent is heavy.

I nod.

"You let me walk away with Dana, and I will give you something in return."

If the stakes weren't so high, I'd fucking laugh at his audacity. "You let her go, and I'll kill you quickly," I counteract.

"I can give you your sister."

CHAPTER SEVENTEEN

DANA

CILLIAN ALL ON HIS own is terrifying in a way I can't really explain. It's like when you fall as a kid. You know how hard you hit the ground. You know the burn along your knees. You know it can happen again. With Cillian, he reminds me of death. I'm not sure why, but I feel like death is constantly breathing down my neck.

That feeling has materialized at this moment, and I'm faced with my mortality. I should be concerned about the gun pointed at my head or the man who's gripped my neck painfully. I'm not. I'm staring at Cillian, who holds a gun, another hoisted over his shoulder like it belongs there. Just like the gun in his hand is an extension of him.

Cillian's features shift, and my breaths are loud as reality slowly seeps through the wall of horror that had transported me to a very dark part of my mind.

"My sister." His brows drag down; he looks angry and confused.

He cocks his gun. The sound sends my heart rate into overdrive.

"Let me take Dana, and your sister will arrive at your doorstep in the morning."

Cillian has a sister? I didn't know that. What's really disturbing is the fact he's looking at me and something shifts in his gaze. Pity. Sadness. His decision dawns on me before he speaks.

"Cillian," I say, but it's too low. He doesn't hear me. "Don't do this." I blink at him. Once again, he doesn't look at me.

"Where is she being held?" Cillian questions.

"That doesn't matter. You will have your sister if I walk away now with Dana." I'm pulled backward, and Cillian doesn't stop the man from taking me.

Cillian hasn't lowered his gun, but as each step takes me away from him, a pain sharpens in my chest. He won't look at me. I'm ready to scream at him, but deep down, I know it won't matter.

This isn't personal.

I'm moving further away, and it's really sinking in that I'm being kidnapped. A scream finally tears from my throat, and it startles my captor. But he tightens his arm across my neck, cutting off the air to my lungs. A bang roars through the forest, and I'm falling backward. I hit the ground, but I'm cushioned by my captor's body. I spin and scramble away. A hole between his eyes oozes blood. The air grows thin, and I can't look away from the man. His brown eyes stare up into the forest canopy.

I hear the noise behind me, but I can't look away. Hands grab me, and I'm lifted off the ground. The smell is different.

Richard.

"Richard."

"You're safe." My brother pulls me into his chest. I should cry. I should scream. I feel sick. But nothing happens.

"We got them all," Shay says. I need to see Cillian.

"I'm okay," I say to Richard.

He puts me down but drags my face toward him. He's half bent so he can make eye contact with me. "Did he hurt you?"

I shake my head. "No."

My brother lets my face go. Cillian is putting his gun away, and I can't stop myself from marching up to him. My hand connects with his face. The sound is as deafening as the earlier gunshots. I blink tears that fall silently. I don't say anything but walk away.

"Dana," Richard calls after me.

"What was that?" I can hear Shay ask Cillian.

I don't wait around.

"Dana." Richard is on my heels. "You nearly died. What are you running off for?"

"You lied to me about everything. Everything." My lip trembles. I'm sick of feeling weak and fragile. "Was any of my life real?"

Richard doesn't flinch, and it's like looking at my father. "Are you as much of a liar as Father is? Are you as..." I want to say evil, but the word leaves a bad taste in my mouth.

"You've been through a lot," Richard starts.

I laugh and continue to walk.

Richard grabs my arm and stops me. "You can't go back to the cottage." His jaw tightens.

"Why?" My heart starts to beat way too fast, and I'm wondering how much more I can take.

"You just can't, Dana."

I join my hands together and raise them to my mouth to try to push everything down. Having Richard here is giving me moments of joy at seeing my brother, to moments of anger and horror at who he is. I fold my arms and wait.

He nods—like my being docile is what he needs right now.

"My car is ready to go," Richard calls over my shoulder.

"Good." Shay's voice is closer.

"You got a place to go?" Richard asks.

"Yeah, we can go to mine." Cillian's voice has me tightening my folded arms.

"Where the fuck was your phone?"

I glance at Shay. He won't meet my eye, and of course I'm wondering how much he saw.

"I left it in the house." Cillian speaks through his teeth. I don't want to look at him, but I'm drawn to his voice. I'm drawn to everything about him.

"You need anything from the house?" Richard asks me.

I feel sick in the pit of my stomach. I shake my head.

The three men are silent as we continue to the car. My father's Bentley. "You took Father's car?" I say to Richard.

"I was with him when Shay rang."

"He couldn't come himself?" I swallow more pain.

Richard gives me a sideways glance. "He's always at high risk, Dana."

I laugh. "So he'd leave me here to fend for myself."

"You had Shay and Cillian," my brother reminds me.

Cillian, who was going to hand me over. I saw it so clearly in his eyes. Only for Richard showing up and taking the shot, I'm not gone. Richard killed a man. I take another peek at my brother, who's watching me.

"If Father thought you were in danger—"

I cut Richard off. "Don't." My voice is low, but he stops.

My father knew I was in danger, yet he didn't come.

I get into the back of the car. Shay joins me, and the door closes as Cillian gets in the front.

Coward.

Richard rolls down the dividing window and turns to me. I don't know what he wants to say, but I don't want to hear it.

"Just go, Richard."

A heavy sigh and a turn of the key, and we are leaving the forest behind. We pass the cottage, and the door is half-open. My stomach twists. What horrors would I witness inside?

"How many were there?" I hear Cillian ask before the dividing window rolls up.

Shay lights up a cigarette. I roll down my window and glance at him as he offers me the box. I give a shake of my head, and he puts them in his breast pocket.

The awkwardness grows as Shay puffs away on his cigarette. When he finishes, I wait another few minutes before rolling up my window. I try not to think about Cillian's decision in the forest. My heart can't take much more. It makes me realize how hard I'm falling for Cillian. Why him? Why not some normal boy who will treat me well? Who wouldn't get weird about having sex in a bed?

Shay lights up another cigarette, and I roll down my window again. "Are you nervous?" I ask him. He smokes, but he doesn't chain smoke.

"No."

I'm so used to him calling me 'love' that I face him. His short answer hasn't gone unnoticed. "Cillian and I are both adults. I can have sex with whomever I want. So don't make this awkward." There, I said it.

Amusement flashes in Shay's eyes. "I don't care who you have sex with. I'm wondering why you hit him."

I look away from Shay, not ready to share that information. He accepts my silence. My fingers sink into the leather seat beneath me. *My father knew I was in danger, but he didn't come.*

Three cigarettes later, the car starts to slow as Shay fires his recent cigarette out the window. "You smoke a lot," I find myself saying.

"It comes with the job." Shay rolls up the window.

I keep my window down and fold my arms across my chest. "What exactly is your job? You work for my father?"

"I don't work for your father, love."

The endearment doesn't sound like one. "So you aren't Mafia?" I don't think I'll ever get used to that word—Mafia.

"I was raised up north, so my loyalties fall there."

The car starts to move again. "The North has different Mafia?"

"It's not Mafia. We don't label ourselves like down here."

The way Shay says 'down here' makes it sound like he has no dealings with the rest of Ireland.

"It's one island, Shay. There are no borders, nothing stopping us from crossing over. So what divides it? Especially your being an O'Reagan."

Shay grins and exhales. "The mind is more powerful than any border. People can't let go of our history. But I happen to agree with you. We are one nation." Shay trails off and looks out the window. The car slows in front of a hotel that must have once been an estate home.

"I thought we were going to Cillian's house?" I say.

"Yeah, this is it."

This is his house? The door opens and Richard tries to smile at me, but the look is so wrong on my brother's face. I get out, and already I'm looking for Cillian, who jogs up a set of wide steps to the front door.

The gray stucco building is enormous. Ivy covers a large section of the front of the home.

Shay and Richard wait for me to go first. I don't know what they are worried about—my running off? I'm too tired to run, and I have nowhere to go.

A wide golden door knocker grows larger as I climb the steps. The large lion's head with an open mouth isn't the most welcoming, but I find myself seeing humor in the knocker.

When I enter the foyer, Cillian is nowhere to be seen. A male and female dressed in the same uniforms greet me with genuine smiles.

The foyer is huge; you could have a ball in the space. The oddest part is I can't see a stairway. With the grandness of the hall, I expected to see a sweeping staircase.

The high ceilings and curved gold trim bring me back to my travels in Rome. I remember my awe at seeing the Vatican. Cillian's home is scattered with the same interior. Now I wonder about his travels and his job.

"I might start working as a bodyguard," Shay says behind me.

I glance at Shay as he takes out his cigarettes and removes one. He doesn't light it up; instead, he places it behind one ear.

"I couldn't picture you around a politician or celebrity. You look..." Richard trails off.

"Dangerous," I fill in, and Richard grins at me.

"I was going for scruffy," Richard teases, and I want to enjoy this moment with my brother, but I can't.

"Mr. O'Hara asked me to show you to your room." The woman steps forward. *My room?* My gaze scans the area for Cillian. Maybe it's a good thing he's disappeared.

I look at my brother again and he nods. I hesitate to move. "Go freshen up. I'll still be here," Richard reassures me.

I follow the lady across the foyer. Several rugs are scattered across the beige tiled floor. It shouldn't look right, but it does. I see the elevator before we stop at it. The gold doors don't reflect us. The design that's carved on the doors is the same as the door handle. The lion's head, with his mouth open, is repeated in a pattern.

I take a look back at Shay and Cillian, who are walking off in the other direction. The ding of the doors makes my heart jump. The lady holds out her hand for me to go first. I step into the elevator, and once she's in, she hits number three.

To the third floor, then.

Everything is starting to become too much. "I'm Dana." I hold out my hand and when the woman turns, she takes it. "Jo." Jo has kind eyes and a soft smile. Small blonde curls are tight to her head.

The elevator doors open, and I follow her down another impressive hallway. "This is an estate house?" I ask. I notice red ropes in front of a few rooms that stop entry. I can only imagine an estate house having this.

"Yes. We have guests on Sundays and every second Wednesday. Parts of the house are off-limits, per Cillian's request."

Jo stops at a set of white double doors and opens them into a bedroom. My bedroom.

The soft mint green walls meet with the back wall. The moss green wallpaper covering the back wall is strong with its small pink rose buds—in this room, it works.

Everything in the room is mahogany, from the four-poster bed to the large linen chest that sits at its end. My mind is picking up little bits. The longer I'm in the room, the more I notice small things, like how carvings on the posters of the bed are the lions' heads again.

Or the fact there's a freestanding bathtub near the large window. Everything is huge and spacious, yet the room holds warmth. Jo passes me and opens another set of double doors. "I've left fresh towels and all the toiletries for you."

The bed linens match the wallpaper. My gaze is drawn to the high ceiling; the molding is sprinkled with gold.

"Thank you," I say to Jo.

She walks around the room, and I notice the source of the warmth. A fire has been lit, and it appears it's been lit a while.

"Your clothes are in here."

I spin, my mind buzzing. Jo has opened another door that was camouflaged among the wall of wallpaper. She flicks on the light, and I step a little closer to see into another room that holds rows of clothing.

"My clothes?"

"Yes. I'm sure they are all your size. Mr. O'Hara gave us the measurements."

Mr. O'Hara.

"Cillian," I spit out.

Jo flicks off the light and closes the door. "Yes." She walks back toward the main door. "If there is anything you need, just dial one on the phone."

Phone? Jo points and I see it—a slick black phone on the bedside table. Now that I see it, it looks so out of place in the room. The door closes, and I turn to see that Jo has gone.

My heart starts to race. What now?

I walk across the wooden floor, which is also decorated with several different rugs. I pick up the phone and punch in my father's number—all but the last one. My hands start to tremble, and I drop the phone. What would I say? Why did you leave me to die? Where were you when Cillian was about to hand me over to the enemy?

The enemy? I had no idea who that was anymore. I had no idea of anything.

I'm staring at the phone when a soft knock on the door pulls me away. I'm tempted to hide it in case it's taken away from me. A last second decision, I push it under the pillow and turn as Richard enters the room.

"You got the best room in the house." He tries to smile, but it doesn't work on him.

I want to tell my brother that I want to go home, but do I? "How's Mother?" I ask.

Richard's jaw tightens. "Good. Dana, I know this isn't easy." Richard steps into the room, inspecting the space. Maybe he's doing it to avoid eye contact. "Mother thinks you went back to Italy."

"She's very gullible," I bite back.

Richard grins. "I agree." Is that pain I see in his eyes? Seeing any vulnerable streak in him has my walls crumbling.

"Tell me what's happening. I feel like I've stepped into another world, Richard. I'm trying to understand all this, but I can't tell what's real anymore."

"Father got a tip that you were a target. Honestly, I think it was our own doing. Like a reaction of putting you in Cillian's care."

I half snort at Cillian's name. Care my ass. "Thank God you showed up and stopped that man from taking me." I step closer to my brother. "Thank you." Richard has never been the hugging type. That was Jack, who I miss so much.

"I didn't do anything. I'm so grateful Cillian was there and killed that man."

I'm shaking my head. "Cillian didn't; you did." My heart starts to race.

"It was Cillian. I'm just glad you're safe, Dana."

But I saw him look at me with such pity. I saw it in his eyes, that he was letting me go. I keep replaying the scene in my head, trying to picture Richard at that moment. Had I seen him take the shot? Had I seen anyone take the shot? No, I hadn't.

"Why don't you freshen up and have something to eat?"

"I don't need to freshen up," I bark at Richard. A shower and a meal won't fix this.

"Have you looked at yourself?" Richard asks.

"How long do I have to stay here? When will all this end?"

Richard exhales and steps up to me. He grips my shoulders and dips his head. "I'm going to be honest with you. This never ends. This is our life. I'm sorry." He releases me.

But for the first time since all this started, I'm so grateful for his honesty.

"I'll go wash up," I whisper.

He nods but doesn't walk away. "I have to go, but Cillian has assured me you can ring us anytime you want."

"Can I ring Jack?" I ask. I want to ask about Maeve.

"Of course." Richard doesn't leave.

"You look just like dad." The moment I say the truth, my vision wavers. "Why didn't he come, Richard?" I blink the tears.

"He's a target all the time. I told him I would go in his place."

"Liar." I fold my arms.

"You've had so much to take in already. Please rest."

I nod. My mind feels more exhausted than my body. I nod. Richard clears the distance and places a kiss on my forehead. "I'm sorry, Dana."

His words have me reaching up and wrapping my arms around him. He hugs me back, and I hold on to him far longer than I should.

"I love you, Richard." He's the one that came when I was in danger today.

"I love you too." He presses another kiss to my forehead, and I release my brother.

"I'm going to freshen up," I tell him before he says it again. "I'll see you soon." I say the words like that's what's going to happen. I have no idea when I'll see Richard again, but I need some reassurance.

"I'll ring you later," Richard says, but I know it's a way of ending our conversation. He leaves the room, and I appreciate how hard he is trying. We aren't a family that talks about our emotions. Having two manly brothers and a father who often struggles to express himself, my mother's the only one I've had to lean on.

Now I can't.

I enter the bathroom and take one look at myself in the large golden-framed mirror that's directly behind a tub that's similar to the one in the bedroom. I'm covered in mud. The girl in the mirror reaches up and pulls a twig and some leaves out of her hair.

And as I look at myself, I wonder if anything will ever be the same again.

CHAPTER EIGHTEEN

DANA

I'M SITTING IN THE bath. The mirror that covers the wall is steamed up. My skin has turned pink from scrubbing it. I keep hearing the gunshot over and over in my mind. I rest my head on my knees as I keep replaying that moment in the forest when I thought Cillian had handed me over to the enemy.

He hadn't.

A knock at the door is quickly followed by Cillian stepping into the bathroom. I pull my legs closer to my chest, very aware that I'm naked.

He's washed too. His dark hair is damp. Cillian is always confident, but right now he appears unsure as he walks over to a stack of towels and picks one up. I want to ask him what he's doing, but if I start talking, I'm sure nothing good will come from it.

He holds the towel wide and close to the bath and turns his head away. The water is almost cold, and I'm wondering how long I've been there. The room is warm as I stand up. I pause, but Cillian keeps his eyes diverted as I step out of the water. The towel is warm that he wraps around me, and once he has it tightly around me, he walks over to the stack of towels. I fix the large one on me and tighten it at the front. The second towel is smaller, and Cillian doesn't hand it to me but picks up strands of my hair and starts to dry the long tendrils. He moves around me, and his gentleness is almost painful.

"You hesitated," I find myself saying.

His hands pause. "My sister, Aoibhe, was kidnapped by the Russians. I've been trying to get her back for a long time. So when they offered her back to me..."

I turn so I can see him. "Jesus, Cillian." I want to tell him that he should have made the exchange, but I'm glad I didn't end up in their hands. "I'm so sorry."

Cillian touches my face, but the crushing pain in his gaze nearly undoes me. "I hesitated," he whispers. "But I couldn't." He drops his hand.

"What about Richard or Shay? Or my dad. Can't they help?"

Cillian's gaze is zapped of any pain, and his eyes grow hard. "Your dad is helping me in exchange for keeping you safe."

I nod. "That's good." But it doesn't look like Cillian thinks so. His jaw is tight, and I reach up and touch his face. "What can I do?" I ask.

"Nothing, Dana." I see the monster lurking behind Cillian's eyes. I don't want to see him in pain.

I have no idea how all this works, but the next time I speak to my father, I will make sure he's doing everything he can.

Cillian returns to drying my hair, and I let him. His fingers brush my shoulders and the back of my neck. The contact sends shivers across my skin. After a few light touches of his hand, I start to think it might not be an accident. Cillian spins me until I'm staring in the mirror behind the tub. He's a head taller than I am, and his dark green eyes are sending my belly squirming. His touch to my shoulders is gentle, but I feel it all the way down into my soul. It eases some of the pain; it lets my mind take a break from the horror of my life, and right now, I'm just me.

Cillian's hand moves around to the front of the towel. Watching him in the mirror is exhilarating. He pulls the towel slowly, and my heart ping-pongs as the towel tumbles to the ground. I'm naked. The air in the room is warm, and the tiles under my feet are warm. Cillian doesn't take his eyes off me as he reaches around and runs his knuckles across my core. His fingers glide closer to my opening, and I inhale a breath in anticipation. I'm not prepared when he slides a finger inside me. His other hand trails along my spine. I never knew someone touching my back could feel so good. His fingers run up and down my spine, and I arch my back, only to straighten as he plunges his finger inside me again.

I meet his eye in the mirror. He's all twisted up with wrath and desire. I want to ask him what's wrong, but he adds another finger inside me. His hands work expertly, dipping in and then running his fingers along my clit.

I reach behind me and touch his hard cock. The idea of him inside me has me turning. His fingers slip from me. When I look up at him, he's still watching me in the mirror, and the look in his eyes makes me feel like a goddess.

I start to lift his T-shirt, and his gaze snaps to me. He helps me remove it. I'm staring at all the artwork on his chest that covers his scars. Each one must have their own story. Cillian doesn't let me linger but stands back and removes his trousers and boxers. I reach for him, but he moves away out of reach.

"Sit on the side of the tub."

I do as he says. My stomach clenches as he kneels down and touches my knees. He grins before spreading them. The air against my core and the anticipation has me throbbing. Cillian runs his hands up my thighs before burying his head between my legs. I push forward, giving him full access. He's sucking and licking my clit, and I'm so close to coming when he stops. His mouth is wet with my juices, and each kiss he presses to my thigh sends my want for him skyrocketing. His fingers sink into my core, and I grip the side of the tub so I don't come off it.

When he dips his head this time, he moves past my clit, his tongue inching further back. New sensations arise and I want to stop him, but I don't. I find myself giving him more access, and his tongue skims the ring of my ass. Long fingers continue to plunge inside me, and with my eyes closed, it's like there are two people touching me, licking me.

Cillian drags his tongue back up to my clit, and one lick sets my nerve endings on fire. He extracts his fingers and rises up, peeling my fingers from the side of the bath and helping me rise so I'm standing in front of him. Everything in me throbs with a want I can't quite explain.

Cillian spins me so I'm facing the mirror. He's like a giant behind me. His hand runs up my spine and stops at my neck, where he grips it tightly before pushing my head down. I bend over, grip the bath, and look back into the mirror. He's watching me and my heart slams into my chest with anticipation. He runs both hands across my back, and I arch toward him, wanting more of his touch. His hands run further down and stop at my ass; he squeezes the cheeks painfully. The burn is instant across the sensitive flesh. His thumb dances along the opening of my anus. I meet his gaze in the mirror, and his eyes have darkened to a green that grows on the floor of the deepest forest.

His large cock touches my opening as he continues to run his thumb along my ass. I keep my eyes open as Cillian pushes his cock deeper inside, and his thumb sinks into my ass too. I cry out and he gives me a wicked grin that's filled with sin, lust, and a whole lot of wrong. He pushes even deeper into me, and I cry out again. I want more, but I'm already stretched. I thought his cock was fully in, but I was wrong. He pushes further in and my cry turns to heavy gasps as he pulls out to plunge in deeper. He keeps eye contact, and I'm swimming in a dark pool I don't mind being in. His thumb sinks deeper, and when he wriggles it around inside my ass, I'm sure I'm about to come. But it's like Cillian knows my triggers and he extracts it slightly, only to give me more of his cock. When his balls hit my flesh, I know he's fully in.

His pounding grows faster, and I close my eyes as his thumb sinks back inside my ass too. My tits bounce and slap against me. I'm feeling too much, but not enough.

"Open your eyes. Watch me come inside you." Cillian's words have me nearly hitting my own climax. I open my eyes and stare at him. My gaze darts to myself and I'm unrecognizable. There's a mix of awe and pleasure painted across my flushed face. My gaze is overcast, like I'm drunk.

Cillian's pounds grow frantic, his thumb fully in my ass, and I can't hold on. Watching him push me over the edge, I call out his name on a long exhale. My shouts have Cillian's pace go berserk before he halts rapidly as he empties his seed inside. His face is twisted in ecstasy, and I'm still rolling in my own pleasure. He gives several final juts before he stops completely. I'm not sure what he removes first, his thumb or cock, but when he leaves me, his seed trickles down my leg, and it's a feeling I never want to go away. As he backs away, I stand up straight. My back rebels with pain when I stretch out my hands. The death grip I had on the bath made them almost numb. I look up to find Cillian still watching me in the mirror. He walks back and I don't know how he can still make my heart pound, but he does. His gaze is softer as he reaches me and presses a kiss to my shoulder that I feel right down into my toes.

He steps away and walks over to a large shower that runs a quarter of the bathroom. He turns on the spray. "Are you going to join me?"

I don't answer with words but step toward him. I want him all over again, and I'm not sure how that is even possible. But I do. He steps under the spray of water, and he's like a god. An immortal. Something a mortal like me shouldn't want, shouldn't have.

He doesn't move as my hands glide across his abs. All the artwork fascinates me, and I see a lion's head buried among the other designs. "What does the lion mean? I've seen it all around your home? Now here." I run my fingers across it—across the scars that are hidden under them. I look up at Cillian to find him watching me.

"It's my family's crest. It represents a brave warrior. We are all special forces or army, so we like to think of ourselves as warriors." He brushes his hair back, pushing water along with it. He steps out from under the spray and swaps places with me. The warm water covers my body, and I close my eyes. After a moment, I dip my head out of the spray and open my eyes to find Cillian staring at me.

"The scars on your body? What happened?" I ask.

His jaw tightens, but he doesn't leave. Instead, he focuses on the cloth and bottle in hand. He lathers the cloth. "Turn around." His eyes are soft.

I do as he says. I almost sigh as he runs the cloth along my back.

"Davy placed all of them on my body as part of his discipline."

I want to see Cillian as he speaks, but he keeps me still by gripping my shoulders. "It was a long time ago, Dana. They don't hurt anymore." He's trying to reassure me.

I try to turn again, only this time, he lets me.

"The scars might have healed, Cillian"—I reach up and touch his temple—"but the pain often gets trapped up here." He doesn't budge, and I push up onto the tip of my toes and press a kiss to his cheek. "I'm here if you want to talk."

We stare at each other before Cillian turns me around and finishes washing my back. Once we are done, he turns off the water and wraps me in a towel.

"Get dressed. I want to show you something." He presses a kiss to my forehead and leaves the bathroom, naked and dripping water. I watch him until he disappears from my sight. When he does, I start to get dried quickly, intrigued to see what he wants to show me.

CHAPTER NINETEEN

CILLIAN

I'M WAITING FOR DANA downstairs. Every time I think of her bent over the bath, my cock grows hard. Staff enter the hallway. They give me quick nods before scurrying off to their jobs.

The elevator doors open, and she looks up and right into my eyes. She's fucking gorgeous. She's wearing a red dress I knew would be perfect on her. It's a bit fancy for what we are about to do, but I don't care. My gaze trails down her bare legs until I stop at her small black boots.

"The boots have got to go," I say as she steps out of the elevator and reaches me.

She's smiling widely, her blue eyes alive. She's stunning. "What's wrong with my boots?" she questions.

I start to walk. "Nothing, but they won't be suitable." I glance at her and her smile widens. I release her from my gaze, and she looks around the large foyer that we walk through.

"So what exactly do you do?" she asks.

"I'm a bodyguard to some extremely wealthy people."

"Anyone I'd know of?" she asks.

"Lots of celebrities. But mostly politicians."

"You aren't going to name-drop?"

I grin at her. "No, I'm not. Just be assured they pay very well."

"Obviously." Dana continues to gaze around. I know how impressive all this is.

"This estate has been in our family for generations. It was bought with old money."

I steer her to a door to our left. We enter another hallway. The carpeted flooring makes our footsteps soundless. The golden sconces on the wall are dimmed, just lighting the hallway that has no windows.

It's almost intimate, and I glance at Dana, who's looking around again. I cut to the right, and we enter an arched hallway that slopes downward—the carpet disappears and tiles take over. The noise of Dana's boots is loud.

"It's a maze," Dana says.

She's right. It took me years to learn the whole layout of the house. I take the door to my right, and we enter the washroom that leads outside.

The glass canopy admits sunshine that Dana steps into.

I take out a pair of wellies from a closet and remove my shoes. Dana smiles at me.

I take out a second pair and hand them to her. "These are for you."

She raises a brow but removes her boots and puts on the wellies. We go outside. "I look ridiculous."

"You look adorable," I say. She looks fuckable, and I'm sure she can read it in my eyes. I'll take her again later.

We've entered the courtyard, and I make my way to the third shed.

"I want you to meet Sally and her crew."

Dana's steps aren't as quick, and the enthusiasm slowly leaks from her eyes. "Sally?"

I nod. "Yeah. She's my favorite girl." I'm grinning as I approach the shed. I get a bucket and fill it with seeds. As I am shaking it, all the girls pour from the shed—Sally leads them toward me—and they're all cackling.

"Meet Sally and her crew," I say as I scatter the seed across the yard.

"Hens. Sally is a hen?" I like to think I hear relief in Dana's voice.

"Why, what did you think?" I hand Dana the bucket.

She takes a handful of seeds and scatters them close to the girls, who cluck and race, gobbling them up quickly. I could stand here and watch Dana all day.

My phone rings and Dana's smile dies a little.

"One second." I take it out and see Skinner's name flash up on my screen. *My father.*

I answer. "Yes?"

"I need you to meet me. I'm sending you over an address." He hangs up.

I open the text that comes in immediately. The address is in the same zip code as I am, so he isn't far.

Dana's watching me. "Everything okay?"

I put the phone away. "Yes. I need to step out for a while."

Disappointment floods her blue eyes. "I won't be long. You can go inside and check the place out."

"I think I'm good here with Sally and her crew." She grins, and I love seeing the light return to her eyes.

"I'm leaving all my girls together."

Surprise lifts Dana's eyebrows.

"I won't be long." I leave before she can further analyze my statement. I leave before I can overthink it, too.

***

The tennis court was spectacular in its glory days, I'm sure. But now weeds have managed to squeeze through cracks in the tarmac. The lines are faded and the green chain link fence has several holes in it. I pass through the tennis court to enter the old courtyard. This part hasn't stood up to time well either. To my right is the back door to the old house. White paint peels off the walls. I push open the back door. The kitchen's seventies décor corresponds to how dilapidated the outside and inside are. The smell of rot and dampness is heavy in the air. Two men are stationed at the kitchen door that leads into a modest hall.

I get a salute, no one speaks, and I pass both men. Another man is stationed outside the third door down in the hallway.

"He's inside." The door is opened, and I step into what once upon a time was a sitting room. The room is grand. The curtains that have been dragged across the rails are moth-eaten, and spots of light shine through the small holes. The room is empty of furniture except for a large open fireplace. I don't look at Skinner; instead, I'm staring at the man who's tied to one of the yellow kitchen chairs. He's been beaten already. He spits blood out in front of him and glares at me.

"What is this?" I ask, not taking my eyes off the man.

"This is Bednar Novak."

I look at Skinner for the first time, and I hate what I see. I see similarities. "You wanted a meeting with him, so here he is."

Not what I meant. But I'll take it.

"I'm looking for my sister. Aoibhe O'Hara." I'm glaring at Bednar.

He's looking around with a snarl on his face. I kick his chair, and he finally looks at me. "I'm speaking to you." I grab his face. "You remember me. You remember I sat and waited to speak to you."

I release him before I break his fucking jaw. "My sister. Aoibhe. Where is she?"

Everything in me tightens—my hands, my shoulders, my jaw. Even my mind. Everything zones in, and all I want to do is kill this motherfucker.

Skinner steps up beside me. "It would be in your best interest, Mr. Novak, to answer him."

Bednar doesn't speak, and I want to strangle the words out of him.

Skinner takes out his phone and zooms through it before stopping at an image of a young girl tied up. She looks about fourteen. He steps to Bednar and holds out the picture.

"I will have her killed if you don't answer Cillian's questions."

Horror chokes Bednar's features, and he keeps staring at the picture. "If you harm her—"

Skinner cuts him off by taking the phone away. "That is entirely up to you, Mr. Novak."

"I don't know anything about your sister."

My fists collide with his face. "Where is she?" I'm roaring. I can barely contain the rage inside me. This bastard buys and sells women. He doesn't deserve to live.

"I think having his daughter is incentive enough, Cillian. Beating him won't help."

I want to tell Skinner to fuck off, but I remember my place. I remember who he is. I remember who I am.

I stand back and compose myself. I hate the flicker of respect I see in Skinner's gaze. I want to tell him I know who he is and get it over with.

"So your daughter dies. What a shame." Skinner opens a pen knife and walks toward Bednar like he's just going to let him go. I can't let that happen. I can't let hope of finding my sister slip that easily.

"I can find out." Bednar speaks up in a huff of panic. "I will find out who took Aoibhe."

I'm already shaking my head. "You aren't fucking listening. I don't just want to know who took her; I want her back. I want everyone who took part in this to die."

Skinner holds out his hand for me to calm down. "We also want a name of who killed Davy O'Hara."

I hate not seeing any recognition of the names in Bednar's eyes. I had hoped for something, but I think we plucked the wrong guy. I didn't pick him. Liam offered him up.

I exhale.

"I will get you the information."

Skinner releases Bednar, and it goes against all my instincts as the ropes fall to the floor.

"You have twenty-four hours," Skinner warns him.

Twenty-four hours. That's a lot of time, yet I've been patient for months. So twenty-four hours shouldn't feel this hard. Bednar is pulled from the room by one of Skinner's bodyguards, leaving him and me alone.

"He said he had nothing to do with Davy."

"He said he would get us the information."

Skinner turns to me and removes his glasses, showing me his missing eye. My gut curls. "Before you got here, I did my own little interrogation. He's not high-ranking. I think he's a dangerous man who sees a lot, but he isn't behind any of this."

I agree with Skinner about Bednar not having a hand in this. He didn't recognize the names. "You think he can find out?"

Skinner walks up to me and places a hand on my shoulder. "We will find out soon."

"And if he doesn't have answers for us?"

"Let's wait and see what happens first."

Skinner removes his hand from my shoulder and leaves with his men. I stay in the room longer than is necessary. Bednar's blood stains the old wooden floor. The cut rope and chair, I pick up. I pocket the rope and put the chair back into the kitchen.

I check under the sink for some bleach. I didn't really expect to find any and I didn't. Closing the cupboard, I know worrying about a drop of blood is stupid. Skinner leaving here without a glance over his shoulder told me he either owned the property or he would send men over to clean up. I don't want to think about my sister, but getting this close to him is making my skin itch on the inside. I'm jittery and just want this nightmare to fucking end.

I return to the house. Dana, of course, isn't in the yard. I've been driving around for hours, trying to get away from my thoughts. But that's impossible.

I keep taking out my phone, tempted to confront Skinner about being my father and to confront my mother on being a liar. She hid that truth from me, and I'm not sure why. I think that knowledge would have helped me more than hindered me.

"Are you okay?"

I didn't hear Dana approach. She's still in the red dress, but she's no longer wearing her wellies. She's put the small black boots back on. Seeing her does something to me.

"I am now."

Her cheeks turn a nice shade of pink.

"Have you eaten?" I ask.

"No. I wasn't really hungry."

"I'm sure you're hungry now." I start to walk and Dana follows.

"I am a little."

"I'll get Frank to make us something. Why don't you go ahead to the dining room?"

She points in two directions. "Which way?"

I take a step closer to her, just so I can see her eyes widen and her cheeks turn a little pinker. I inhale the smell of her without embarrassment. I want to fuck her.

I'm considering dragging her off to the bedroom. I negotiate with myself—feed her first. "The last door on the left."

She looks up at me. Our shoulders brush and I glance at her lips.

"Okay." The pulse flickers in her neck as she speaks.

I release her from my gaze and she walks away. I watch her until she disappears into the dining room.

I find Frank in the kitchen. "I heard your arrival, Master O'Hara. So I've started to prepare your favorite."

"I can smell the lamb. I just hope it's for two."

Frank continues to check pots without looking at me. "I always make it for two."

"That's wise," I reassure him. "How long until dinner, Frank?"

"Fifteen minutes."

"I'll be in the dining room." I leave the kitchen and find Dana sitting at the head of the dining room table. She rises the moment I enter.

"I was just checking it out."

"Sit down, Dana. You look good there."

She looks unsure but sits down when I pin her with a stare. All I can think about is fucking her on the table, or her underneath the table, giving me a long blowjob.

I pull out the chair to her right and sit down.

"I really don't mind moving."

Jo arrives in the room, and without a word, sets the table. I can't take my eyes off Dana, and I realize I don't know much about her. Only the small snippets I've seen and what I know about her family. Her father said she was manipulative. I was starting to doubt that.

"You mentioned you lived in Rome for a while."

Dana nods, but she's watching Jo. I want her to look at me. "Thank you."

Her attention returns to me once Jo leaves. "Yeah. I traveled a fair bit, then I settled down in Rome."

I don't ask why she had settled there. I assume it had to do with Philip. I'm glad he's dead. "Where else did you travel?"

"Jersey, England, France, Australia, Italy. And the Czech Republic, as that's where my mother comes from."

Dana focuses on the cutlery in front of her as she speaks. "I think I was always running from something. I just never knew what exactly. Now I do." She glances up at me.

"What were you running from?" My real question is who do I have to kill.

"My family lies." She doesn't blink but shrugs like it's no big deal, but I see her pain. "They lied to me my whole life—lied to me about who they are." A half-bitter laugh falls from her lips. "I really believed my father ran hotels. That was it." More pain flashes behind her eyes.

I find everything she's saying hard to believe. "You're telling me you never knew your family was Mafia?"

"No. I never knew."

I'm staring at Dana, wondering if I had it all wrong. If she is as manipulative as her father said. My gut churns. Had she fooled me?

It isn't possible to hide something like that, to keep her in the dark about her family being in the Mafia.

"What did you think Richard and Jack did?"

"Work for my father." She shrugs again.

I say what I feel. "That's a little hard to believe."

Her face turns red. "Sadly, it's the truth."

We stare at each other. "You don't believe me." Sorrow clouds her pretty face.

"Can you blame me?" I want her to convince me that she's the victim in all this.

Frank arrives with the food, and we fall silent again as it's placed in front of us. Jo brings in drinks, and when they finally both leave, I'm waiting for Dana to explain herself.

I don't want to feel this way toward her. "If you are lying, it's okay. I can look the other way," I say and start to cut up the lamb. There. I've given her an out and pray to God she takes it. I like her too much, and I'm willing to overlook her small lie.

She laughs and I stop cutting my lamb.

She nods several times before looking at me. "You can look the other way?" she questions.

I grit my jaw. I don't want to, but I will. "Yes," I clarify.

"So you're fine with my being a liar?"

"No. But I'm willing to overlook this lie as long as we have no more of them."

Her smile is too wild, and something is telling me to hold on, that she's about to go full throttle.

"Lies." She says the word with a twisted smile. "That's been my fucking life, Cillian. Lies from the people I've loved the most." Disappointment gouges itself into her features, and she gets up ready to march away. But I'm not done yet.

Not even close.

CHAPTER TWENTY

DANA

HE IS WILLING TO look the other way as I lie. I can't believe he just said that.

"Running won't fix this." His words are sharp. Authoritative. Controlled.

My chest tightens, and a pain flickers to life in the center. I stop walking. I stop running.

"My best friend, Maeve..." Pressure gathers at the back of my eyes. "She killed my cousin." Saying it out loud makes me think she never lied to me. That Maeve isn't sick.

My father is.

"Shay and Jack were there. They all covered it up." I blink and tears fall. "I went to Richard for help..."

The pain grows, and it's like something I've never felt before. "They told me they were Mafia." I swallow. "They handed me to you."

I turn and face Cillian for the first time throughout this conversation. I wipe tears off my cheeks. He's turned in his chair and watches me. "I wish I was lying. I wish Maeve hadn't told me what they did. I wish I hadn't gone to Richard. I wish..."

I wish my father was the man I had believed him to be.

The world around me starts to crumble. "If you have an ounce of respect for me, don't tell me you accept lies."

Cillian doesn't flinch, and a crushing sensation grows heavy on my chest. "I'm not lying Cillian. So your words"—I sniffle—"fucking hurt."

I have to leave or I'm going to cave right there on the floor.

I'm walking at full speed from the room. I don't even make it to the door. Arms circle my waist, and I'm dragged back against his chest. It's an odd moment. My heart still roars in my chest, my mind still races, and his smell grows heavier around me.

Cillian keeps both arms around my waist and just holds me against his body. A giggle starts to bubble up my throat, and I'm waiting for it to release, but a different sound pours from my mouth. One filled with agony and loss. My soul starts to change in Cillian's arms, and only because his arms are around me, I'm not on my knees with the pressure of truths that rest on my shoulders.

"They killed Cian," I whimper. My cousin. A boy, a man. A human. "Shay shot him." I'm bending over trying to force the pain to stop, but Cillian continues to hold me. "They sent me away."

That moment back at the park, when Richard, Jack, and Shay decided to hand me over to Cillian, I had no idea what would happen to me. Would they dispose of me? Since my family is Mafia, anything is possible. Fear had gripped me so hard that I now realize it changed me. It altered my mind where something simple might not be simple anymore. The world is far darker than I could ever imagine. My mind springs to the castle, to my father. "My father, he's a liar." More pain rips through my abdomen. A piece of me breaks further. I'm learning my life all over again, and it isn't one bit pretty.

I'm turning, and Cillian pulls my head into his chest and holds me. Pain, pain, and more pain—that's all I feel as my mind jumps through all the hoops that feel like they are on fire, burning me up.

I'm in the forest again, and I'm falling backward. The man's dead eyes stare up into the sky. I push away from Cillian. The movement is unexpected, and he releases me easily.

"You shot a man."

Cillian's jaw is tight.

"You killed him." Tears drip into my open mouth as I point an accusing finger at Cillian. "He's dead."

"Would you have rather he took you?" Cillian's words are controlled, and it's like they reach out and shake me. Some of my hysteria dies.

"Maybe. Maybe all this will end." I lie so easily.

"You don't mean that," Cillian says.

"Exactly, Cillian, I don't. But I'm glad you can spot a lie when you hear one."

"You're not lying about your father. I'm sorry."

I give Cillian a second look. "Why would you even say that you could look the other way as I lie?" What the fuck is that? Who says that? Who accepts that?

"I just did." His jaw hardens.

I'm shaking my head. "No. Explain to me how you would sit and eat with a liar."

"Because you matter to me."

I'm shaking my head. "That's not good enough. If I matter to you, you don't look the other way."

Cillian exhales. "I apologized."

He did, yet it doesn't feel like enough for me. I don't understand his saying he would look the other way. What relationship is built on those kinds of foundations?

It hits me hard and fast. I understand why this is becoming so painful for me. I want more with Cillian. I don't just want a tumble in the forest or some quick fling. I want him, and I want him to want me.

"You matter to me." I swallow, trying to get my words right. "I don't want us built on lies." I can feel my cheeks heat up. I know I'm putting myself out there. Cillian said once that this isn't personal, so my body is stiff as I prepare for the backlash of my words. I'm expecting him to say there is no us.

He takes a step toward me. "You're right." He eliminates the space between us, and I'm in his arms.

I'm falling hard for Cillian, and I'm not sure if it's due to circumstances and the craziness of my life. Each touch he places on me sends me into a frenzy. Each time he shares a small snippet of his life, I crave more. Each wound with him is amplified, each smile feels like ecstasy. I have no idea what all this means; only that he matters.

"Pardon the intrusion, Master O'Hara."

"Yes, Frank." It's an almost growl from Cillian that rattles his chest. I slowly leave his arms.

"Jack O'Reagan is here."

My body stiffens. Jack is here. I look at Frank, trying to see behind him, but I don't see Jack.

Cillian doesn't speak, but Frank nods, like he got some unspoken directions, and leaves.

"Do you want to see him?" Cillian asks, getting my attention.

"I need to see him." I wipe my eyes and try to work on my appearance. I'm fidgeting, fixing my dress. Brushing my hair with my hands.

"I'll come with you," Cillian says.

"He's my brother. He won't hurt me." The moment I say the words, another wave of shock sends sparks to my nerves. I tighten my fists to stop the small tremble. *Would he hurt me?*

"I know he won't, Dana." Cillian reaches out and tucks a strand of hair behind my ear.

I look up into Cillian's eyes. "I think it's something I need to do myself. I need answers."

Cillian doesn't look happy, but he agrees with a nod of his head.

"Frank is outside the door. He'll take you to him. I'll be here when you are done."

I'm ready to walk away, but something lingers in Cillian's eyes, and I rise up on the tip of my toes and press a kiss to his lips.

His lip tugs up into a slight smile as I place a second quick kiss on his lips. I leave before my body grows more aware of Cillian's existence.

Frank is indeed waiting for me outside the door. "This way."

I follow him across the foyer. My stomach squirms as Frank opens a large set of double doors. The sitting room is exquisite, but my brain skips all the luxurious furniture and soaks up my brother. Jack rises off the couch. Eyes the same as mine examine me from the tips of my toes to the top of my head. I want to run into his arms, but something has changed. I step into the room.

"Thank you, Frank," I say as Frank gives a brief nod while closing the doors behind me.

My heart won't settle as Jack continues to stare at me. He frowns. "How are you?"

I'm sure my eyes are red and puffy. "I'm okay." I look away from Jack. I'm unsure about him. I know he would never hurt me, but we were close, and all of this has knocked me off-kilter. I want to ask him so many questions, but they've never gotten me far in the past.

"Father came to see me," I start and sit down on the couch. I sit on the edge furthest away from Jack. He slowly sits back down, but he wears a troubled look.

"Did it go well?" Jack asks. He's thinking before he speaks.

I move closer to Jack. My heart tells me not to, but I listen to my head—I need to. "I'm sorry about Maeve."

Jack sits back slightly. The movement is minimal, but it's a loud noise in the quiet room. "What do you mean?"

Is that a slight thread of panic I see? "Father told me how sick she is. That she's unstable and imagined everything with Cian."

I stare at Jack, daring him to lie to me, praying that my brother hadn't failed me too.

"That's what he said?" Jack questions.

"Isn't that what I just said?" I fold my hands in front of me.

Jack's face hardens, and he looks away.

"Is it the truth, Jack?" My voice rises, but I can't let him see my pure desperation. I need the truth so much. So badly.

My brother looks back at me. "What do you think?" he asks.

I know what I think. I shake my head slowly. "I think he's lying."

"You're far smarter than I was, Dana." Jack looks pained. "I wish I saw through his bullshit when I was younger."

I still need him to confirm it. "So she killed Cian?"

Jack's face grows hard again. "It was self-defense."

It doesn't matter. All that matters is that Maeve's mind isn't fractured like my father had claimed.

"How can you look at Shane and Una?" I ask and realize the unfairness of the question the moment I speak it.

"It fucking kills me," Jack barks.

I have no idea how Jack lives like this, but now I realize that I'll have to, too. I'll meet Una and Shane and have to act like I don't know what happened to Cian. Can I do this?

Something shifts in Jack's eyes. "I didn't come here for a visit. We got some bad news today; that's why Richard came to you earlier and Father couldn't."

"What?"

"Finn is dead."

I'm glad I'm sitting down. "What happened?"

Jack won't look at me. "They aren't sure yet. They found him dead in his home." Jack still won't look at me.

My stomach sours. "Did someone kill him? Is this because of Father being in the Mafia?" My questions sound silly. Of course it is. This is what happens to people who are in the Mafia. They live short, high lives and die.

"No." Jack looks at me as a new wave of agony strains his face. "Dana, he might have taken his own life. They found an empty bottle of pills in his hand."

My nose and throat burn. "Oh my God. Finn." He was always happy, but ever since the accident that put him in a wheelchair, he has been different. It hits me like a fast-speeding truck. "How did he end up in a wheelchair?"

Jack's lips twist. "He was shot."

I grip the couch. "Because of Father?"

"No, Dana. Finn also worked with Father. It's a family business."

"Finn is Mafia too?" *Was* is more appropriate now.

Jack nods, and I drop the line of questions. Finn is gone. That fact keeps circling in my mind.

"Father okay?" It was his baby brother. He must be devastated.

"He'll be fine," Jack reassures me with too much venom and uncertainty in his voice.

"What is it, Jack?" *What more could be wrong.*

He moves closer to me. "The funeral will be in the next few days."

Jack reaches out and takes my hand, and it opens the doors that have been keeping me at bay. My vision wavers. "So you will have to be there."

I sniffle. "Of course."

Jack isn't showing any emotion, and I pull my own back.

"Shane and Una will be there—"

I take my hand out of Jack's. "That's why you're here. To make sure I keep my mouth shut."

Jack exhales. "No, Dana. I wanted to make sure you were okay."

"Don't worry, Jack. Your secret is safe with me. Never fucking mind that Finn just committed suicide. Let's all make sure you don't get into trouble." I'm becoming irate. My voice rises significantly as my heartbeat soars. "Wouldn't want to upset Maeve." I have no idea why I'm blaming her. But if she hadn't pushed Cian to his death, what would my life be now?

Jack is pulling me into his arms, and my fists collide with his chest. "Every one of you are selfish fuckers." I'm screaming as I continue to hit Jack. He doesn't stop me. I hear the door open, but I'm too lost in my own anger to look.

"You use people." I'm still shouting as Jack pulls me closer to his chest. His hand is tight on my head like he can silence me.

"You kill people." These are my final words before I sob.

"Finn is dead," Jack says, like I don't already know.

"What happened?"

Through my turmoil, Cillian's voice pulls me back.

"They think he took his life," Jack confirms.

I stop crying, but I'm ready to leave Jack's arms. The image of Finn lying on the floor with an empty bottle of pills... How far did someone have to go to end their life? "He must have been so lonely." My eyes, throat, and nose burn. I swallow saliva and tears. "He had nobody," I continue.

"Do you think he took his life?" Cillian asks.

"I'm not sure." Jack's response has me looking up at my brother.

"What do you mean? You said he was found on the floor with an empty bottle of pills. What, you think he took one too many?" My voice is rising again.

"I don't know." Jack grips my shoulders. "No one knows yet." The vein on the side of his neck throbs. I've seen that happen a few times in our lives.

"Okay," I answer, and Jack seems a little satisfied.

"You could have rung," Cillian continues.

Jack rises off the couch. "She's my sister."

I turn to Cillian. He's struggling to stay still. His body leans forward, his hands clenched, his jaw tight, his eyes on fire. "It's okay," I say to Cillian.

He's about to speak when his phone rings. He takes it out of his pocket and takes a look. "I'll just be a minute." He leaves the room.

I turn to Jack, who is staring at the door as he rubs his jaw. I can see the strain around my brother's eyes. "I won't say a word."

Jack robs me of air when his eyes land on me. They ache, and I walk to my brother and wrap my arms around his waist. Instantly, Jack hugs me back. He's always been the hugger. He's always been my rock, my brother, my friend.

"Tell me all this is worth it, Jack." I swallow the agony that throbs inside me. I've never felt so beat down.

"It will be," Jack says.

I cling to my brother because the truth lies in his words.

CHAPTER TWENTY-ONE

CILLIAN

I DON'T KNOW WHO I want to kill first. Jack, Richard, or Liam. The torture in Dana's eyes is too much.

"I'm assuming you're calling about Finn," I speak to Shay the moment I answer the phone.

"You heard?"

"Jack is here," I growl, not liking him in my home, upsetting Dana. Her shouts had me nearly breaking down the door. I've never had to hold back so much. My training is the only thing that kept me from pulling Jack away from Dana.

"Yeah, it's shit. But that's not why I'm calling."

No love lost there then.

"The men in the forest weren't part of Novak's group. They aren't part of any group, Cillian."

I walk through the hall. "Mercenaries?"

"Yeah. Hired by someone."

I stop walking. "Who?"

"I don't know. But it's someone who knows where we were. That's a safe house. No one would know about its existence unless you told someone?"

I half laugh. "You took a long time to get to your question, Shay."

"Did you tell anyone?" Shay asks directly.

"No." I hadn't. But I had mentioned having Dana in a safe house to Robert. I wasn't followed, and he would have no want for Dana.

"I'm still trying to gather intel on the group. But so far, we know they don't belong to anyone. So whoever hired them wanted it to be untraceable."

I'm walking to my office, but I don't want to be too far away from Dana, so I linger in the foyer. "You want to tell me what happened to Finn?" Shay would know.

"I have my suspicions," Shay says.

I know talking on the phone isn't safe.

"So it wasn't suicide?"

"No." Shay confirms it. I could see something in Jack; he knows something too. Someone made it look like a suicide. I didn't know Finn at all, but I did know that he was Darragh's twin, and they were close.

"I'm sorry for your loss," I say.

"Thanks. I'll be in touch." Shay hangs up, and I walk back to the door, listening. They are still talking, their voices low. But Dana doesn't sound distressed like she had only moments ago. I had pushed her too far at dinner. I couldn't blame her, but she mattered to me more than I thought, and I was willing to overlook lies so that I could keep her.

And I was keeping her.

The door opens, and I come eye to eye with Jack. He breaks eye contact and closes the door behind him.

I want to march in there and make sure Dana is okay.

"She will be okay. It's a lot to take in." Jack says.

"Your family kept her in the dark about what you all did?" I ask.

"It was our mother's wish. Stupid, I know." Jack confirms everything that Dana was saying is true. Her whole life, she didn't know about her family.

It was beyond fucking stupid. My blood pumps too fast through my veins. They should have told her.

"When is the funeral?" I ask before I lash out.

"I'll let you know. We are still waiting for the post-mortem."

I snigger. "One of your own?"

Jack takes a step towards me. "What the fuck are you implying?"

Shay liked Jack, but straight away, I didn't. He was cocky and arrogant, that's the feeling I got off him, and he also upset Dana. Richard hadn't left her in a fucking state. But this prick--.

"Let's not pretend." I grin.

"If you have something to say, Cillian. Say it."

He's waiting, I'm waiting, and the door opens. Dana looks shaken.

"Do let us know when the funeral is." I step around Jack and go to Dana.

"I will." Jack growls and turns around as I wrap an arm around her shoulder, pulling her closer to me. Jack's mouth forms a line, and Dana is stiff in my arms.

Fire burns up his eyes as he glares at me. They soften when he looks at his sister. "I'll talk to you soon."

"Bye, Jack," Dana whispers.

Jack hesitates, not sure what to do. He's looking at me like he wishes I would fucking disappear. No luck. I tighten my hold on Dana, warning him not to upset her further.

"See you soon. "Jack says before leaving.

I don't let Dana watch him walk to the door; instead, I lead her to the bar. I think we could both use a drink.

"I'm sorry about your uncle." I finally let her go as I walk to the bar and take down two glasses.

"Me too. I wonder how lonely he was to do something like that. How does anyone get that far?" Her brows drag down as she speaks.

I fill two glasses with whiskey. "Everyone has demons," I say.

Dana looks up at me and walks to the bar. I hand her one glass. Maybe believing he took his life is the lesser of two evils. But behind her worry, I see something deeper, like it has crossed her mind that this could be murder.

I pick up my glass and drink it down. Dana does the same. I could think of a few people who could have done this, but it really didn't matter to me.

"I need to ring my father. Make sure he's okay." Dana looks into the glass.

My phone vibrates in my pocket, but I keep my focus on Dana. "You want another drink?" I ask.

She nods, and I refill both our glasses. "I'll take it with me up to my room."

"No need. You can make the call here. I'll give you some space."

She hugs her glass, and I drink down mine as my phone starts to vibrate again. I walk around the bar and press a kiss to her forehead. I linger for a while, and she leans into me. "The phone is behind the bar." I finally release her.

"Thank you, Cillian."

The moment I vacate the room, I take out my phone and read a message from Robert.

We have information about Aoibhe. Meet me at my home.

I look back at the door that Dana is behind. I consider telling her that I'm leaving for a while, but I hear her low words as she talks to her father. I leave word with Frank that when she's off the phone to tell her, I won't be long.

I'm trying not to think about my sister as I drive to Robert's home, but of course, I can't stop all the bad thoughts that pool in my mind. Finding her has been everything, but getting closer to having my sister back brings with it its own set of problems. What did she suffer? Would I get my sister back or a shadow of what she was? Did they hurt her? Rape her? Make her sell her body?

The air grows thick, and I open the top button on my shirt. Thoughts like that kept me awake most nights, but I kept reassuring myself that Davy would get her back.

I slow down as I near Robert's house. The gate is opened, and I drive up to the house. The same young man is at the door. I'm ready to tell him I'm not fucking trudging across fields.

"Mr. Jordan is waiting for you inside."

I enter the house and am directed into a small kitchen. It surprises me to find him sitting in this room, based on the sheer size of the house. It must have been staff quarters, but it's here I find Robert at the stove.

"Sit down, Cillian. I made some soup." He glances at me over his shoulder. "Will you have a bowl?"

"I will."

He nods and dishes out two bowls of soup, and brings them to the table. "This is my mother's recipe. So don't fucking insult her."

I take a spoon full. "It's delicious." The soup is thick but sweet. It's a nice combination, and I continue to drink it.

"Bednar Novak gave us an address. Your sister will be there tomorrow night at eight."

"That sounds like a fucking setup," I say, but hope does something funny to my stomach.

"I agree." Robert takes another swallow of his soup. His gaze travels back up toward me. "That's why I think it's best you don't go."

"I'm going," I answer. Setup or no setup, that chance that she might be there is enough to make me go.

"We'll be ready."

"I appreciate that."

Robert finishes his bowl of soup. "They had no hand in your father's death."

I hadn't asked. I hadn't cared. All I wanted was my sister. I can't say they are lying because I don't know anymore. Liam could be lying; Liam could have killed him, but why?

"Don't worry, Cillian, we will find who's responsible."

"I know." The Jaguars will go to every length possible to bring to justice the person responsible for my father's death.

"Are you sure about tomorrow night?" Robert asks as I finish my soup.

"Yes." I push the bowl forward. "If it were your sister, wouldn't you do the same?"

"I would." Robert sits back.

"Then why are you questioning me?" I lean in on the table. Something has been bothering me about the attack at the safe house.

Robert half grins. "I can't ask a question?"

"How about I ask a question, Robert. How did you know where I was?"

His grin slides from his face.

"No one knew I was looking for my sister. I hadn't spoken to Bednar Novak at that time, but here mercenaries arrive, offering me my sister at a safe house that no one knows the location of."

Robert doesn't respond, but the truth is plain on his face.

"You bugged my car the day I arrived here to speak to you. That's why you made me walk across all those fields; to buy yourself some time."

Robert still hasn't responded, but his silence is an answer enough.

"Those men weren't ordered to shoot to kill, were they?"

"No." Robert answers.

"The offer of my sister wasn't real?"

"No."

Relief swims thickly in my veins, relief that I didn't actually throw the chance away at saving my sister.

"What did you want with Dana?"

Robert looks away from me.

I reach across and grip both his hands, dragging him closer to me. "Get your fucking hands off me."

"What did you want with Dana?" I repeat.

We stare at each other, each of us firing off threats that should have us stopping this. I pull his arms.

Robert growls. "She's valuable and can be used against Liam."

"For what?" She's a fucking girl. I want to scream. She's mine. No one has a right to touch her.

"Answers. Now take your fucking hands off me."

I release Robert. He rubs his wrists.

"She's off limits." I bark.

His laughter has me clenching my fists. "Is she now? I'm sorry, me boy, but she's not tied to anyone."

"She's tied to me. If she's harmed, I won't fucking stop, Robert."

Robert laughs again. "She's tied to you. Are you married to her?"

"No."

"Then you're not tied to her, Cillian. You know how this works. You know she's valuable."

"She's off limits, Robert." I stand and growl down at him.

"I'd take all that energy and use it to find my sister."

I'm moving, and I don't think as my fist collides with Robert's face. It's a mistake, and I know it the moment I do it.

I stand back, and I'm ready to take a blow from him. He glares at me from the corner of his eye as he wipes blood from the corner of his mouth.

"Go home, Cillian."

He won't stop going after Dana, and it's not just Robert or the Jaguars. The knowledge of Dana will have more people seeing the potential in having her. The control they believe they would have over Liam.

"When you sent your mercenaries to the house, word traveled back to Liam O'Reagan. So you have a snitch in your house." I warn Robert.

His eyes light up with surprise.

I'm not done. "He knew his daughter was under attack, and he knew she might die. He didn't come, Robert. He sent Richard instead. Think about that." I bark, hoping I'm driving my point home.

I leave Robert's home and make my way back to my house. Tomorrow I might finally get to see my sister again. That should have me elated, yet my mind is spinning with the danger that Dana is in. I know no matter what I say to Robert, it won't stop him or anyone else from trying to use Dana as bait for her father.

I know there is only one way of stopping anyone from harming Dana.

CHAPTER TWENTY-TWO

CILLIAN

Dana is still in the bar when I arrive home. She's curled up on a couch, an empty glass still in her hand. Her red puffy eyes show me her pain. I walk to her and kneel down. Her face is soft as she lies asleep on the couch. She's precious. I trace her face with a single finger, and she sighs. Removing the glass from her hand, I place it on the coffee table.

"I was looking for you."

Her voice draws my attention back to her. Her eyes are open. "I'm sorry. I had to step out for a while."

"Frank told me." Dana sits up.

I stay kneeling in front of her. "How is your dad?" I ask. I don't give two fucks how Liam is, but clearly, Dana does.

"He isn't one to show much emotion, but I'm sure behind it all, he is hurting." She nods like she's trying to reinforce her words.

I highly doubt that Liam is in mourning.

"What was wrong earlier, that you had to leave?" Dana's blue eyes are wide and expectant.

I reach out and take her hand. Her gaze darts from me to our entwined fingers.

"No, everything isn't okay. I found out you are a target."

Her lips drag down, and she sits a little straighter. "A target?" She blinks.

I tighten my hold on her hand. "I won't let anything happen to you, Dana."

Her brows drag down, and she glances at our fingers. "Is this because of who my father is? Because I'm his daughter?"

I nod. "Yes. But there is a way to protect you."

She's looking at me again expectantly.

"You can marry me."

Her laugh is short and unsure. "Marry you?"

I release her hand and sit up beside her. "Yes. You could marry me, and that way, you become protected."

She's looking at me like I just lost my mind. My phone vibrates in my pocket.

"I don't even know you."

"You can get to know me," I answer.

Dana gets off the couch. "I would never marry for protection."

"What? You would marry for love?" My words are dry and bitter.

Dana throws her hands in the air. "Yes, of course."

"I just want you to think about it."

"No." I don't like her instant answer.

Marrying her isn't something I'm ecstatic about, but I didn't expect her to say no to me, and I don't like that, either.

"You have someone better to marry?" I get off the couch.

"I'm not saying that. I don't know you, Cillian."

"What do you want to know?"

Her mouth opens and closes, and she folds her arms across her chest. "You're serious about this?"

"Your life depends on it, Dana," I answer honestly and take a step towards her. Marrying her is the only way to keep her safe from all the vultures, and marrying her isn't as unappealing to me as I would have thought.

"No." She says again, only her voice is lower and doesn't hold as much conviction as it had before.

"You would rather put your life at risk than marry me?" I take a step towards her.

Her blue eyes widen. "It's not that, Cillian. I don't want a marriage based on necessity. I want someone to ask me because they want me."

I reach for her and touch her face. "I want you."

She tilts her head, but I see the smile in her eyes. "You know what I mean."

I focus on her lips. "Just think about it."

Her small pink tongue flicks out, and she licks her lips. "Okay." Her word brushes against my lips, and I don't hold back as I press my lips to hers.

Her mouth is warm as I push my tongue in. I run my hands down to her plump ass, and instantly my cock starts to grow.

"Marry me," I whisper against her mouth. Her breaths are fast against my lips. Her eyes narrow as she tries to control her breathing.

"No."

I grin and drag her mouth back to mine. My hands dig into her ass, and she groans into my mouth. I pull her up in my arms, and she wraps her legs around my waist. The red dress shifts easily, giving me access to her bare thighs that I grip. I squeeze, and she hisses in pain.

"Marry me." I say again.

I don't allow her to answer but kiss her hard as I walk us toward the bar.

Her teeth graze my lip, freeing her mouth from mine. "No."

My cock grows heavier, larger, and I want to bury it in her pussy and mouth.

I stop at the bar and sit her up on it. Breaking the kiss, I release her. Her breaths are still frantic, and I love watching her gaze dance across my face and the room. "The door isn't locked."

I grin. "I know. Anyone could walk in while I'm doing this to you." I pull up her dress and bury my face in her sweet, smelling pussy. Her panties are damp, and I grip the edge with my teeth moving them aside before gliding my tongue along the bare exposed skin. Dana's hands sink into my hair. I reach up and push her legs further apart while running my mouth across her damp panties.

I step back and grip the edge of her panties. I don't look away from her as I drag them down. Her cheeks turn pink, and she's fucking perfect. The moment I have her panties off, I return to her pussy and sink my tongue inside. She arches back, and her groans have me sucking her clit; she's already soaking, and my cock aches to be inside her. But I want something more now. Something I didn't even know I wanted. I suck and nip her clit before coming up and pressing my wet mouth to her thighs before standing up and dragging her closer to me. Her gaze snaps to mine.

"Marry me."

She's breaking. She's wavering; I pull her off the bar, so she's standing on the floor in front of me.

She rises up slowly, and the smile she gives me has my cock straining against my trousers. She runs a hand to the back of my neck and pulls me closer to her mouth.

"No.

Fuck Me. She's so sexy.

I move her back toward the arm of the couch. "How many times do I have to ask you before you say yes?"

"Keep asking me, and you'll find out." Dana's answer has me spinning her. She knows what I want and holds onto the arm of the couch, bending over.

I gather her red dress in my hands as I pull it up over her exposed ass. She shifts as I open my belt, and I can't stop myself from running my fingers along her opening that drips with her juices. With my other hand, I push down my zipper and let my trousers fall to the floor. Moving closer to her, I sink my finger inside her pussy while pushing my boxers down. My cock aches as my fingers brush against the head.

I add another finger to her pussy, and Dana throws her head back, her long black hair flowing down her back. I grab a handful and remove my fingers from her pussy. She turns to look at me.

"Marry me, Dana."

Her blue eyes are wide, and she's swimming in a pool of lust and want. I place my cock at her opening but don't put it in. I'm waiting for her answer.

She's weighing her words and that, to me, is fucking progress. "No."

I release her hair and grip her hips. She drags in a breath waiting for me to enter her. I do it in one slam. She cries out, and it's fucking bliss as her warm, wet pussy clenches around me.

"You're so tight." Her pussy was made for my cock. I pull out and slam back into her. She cries out again, and I sink my hands into her hips. I know my fingers will leave a mark as I tighten my hold on her and pump heavier inside her.

Her cries grow louder, and she's forgotten about the unlocked door. I never gave a fuck. Her groans of pleasure loosen my own as my flesh slaps against hers.

"Marry me," I say again as I continue to fuck her. I don't care to hear her answer. All I want is to keep sinking my cock in her sweet wet pussy.

She's crying out, and when her voice rises and her pants grow more frantic, I know she's close to coming, and I want to come with her.

I move faster and harder against her. My body roars as I push past the final barrier, and I'm coming violently inside her, her cries pierce my own pleasure, and I feel her juices flow all over my cock. If I hadn't come already, I would have as her juices continued to flow across my cock. I slow my pace, but I don't pull out of Dana as our heavy breathing continues to be the most dominant sound in the room. When my breathing is more under control, I slip out of Dana. My phone continues to vibrate in my pocket, but I ignore it as Dana pulls up her panties and fixes her dress. Her cheeks are red, her eyes alive.

"Marry me," I say once I have my boxers and trousers back on.

"No." She doesn't smile as she gives me the same answer. "I'm going to tidy up."

I don't want her to wash my cum off her pussy. I like to know that underneath her pretty little dress, I've stained her.

"Think about it," I call as she walks away.

She doesn't answer, and I'm staring at the door long after she leaves. My phone continues to vibrate, and I take it out of my pocket; Shay's name flashes up on the screen. I accept the call.

"I have a location as to where my sister is. I need you tomorrow night." I walk to the bar and pour out a shot of whiskey.

"I'll be there. How did you find her?" Shay asks.

"The Jaguars found her. They are coming too. But I want you at my back."

"We can talk more tomorrow night." Shay answers.

I'm glad he is with me, but I'm sure he didn't ring for the chat. He must need something from me, too. Tomorrow night I'll find out.

"Come to my place around nine tomorrow," I say to Shay.

"Okay. I'll be there."

I end the call and see the address from Robert. I didn't fully trust him before, and now after his sending mercenaries after Dana, I really had little faith left in him.

I could tell Skinner, but that sounded a little too much like running to daddy.

I find Dana in her room. She's changed into another dress, and this one is bright yellow. She's sitting on her bed, looking at a phone in her hand. I stand at her door and just watch her.

"Who are you calling?"

Her head snaps up to me. "My mother." She gives a watery smile. "I was thinking about it, but I'm not actually going to call her."

I stay at the door frame. "Why not?"

She swallows and glances at the phone that she still clutches in her hand. "Because...." She shakes her head. "Because she lied to me, and I don't want to be mad at her."

Funny how my mother had lied to me, too.

"She's your mother. She did it to protect you." I think I'm telling myself the same thing. My mother never told me about Skinner for some reason that I'm not sure of, but I have to believe at the time she thought she was protecting me.

"But she didn't protect me."

I step into the room. "You had a good childhood?"

Dana's gaze travels to my abdomen like she can see through my shirt and see all the scars that tell my childhood story.

"I know, but..." She drops the phone. "She didn't hide something small, Cillian."

I walk to the bed. "My mother hid my true father's identity. She still doesn't know I know. But I can only assume she did it for some reason she believed was the right one at the time. You have to believe that too."

"Why?"

I sit on the bed. "Because they are our mothers, and you are her daughter. She would never hide something to harm you."

"I know that." Dana glances away from me. "It's just not easy."

"You don't have to forget Dana, but you should forgive her."

Dana looks at me. "Will you forgive your mother for lying to you?"

The truth is simple for me. "I already have."

"Ring her." I dip my head so Dana will look at me.

"I'm not ready yet." She admits.

I nod. "Okay."

She's lost in her own thoughts. I assume she wants her space. I get off the bed.

"Don't go. I don't want to be alone."

"You aren't alone, Dana."

"Stay with me." She touches the space beside her.

The last time she had offered me to share a bed, I had upset her. She's thinking about the last time.

"Marry me."

Her nostrils flare. "No." She whispers.

I get back on the bed, much to her surprise, and pull her into my arms. She rests her head on my chest, and I tighten my hold on her. There is no way I will ever sleep with Dana's intoxicating smell and warm body close to mine.

"Your heart is racing." Dana looks up at me.

"That's the effect you have on me." I press a kiss to her forehead.

Dana frowns and looks away before resettling on my chest. I didn't think sleeping was possible, but I woke up in a pitch-black dark room. Dana is still asleep on my chest. I slide her onto her side of the bed. She groans but falls back to sleep as I get off the bed. I walk around and drag the blankets from my side over her before leaving the room.

Taking out my phone, I see I have a missed call from Robert.

It's three in the morning, but I ring him back. He answers on the second ring.

"We move tonight."

My heart soars and crashes all at once. "Why? Has something happened?" I ask as I move to my room to get my gear.

"No, she was moved a few hours ago to a better location."

My sister is alive. That knowledge fully sinks in. I don't know what I truly believed, but for the first time, I fully accept she's really alive.

"Send me the location. I'll meet you there." I hang up on Robert as I enter my room and dial Shay's number.

He doesn't answer straight away. When he does, he's groggy.

"We move tonight. I'll send you the location. Can you meet me there?"

"Yeah, yeah. What time is it?"

"It's three o'clock." My phone dings with a message as I take two guns out of my drawer and   make sure they are loaded.

"Okay, send me the address."

"Give me two minutes." I hang up and drop the phone on the bed as I place the weapons on my body.

I open the address from Robert and send it to Shay as I leave the house.

I'd finally have my family back.

CHAPTER TWENTY-THREE

CILLIAN

I ARRIVE AT THE location. It's an industrial compound. The buildings at the front are barren and unfinished—heavy plastic shifts and moves in the wind. Scaffolding is rotting and falling down from years of being left abandoned. I know locations like these may seem empty but are normally active with prostitution and drug dealing.

Shay's already here. I get out and walk over to his jeep. Robert is getting out of his car and walking toward me.

"You didn't have to involve him," Robert says, jutting his chin out towards Shay as he gets out of his jeep.

Shay lights a smoke, and he smirks at Robert.

"I know. I wanted him here with me."

Robert tightens his lips but accepts what I am saying. Razor, Big John, and about ten more men spread out around us.

"She's with three other girls. We only take Aoibhe. Get in and get out." Robert advises everyone as he shows them a picture of my sister. My stomach tightens as I see a glimpse of her smiling face and dark curls that always had a life of their own. "No shooting. Stay quiet and unseen."

Everyone nods. I notice that I'm not the only one who doesn't. Shay leans against the jeep, smoking his cigarette. He's not nodding along with Robert. He meets my eye, and I give him a nod. I want them all to die.

"Let's move." Robert starts, and everyone enters the sizable gap in the chain-link fence. Shay falls into step beside me, and I enter the industrial estate.

Everyone spreads out, but I stay with Robert. Since he got the tip she was here; staying with him seems wise. We move past buildings that are not abandoned. I hear the sounds of life as we go deeper into the park.

Shay is glancing around him. "Who told you she was here?" Shay asks.

"A source." Robert won't tell him. Shay has got to know that. Shay might not consider himself an O'Reagan, but everyone else does.

Robert juts his chin toward a building that has more structure to our left. "Remember, there are three girls; only take Aoibhe with us."

"Why?" Shay steps closer.

"Because that was the agreement I made with Bednar Novak. He gave us the location of Aoibhe as long as we take her and no one else. This will go unnoticed, and then his daughter will be returned to him. We can cut ties with the Russians. We don't want to get on their bad side." Robert steps away like that ends our conversation.

I have no intentions of walking away unnoticed. I want them to notice me.

Robert opens a side door and enters the building. I grip Shay before we enter. "This could be a setup."

"Yeah, I thought of that."

I release him and follow Robert into the darkened building. Long red lights are placed every few feet. They hang from the ceiling near the walls. Wires are exposed, and it's a fire hazard. We pass a few people who don't even notice us. They are somewhere else. Their bodies are filled with drugs. Robert pauses and waits until Shay and I catch up with him.

"He said the door would have a white X." Robert points at the door that has a tiny x marked in chalk. I go first and wipe the mark away. My heart won't settle as I withdraw my gun and take the safety off.

Robert grips my arm. "I said. 'No shooting.'"

"I'm not going in unarmed," I whisper and shrug him off.

He's not happy, but fuck him. I enter with Shay on my heels. He also withdraws his gun, and having him at my back makes me braver. The room is plunged in darkness. Only the glow of the red light from the open door sheds light on the huddled forms on the ground.

My heart grows frantic as I step closer and reach out. For a moment, they don't look real. They don't even move, and when I touch flesh that's warm, I spin the first girl around. Her eyes are vacant of life. Her thin frame is close to collapsing, and I'm praying it's not her. I shake her, and she focuses on me. Brown eyes. She has brown eyes. She's not my sister.

Shay is at the door with his gun at the ready as I reach for the second girl. I don't waste time but drag her thin frame to the stream of red light. Her eyes look brown, too. "I need light." Pain lances across my chest as my eyes trail down to the thin arms that are bruised and abused from needle holes.

Shay walks towards me and takes out a lighter. He brings it close to the girl's face. She flinches away and cries. Her nose is wrong. "It's not her." I release the girl and pick up the first one who lies on the floor. I kneel, and the light goes out as Shay follows me. I push the girl's hair off her face as Shay flicks the lighter again.

"Aoibhe," I say my sister's name, and I see life behind her blue eyes. It's a flicker. She is barely lucid. "Jesus Christ." I drop the gun and drag my sister into my arms. She doesn't stop me. I pick up her thin arms and fold them around her chest. I can't look at the marks. I rise, and Shay picks up my gun, holding both guns in front of him. He takes the lead.

Robert glances at Aoibhe in my arms, and I pause, looking back at the three other figures.

"Leave them," Robert warns, and I move after Shay. No one stops us. Bednar had kept to his word. I hold my sister to my chest, but I'm afraid of her snapping. She's too small. Too thin. Too quiet. We get out of the building, and I'm walking away, but with each step I take, my heart seems to grow heavier and colder.

Robert lets out a whistle that splits the air, and slowly his men emerge from the buildings and join us. "Mission accomplished." He barks.

I'm at my car. I have my sister, but I can't open the door; it feels wrong leaving those other girls behind. "We can come back," Shay says the words that I need to hear.

The three girls keep flashing in my mind. If someone had come for one of them and left my sister behind, I would kill them.

I look at Shay. He nods like he can read my mind. "I'll go back and get them out."

I tighten my hold on Aoibhe. I can't speak with the fury that burns up my veins.

"We need to leave." Robert is behind us. I can't look at him.

Shay walks to his vehicle, and I finally bend down with Aoibhe in my arms and open the door. I place my sister in the passenger seat. Her head lolls to the side, and I have a moment of thinking I've gotten the wrong girl. I push her hair away from her face, and her birthmark, that's like the map of Ireland, is there behind her ear.

I grip the door as my chest keeps expanding.

Cars start, and with every ounce of strength I have, I close the door and get into the driver's side. I take another look at my sister before I reverse out onto the road. Each streetlamp we pass casts an eerie light over her, and I keep questioning if it's her. I reach across and press two fingers to her neck. She has a pulse. She isn't dead.

I pull over as my mind grows frantic. It isn't Aoibhe. I lean over and push her hair aside, revealing her birthmark. My fingers trace it.

"Aoibhe," I say her name, and it's like everything in me crumbles. I have spent so much time keeping it all in—so much time suppressing every memory with her in it, so much time trying not to cave.

I give in and pull my sister into my arms as I start to cry. I cry for her. I cry for myself, and I cry for my mother.

"Aoibhe," I say her name again, and she groans. I haven't cried since I was a boy, and it normally involved a beating.

I have to pry my arms off her. Letting her go is painful, but I finally restart the car and get my mind focused as I wipe my eyes and run my hand down my face.

I pick up my phone and call our doctor.

"I need you at the house, now."

"I'll be there in twenty minutes."

"Make it ten," I say.

"What's the injury?" he asks as he moves. He must be getting dressed. It's four-thirty on my dashboard clock.

I pull back out on the road as I list what I think Aoibhe might need. "Drug withdrawals, malnourishment, dehydration." I glance at Aoibhe again. She's like a rag doll lying on the front seat.

"I'll need to drop by the surgery, but I'll be with you as soon as possible."

"Be as quick as you can." I hang up and ring my mother.

She sounds alert. "Are you okay?"

"I have Aoibhe." My heart thumps in my chest, and I look across at my sister again just to make sure she is really there.

My mother doesn't answer.

"Mam?"

"Where are you taking her?" My mother's words are controlled, and I think she is in shock.

"To my house. The doctor is on his way."

"I'm getting dressed."

I hit the indicator to leave the main road. "I'll send Frank to pick you up."

"No. I'll come myself." My mother responds too quickly.

"Mam. Just let me send Frank."

"I'm not at the house." She's moving around. "Cillian?"

I think I'm sure of who's house she is at then. "Yes."

"Is she okay?" My mother's voice cracks.

I want to tell her yes. I want to reassure her, but when she sees Aoibhe, I want my mother to be prepared. "I'm not sure. She's lost a lot of weight."

Pain grows inside me as I take another look at my sister. "She's different."

My mother doesn't sob. "I'm getting off the phone. I'll be with you soon." Her control is strong, but I don't think she'll maintain it when she sees Aoibhe.

"I love you," I say. She needs to know, no matter what, that she's loved, and this isn't her fault. She's blamed herself enough.

"I love you too, son." Her words are softer, and the line dies.

***

When I reach the house, Frank and Jo are waiting for me. I'd called ahead to get a room ready for Aoibhe. Picking her up is frightening. She weighs nothing. The odor that rises from her stick-thin body is overpowering as I carry her inside.

Jo's gaze widens, her hand flutters to her chest, but she remembers herself and falls into step beside me. "Her room is ready."

Aoibhe's head lolls to the side, her skin ghostly white under the lighting. I'm tempted to stop and place her on the floor so I can examine her, but I keep moving to the elevator. Jo joins me, and we rise to the second floor.

The doors open, and I follow Jo to the room she set up. The bedroom has a fire lit, and the curtains are drawn. The blanket has been pulled back, and I finally place Aoibhe on the bed. My heart doubles in speed as I see my sister fully for the first time.

Her sunken face holds traces of my sister. I push her hair fully back. Her eyes are closed, the sockets sunken. I'm afraid to touch her face in case it caves in under my fingers. Her lips are dry and cracked. Dirt and marks coat her face and neck. I continue to assess with as much distance as possible. I try to think of my training. I remove the denim jacket.

Her thin arms are covered in bruises. The needle marks on my sister's arms have my mind slipping, and my brain fires off a warning of some impending doom. I'm holding her hand as I fight for control.

"Dr. Alex is here." Jo's voice has me releasing my sister's hand and giving me the strength to continue assessing her.

"Cillian," Alex speaks from behind me, and I glance at him, giving him a nod. Stepping back, I stay close but give him space to assess her.

He checks for a pulse. "She's alive," I say.

He ignores me, takes out a small flashlight, and checks her eyes. "She isn't alert." I fold my arms, feeling fucking useless.

The doctor runs his hands along her shoulders and arms. "There are no broken bones."

"Cillian." My mother's voice has me turning away. She's standing in the doorway, and I can't do anything to prepare her for this. I walk to her, blocking her view of Aoibhe.

I pull my mother into my arms. It takes her a moment to relax. "It's bad, isn't it?" She asks into my neck.

"She looks different." That is all I can manage.

My mother steps out of my arms, and I don't want to see her face as she looks at her daughter. She walks past me, and her sobs start almost immediately.

My gaze meets Jo, who's watching. "You can leave."

She half bows and pulls the door closed behind her.

Aoibhe didn't need an audience. She'd be pissed to know anyone saw her like this.

"What happened to my baby?" My mother's wails grow, and I go to her.

I want to tell her she doesn't want to know. It won't do any good, but I know I want every single tiny detail. I want the information to sink deeply into my brain, so when I go for the people who did this, nothing and nobody will stop me.

I hold my mother, and her sobs don't stop as the doctor continues his examination. Once he is done, he doesn't speak but sets up an IV drip. Two different bags are attached to it, and I hate when he places a needle in her damaged arms.

Once he's done, he faces us. My mother composes herself. "Nothing is broken. The fluid will help with getting the drugs out of her system, but it could take a few hours before she wakes up."

"That's good," I tell my mother.

"I have no idea of the damage done by the drugs, Cillian. We won't know more until she wakes up. When she wakes up, liquid in small amounts before you even consider introducing food."

"Okay." The idea of Aoibhe waking up is both terrifying and elating.

"I'm going to take some blood and run a few tests for now."

"Thank you, Dr. Alex." My mother reaches out and touches his forearm.

We let him finish up and wait for Aoibhe to wake up.

CHAPTER TWENTY-FOUR

CILLIAN

I STEP OUT OF the room, leaving my mother sitting beside Aoibhe. She still hasn't woken. I answer the phone to Shay.

"Did you get them out safely?" I ask.

"No. I left them there."

"I'm in no fucking mood, Shay."

Shay doesn't laugh, and I stop walking.

"Someone will come back for them," Shay responds. He's smoking.

"You left them as bait?" I would have done the same, that is, until the bait has a face and that face is my sister's.

"I'm still here. Someone will show up, and I'll follow them."

I know he's right. "I'm on my way."

IF there is a chance of finding the people who took my sister, I will take it. I check on Dana before I leave. She's still asleep. I'm tempted to wake her, but I let her sleep. I don't return to my mother but leave word with Frank.

I've already got two guns on me, and I take a knife also before getting into my car.

I hit Shay's number, and he answers on the first ring. "Any movement?" I ask.

"No, it's still quiet."

I nod. "I'll be with you soon."

"How is your sister?" His question shouldn't affect me, but I tighten my hold on the steering wheel.

"I need to kill every one of them."

"We won't let one live, then," Shay responds.

He's some friend.

"There's a van arriving." Shay's words have me pushing my foot to the floor.

"I'm nearly there." I hang up and drive to the industrial compound. I park a block away and jog the rest of the distance. Shay is in his jeep. I grab the handle, but the door is locked. He unlocks it, and I climb in.

"Anything?"

"They are still in there."

Guilt at not letting the women go churns in my stomach. I understand Shay's reasoning, but once again, I can't unsee my sister huddled among the other girls.

It doesn't take long for lights to split the air as the van moves through the industrial estate. Shay's jeep is parked along the side. I still find myself ducking down as the van passes us. Shay starts the jeep and follows the van through the empty streets. We lose it a few times because we don't want them to know they are being followed. Shay finds them, and we leave the town and go out into the countryside.

"Finn's funeral is Wednesday. Liam rang my father and made it clear that he would like me there, too."

"So you are forgiven?" I ask and glance at Shay.

His cheek rises as he grins. "I think letting you and Dana stay at the safe house won me some brownie points."

"That's good, then?"

"It allows me to get closer to him." Shay's grin is gone, and hate tightens his features. He glances at me.

"He asked Richard to kill Finn."

"So Richard killed him. Fuck." That's messed up.

"No. Richard wouldn't have. It was Liam, I know it. Richard wouldn't have gone through with it."

I didn't know Richard, so I'd take Shay's word for it.

The van starts to slow as we approach a field. A man jumps out and opens a gate. Shay slams his foot down on the accelerator and hits the back of the van.

"You want to tell me the plan?" I ask, gripping the door.

Shay's reaching for the door while pulling out his gun. "Sorry, I didn't see you stopping." He calls to the man who's walking towards us.

"You fucking stupid fucker."

The sound of the gun is barely audible, thanks to the silencer. The man hits the ground, and Shay steps over him and moves to the van.

"Sorry about that. I had a few drinks." He's talking while walking. I jump into the driver's side, and as he raises his gun, I reverse the jeep back and park it along a ditch.

Shay walks back, and I meet him at the first body. I don't hear the girls screaming and question if they are even in there. We push the body into the ditch, and I open the back doors of the van. Three heads turn to me.

"Get out," I say.

Not one of them moves. I reach in and take out the first girl. The other two follow. They are like zombies.

Once they are out, Shay closes the door. "I'll get the van into the field. Maybe put them in the jeep."

I lead two of them to the jeep and return for the other. Shay has the van in the field, and the gate is closed. I jump over the gate and open the passenger door. I have to jump back as a body falls out. The second man. "You could have warned me."

I climb in and don't even have the door closed before Shay starts driving. "What would be the fun of that?"

Wetness seeps into my trousers. I try not to sit on the blood, but it's pretty much all over the seat. I focus on getting my guns out as I look out the window. I can see a man up ahead. A machine gun strapped to his back. He waves for us to slow down. The darkness blinds him from seeing us. As we near, I'm ready to ask questions. Shay rolls down the window, and the man doesn't have a moment to blink before Shay pulls the trigger. The man hits the ground with a thud.

"It's hard to question a dead man, Shay."

Shay continues driving. "I don't see the need to question him." Shay glances at me. "You said you wanted them all dead."

"Yeah, I did."

Shay grins. "Well then."

Shay stops the van as we near a hedge. "Best on foot from here."

Once Shay turns off the van, the silence seems to expand. The sky is starting to lighten. I'd say we have two hours before the morning will be here. We walk along the hedge line. Once we find a gap, we enter another field. It's at the peak of this field that we look down on several buildings. Lights shine in all directions.

"How many men are down there?" I ask.

"More than the bullets we have." Shay starts the decline.

I smirk as I follow him down the hill. "So, I think we should have a plan now."

"The girls were being delivered here. So, this is either a huge fucking whore house or a sorting area. Either way, these are the gatekeepers. So we release any girls and kill anything else that moves."

"Sounds like a plan," I tell Shay.

As we near the bottom of the hill, we go silent, and like always, I forget everything, and my training kicks in. Shay signals he's going left, so I take the right. Two buildings are here, and I stop close to the first one. Taking out both guns, I check the safety is off and step up to the door and knock. I take three deep breaths and lean against the wall. Blood roars in my ears as my adrenaline peaks. The rush sends a tremble through my body. The door opens, the noise silences everything in me. The man steps out, and I fire a shot into his temple. The gunshot is loud, and I know the timer has started. I remove his machine gun and sling it over my shoulder while entering the building. A man rushes down the stairs, and I fire while I keep moving to the first door.

I kick it open and enter an empty room. A set of cards is sprawled out on the table. A cigar still burns.

Fuck.

I duck out of the room as the door explodes. I hear the shotgun being reloaded and spin in firing towards the far wall. I hear a thud but wait before entering the second room. A man lies dead on the ground. The room is empty. Movement on the stairs has me moving backward into the first room. I hear the creak of the wood as some-one takes another step. Closing my eyes allows me to really listen. It's not just the stairs; someone is in the hallway. I open my eyes and step out. With a gun in either hand, I fire a shot at the stairs and at the man in front of me. His machine gun sprays bullets into the ceiling as he falls backward.

The remainder of the downstairs is empty. I pick up the machine gun as I race upstairs with the two slapping against my back. Two rooms hold several girls. Two of them bleed out on the floor from the earlier gunshots. The other girls aren't screaming. The drugs keep them subdued. I leave them. They will be safer here. I go to the front room and look out the window. Three men are moving toward the building. I open the window quickly and position one machine gun. They don't look up; they are too focused on the front door. I let bullets rain down on them. I don't stop until the three men are on the ground and the machine gun is empty. I throw it on the floor before pulling the second one from my back.

I leave the building and move to the second one. I'm ready to fire when a man appears, but it's Shay. He nods at me and moves up to the door. The rush is different with him at my back. He's gathered his own arsenal of machine guns, and that's all I hear as we enter the building and fire at each and every man without thought. I just know every one of them has to die. When we are done, I get the satisfaction out of walking among all the dead bodies.

"We should have kept one alive," I say. It's an afterthought.

One groans, and Shay drags him off the ground. "You could be in luck."

"Who do you work for?" I ask.

Blood gurgles from the corner of the man's mouth, and he hits the ground as Shay releases his dead body.

"There are several girls in the next building," I say.

"Yeah, there were a few in the one I checked."

I nod. "Let's round them up."

We do. We lead each girl down to a van. They obediently climb in. We leave all the guns behind except for our own.

"You know this is going to blow up," Shay says as we drive out of the hidden site and back up toward the fields where this seedy world is hidden.

"I'm betting on it," I say.

I still want to know who is behind all this. We drive toward town. Shay stops on the main street. The sun is starting to set. I get out and open the back doors. Some of the girls seem slightly lucid. They are still dazed as I order them out of the van. We leave all of the women in the middle of the road and drive off. Shay circles back to where we left his jeep.

"You take my jeep. I'll get rid of the van."

I pause before I get out. "Thank you."

Shay grins. "When the time comes, and I need you to help me kill Liam, I know you will be there."

I nod. "One hundred percent." I get out and jump into Shay's jeep.

Driving home knowing that I have put a huge dent in the Russian's operation makes me smile. It won't end at this, and I'm okay with that. I hope they come looking for me because I'll be ready.

CHAPTER TWENTY-FIVE

DANA

IT'S THE MORNING OF Finn's funeral. I'm staring at myself in a full-length mirror. The black dress is something I would picture my mother wearing. I look just like her. I brush my hair across one shoulder. The long black tunic brushes my ankles, and I take out the leather gloves and hold them. It's too early to put them on. Everything is so black, so bleak.

The vanity set that sits in the room has every cosmetic a woman could ever want. I walk to it and pull out a drawer that has a huge range of eyeshadows. I pull out the next one, and I run my fingers across all the lipsticks. Number 68. A deep red. I open it and look up into the mirror as I apply the stark red lipsticks on my lips.

The door opens, and I meet Richard's eye in the mirror. He's in a black suit, the shirt is black, too, and my stomach tightens. He looks like Dad.

"You look like Mother." He says, stuffing his hands in his pockets.

I pat my lips together and pocket the lipstick while facing Richard. "You look just like Dad."

We stare at each other, and I'm not entirely sure if he appreciates being compared to father because I'm not feeling overwhelmed at being compared to our mother.

Over the last two days, I've thought of ringing her, but words failed me. I didn't even have Cillian to talk to. Ever since his sister returned two days ago, he's been gone. At night I feel the bed dip, but when I wake, he's gone.

"Is she here?" I ask.

"Mother?"

I nod.

"No, she's at home with Jack and Maeve."

Maeve. Hearing her name sends fire through me. "Is Maeve coming to the funeral?"

"Of course. Why wouldn't she?"

I shrug, and I can't hold my brother's stare. All I can think is she killed Cian. "Nothing."

"Are you ready?"

I look around the room like I won't see it again before leaving with Richard. Downstairs is quiet, apart from all the security I see spaced out through the foyer.

"Did something happen?" I ask Richard while keeping my voice low.

"Most likely."

I glance at Richard's answer, and he looks at me. I smile.

"Thanks."

Richard focuses forward. "For what?"

"Being honest. If I had asked Jack, I'm sure he would tell me everything is fine. That there is nothing to worry about."

The front door opens, and I glance back as a man with several bodyguards enters the foyer. His gaze snaps to me, and I pause.

"Dana O'Reagan. I would recognize you anywhere." The blond man, who isn't much older than Richard, walks towards me. Richard has stopped walking too.

"Lucian Sheahan," He says his name while taking my hand. He also says his name like I should know who he is.

"A pleasure," I say, keeping my tone simple.

His light blue eyes twinkle. "Indeed."

"Lucian, today isn't a good day."

The voice coming from behind us, sends every cell in my body on high alert. Cillian walks towards us. His jaw tight, his eyes angry as he looks at my hand in Lucian's.

I immediately let it go.

"Can we talk privately?" Lucian's blue eyes narrow as he stares at Cillian.

I glance at Richard, who's also watching Lucian.

"I'm busy." Cillian steps up beside me, his hand moving slightly in front of me like he's getting ready to pull me away from Lucian.

I'm not the only one who notices the movement.

Lucian raises a brow, glances at me before he glares at Cillian. "I'm not asking, Cillian."

My stomach curls, my heart starts to race.

"I'm not talking right now, Lucian."

Cillian's hand touches the small of my back as he steers me away.

"What you did was reckless." Lucian starts.

Cillian stops walking, and I turn back to Lucian.

He's angry. His security moves closer to him. "You got your sister handed to you. All you had to do was walk away."

Cillian grins. It's carved from anger and so much pain. "I've only started."

Lucian steps closer, and his men circle him. I'm being moved away by Richard. But I don't want to go.

"Exactly. A war with the Russians. Even your father wasn't stupid enough to do what you did."

The room inhales, and I'm waiting for Cillian to unleash all his anger on Lucian.

"Go." Richard releases me and points towards the living room door. I don't want to go. When I don't move, Richard spins.

"Go now, Dana." I hate how I shrivel under my brother's stare.

I have no choice but to walk away.

"You came all this way to tell me that?" Laughter in Cillian's voice sends waves of fear across my flesh. I don't know their world, but I understand that Lucian is important, and Cillian doesn't seem to care. I reach the door and pause. When I look back, Richard is glaring at me.

I enter the living room and close the door, pressing my ear against it, but I don't hear anything. My temperature soars the longer I pace the room, waiting for Richard to come. I shed my tunic and walk back to the door.

I check my watch. It's been fifteen minutes. I turn the round doorknob and open the door slowly. The foyer is empty. I turn back and pick up my tunic. None of the security is in the foyer, and I have no idea where anyone is. I stare at the elevator, thinking of going back upstairs, but the funeral is in thirty minutes, and we will be leaving soon.

I walk to the front door, my heels clicking loudly on the tiled floor. I open the front door. The air is cool on my flesh.

I step out, and I'm surprised to see a limo in the driveway. The back door opens as I pull on my jacket.

Blue eyes smile at me.

"I'm sorry you had to see that. We aren't always as volatile." Lucian doesn't get out of the limo but smiles at me.

I shrug. "It's my uncle's funeral this morning. Business should wait."

Lucian smiles. A flash of white teeth. "I do apologize. My manners in front of a lady aren't something I should ever forget. I'm very sorry about Finn."

"Thank you. Where are you from?" I ask, coming down the steps. He is apologizing, which is more than a lot of men around me would do. Lucian rises, in my estimation.

"Northern Ireland."

That surprises me. "You don't have a Northern Ireland accent. You have a British twang."

"In England, I sound very Irish to them, here I sound British. I can't seem to win." He smiles again, and there is something charming about him.

Lucian looks up at the house. "You should go inside. It's cold."

"We will be leaving soon for the funeral."

"Would you like a lift? I've plenty of space."

He still hasn't gotten out of the car. His eyes are soft, and I find myself looking back at the house. "No. I better wait for Richard and Cillian."

Lucian smiles. "No problem. I might see you later." He closes the car door, and I walk back to the steps. The limo rolls silently down the driveway, and I watch it disappear. The door behind me opens, and it's Richard. I'm looking over his shoulder, searching for Cillian.

"He will meet us there."

I try to hide my disappointment as I follow Richard to his car.

"Lucian seems nice." I find myself saying.

Richard opens the passenger door for me. I get in and wait for him to get into the driver's side before putting on my seat belt.

"Lucian is dangerous," Richard responds as he starts the car.

"How so?" I don't expect an answer.

"He's the leader of the RA now."

"The RA?" I ask.

Richard glances at me. "Keeping you out of all this really wasn't wise. The Republican Army."

"Like the IRA? Aren't they all dead?" I thought that they died a hundred years ago.

"No, Dana. Some things don't die. Like pain and hate."

"He's very young to be a leader."

Richard doesn't respond, and I get that this conversation is over as another one arises.

"What is happening with you and Cillian?"

I'm ready to say nothing. But Richard has been honest with me. "I really like him."

I take a peek at Richard. His jaw is tight.

"I think he really likes me."

Richard's hands grip the steering wheel.

"I want to be with him, Richard."

My brother finally looks at me. "We will discuss this another time."

I don't care when he wants to discuss Cillian and me. I really want to try with Cillian. He isn't someone I can just forget. I don't want to.

We arrive at St. Mary's Church. As we pass rows and rows of cars, I pull on my gloves. The closer we get to the front of the church, the more limos and high-end cars I see until it's just all limos with my father's Bentley at the front.

Richard pulls into a spot that he's being directed into. People file around the cars and make their way into the church.

So many people. Yet, no one was there as he took his life. "Did the post mortem come back?" I ask.

Richard doesn't answer, and when I glance at him, he's looking at me.

"We already knew the cause of his death. He took his life."

"I know. I just." I shrug. "I don't know."

"We better go in."

I don't want to, but I unbuckle myself and get out of the car.

The first person I see is Maeve. She half-smiles at me. She's with Jack, Shay, and a girl with long red hair and another girl with blonde hair who leaves them and walks towards us. She's light on her feet, her blonde hair billows behind her, and when she reaches Richard, she rises and presses a kiss on my brother's cheek. She looks at him like he's the only person here. I clear my throat, and she releases my brother.

"This is Claire. I had wanted you to meet her before; it just never felt like the right time." Richard's hand snakes around Claire's waist.

"Hi, Claire." I extend my hand.

She takes mine. "So lovely to finally meet you, Dana. I wish it were under better circumstances."

"The next time, we will have dinner." Richard looks down at Claire, and it sinks in that I don't know much about my brother. He loves her. I can see it in his eyes. Everything about my brother softens. I've seen it before when my father looks at my mother.

Pain lodges in my chest, and I focus on the four people who walk toward us. Shay bends down and whispers something in the red head's ear. She swipes at him and laughs.

Today is already full of surprises. I'm trying not to look at Maeve. She doesn't stop walking until she's pulling me into her arms. I don't respond.

"I'm so sorry, Dana."

I exhale and wrap my arms around her. It's Maeve. My best friend. I know her inside and out, and I give in and really hug her.

"I'm sorry, too." I find myself saying. Sorry for not being there for her when she needed me. Sorry for freaking out when she told me about Cian.

We release each other, and I find Jack smiling at us. I don't return the smile as our parents walk towards us. My father links his arm with my mother, and I'm aware of how all the surrounding footfalls slow down.

My father's gaze touches each of his children, and we each get some nod of approval. His gaze lingers on Shay, who takes out a packet of cigarettes.

"You said you would quit." The red-headed girl whips her head up to Shay. She's so much smaller than he is. And I don't know who's more shocked when he puts the packet away.

Richard grins at him, and I see the smile in Jack's eyes.

"What?" He questions. Being uncomfortable is an odd look to see on Shay.

"You look great." Pain. That's what I hear in my mother's voice when I finally look at her.

I have an overwhelming urge to wipe off the lipstick. Maybe it's because my mother's focus is heavy on my lips.

I take a quick look at my father, but his focus is beyond my shoulder. I hear the footsteps behind me, but I don't turn around.

"You, too," I say to my mother.

A hand touches the small of my back, and becoming familiar with someone is a funny thing. I don't have to turn to know Cillian is here. He presses a kiss to the side of my head, and I want to smile up at him.

"Get away from my daughter." My father's anger is jarring, and it kills my smile.

"Liam." My mother's eyes widen in shock at his demeanor as he leans closer to Cillian.

"No." Cillian's response is warranted, and I feel the surrounding pull from my brothers.

"Liam" My mother repeats my father's name.

She always is the one to pull him back, yet when I think about it, he doesn't usually get angry.

"Dad." My father looks at me, and I widen my eyes for him to stop this.

"We better go in." Jack, ever the diplomat, speaks up. My mother nods, agreeing with him. I can't see Shay or Richard as they are behind me, but I'm pretty sure they aren't agreeing.

"I don't want you near her." My father continues. My heart starts to race. This isn't like my father, and we are in public.

I spot Uncle Shane walking toward us, and the blood pools in my shoes. All I can think about is Cian. My father is forgotten as Shane walks towards us. This is my first time seeing him since I found out that Maeve and Shay killed his son.

Bile rises in my throat, and I remember all of this is happening to me because of the secret. I clear my throat to try to ground myself. I find myself reaching behind me for Cillian. My father is still speaking, but I have a horrible sense of floating.

"What's wrong?" Cillian reacts to me straight away.

"Shane, is Una with you?" It's my mother's voice, but I need to walk away.

"I need a minute," I say to Cillian, and we are walking away from the group.

I know everyone is talking around us, but I don't hear their words. All I see is Shane, Shane's pain the day he buried his son.

My vision waivers as Cillian leads me over to the side where an old convent building is. The fence that runs around it has a small concrete wall. Cillian leads me to the wall and sits me down before he kneels in front of me.

"Funerals are shit. I know. Take a few deep breaths." Cillian's hands touch my face, and I focus on his touch. It keeps me here, and the world around us disappears.

I can't speak about what is really going through my mind. "You buried your father?" I say, remembering the day in Cabra Castle when I had pushed him too far.

"Yes. Just stay focused on me." Cillian smiles.

Everything sheds off me, and I find my smile for him.

"I'm sorry I haven't been around."

I raise a hand. "I know you had your sister to take care of. I get it." *I still missed you.* "I'm so glad you found her, Cillian. How is she?" I take his hand, and he stares at both our hands before his green eyes shoot up to my face.

"Marry me."

I laugh. The noise is low, but I can't stop it from coming out. I smile as he waits. "No."

He nods like he expected me to say no and helps me stand. I find everyone watching us. Shane is saying something in my father's ear, and they turn with my mother in tow and walk toward the church. My brothers and Shay wait for me, and I join them, holding Cillian's hand. No one seems happy. But I'm not thrilled with my family either.

Stepping under the church's arch sends tingles across my flesh, and I feel wrong with the knowledge I have stepped into a house of God.

How easily I have become a sinner like my family.

I zone out of the funeral, and I can't stop watching Una and Shane. They sit with my parents in the front row with the rest of my uncles and their wives. Throughout the whole thing, Cillian doesn't let go of my hand, and when the bells ring announcing we can leave, I stand up. I'm surprised because it feels like we just arrived.

After the funeral service, everyone gives their condolences, and I feel like I've moved around most of the churchyard.

"How are you?" My mother appears at my side. Cillian is across from me, and he looks at me now. I give him a nod to let him know I'm okay, and he returns to talking to a group of men.

"Shocked. You hid everything from me my whole life. You made me believe we were good, decent people. But that's not who we are." I keep my voice low, but I hear the anger laced through my words.

"I thought I was protecting you, sweetheart. I didn't want you to grow up in a world..." she trails off.

"Of what? Corruption? Greed? A world with no morals, mother?"

"That's not fair." My mother tilts her head, pleading with me.

"Tell father to lay off Cillian." I know it's wrong to use my mother's guilt that is so visible in her eyes, to my own advantage, but I don't fully understand my father's hostility. Then again, I'd never brought a man home before. My stomach squeezes when I think of Philip.

I find my mother looking at me. "I will speak to your father. He just has a lot on his plate with his brother."

Did she know about Philip? I look back to Cillian and don't see him. My heart starts to race, and for the first time, I see my family as strangers and Cillian as my family.

"I have a lot on my plate, too," I say.

My mother rubs her arms. "I'm so sorry, Dana."

I don't know what possesses me, but I lean in and press a kiss to her cheek. I suppose I think of what Cillian had said about forgiving her. That she did it all with good intentions, even if it wasn't the right call.

"I love you, Mum."

The relief swims in her eyes. "I love you, too."

"I better go look for Cillian."

My mother smiles and nods. "I better look for your father. I'll have a word."

"Thank you." I give my mother a final hug before I start looking for Cillian. Anyone who steps close to me to give their condolences, I quickly veer away from and keep walking.

I reach the church gates, and someone across the road in the fair green car park waves at me. I recognize Lucian and wave back.

He's saying something, but I can't hear him. I take a final look at everyone in the churchyard, but I don't see Cillian before I walk across the road to Lucian.

CHAPTER TWENTY-SIX

CILLIAN

THE SMELL OF PISS assaults my nostrils, but I've been in worse places. The part I don't like is the gun that Liam O'Reagan presses under my chin.

He's losing control! This is the man who NEVER loses control.

"I warned you not to touch my daughter." His tone is calmer, but it's a bit late for that. I think everyone saw him snap in the yard when he pushed me into this rank bathroom.

I don't answer, and he pushes the gun tighter to my chin. I'm pretty certain Liam will not fire a gun here. There are too many witnesses.

"I know what grief does to a person," I say.

He steps away from me, and I am not expecting the action as he puts his gun away. Now I'm unsure.

"This is a warning you refused to listen to." Liam straightens his jacket and, with each small motion, it's like he's putting his composure back together.

I reach for honesty. "I'll treat her well." I don't want to have this kind of chat with him.

"No."

I raise a brow. "No?"

"My daughter is worth ten of you. This ends, and I will see a fitting punishment for your disobedience."

I step away from the wall. "I think you should be more concerned with burying your brother." I step closer. "Who ended up in the fucking ground because of you." I know Shay won't be pleased, but fuck Liam O'Reagan.

He doesn't even flinch. "What would Shane think?" I say.

"About what?" I hadn't heard Shane come in, and neither had Liam from the look on his face.

Liam recovers quickly. "About Cillian wanting to date my daughter."

Shane looks out into the yard before turning back to me. He looks me up and down like he can see what makes me up.

"I'll let you know when I have a drink with him later."

Liam smiles. "That's good enough for me."

He's a fucking snake.

"They are getting ready to move." Shane fires one more look at me before leaving the bathroom. Liam is walking away, too, but pauses in the doorway. I'm waiting for his threat, but he doesn't give one. Instead, he walks away.

That is worse than a threat. I have no idea what to expect. I'm out of the bathroom, and the light of the day seems sharp as I move through the crowd. I spot Shay and a redhead who has been at his side the whole time. "Have you seen Dana? She was talking to her mother the last time I saw her."

Shay glances around and shakes his head. He reaches for his cigarettes on auto-pilot, and the redhead clears her throat.

He puts them back in, and I take a moment to look at the redhead. I hold out my hand. "I'm Cillian. Shay's best friend. I'm sure he's mentioned me."

She smiles and takes my hand. "Emma, the better half of Shay."

I smile at Emma. "I believe you."

Her laugh is gentle, and she smiles up at Shay.

"Where have you been hiding her?" I ask Shay, teasing.

"I don't like her out in the open. But she wanted to come." He looks down at Emma.

"I swear people were starting to think I had an imaginary boyfriend."

My smile widens. "You make a lovely couple, and we should have dinner and drinks one night."

"There's Svetlana." Shay drags my attention away from Emma, and I see Dana's mother. She meets my eye, and I want to tell her what a bitch she is for how she treated Dana, but the only thing I notice is that Dana isn't with her.

"Thanks. I better keep looking." People are filing out of the churchyard, and I stop at Richard and Jack, but they haven't seen Dana either. The smaller the crowd gets, the more I worry. Liam and Svetlana are climbing into their car, and I hate going to him, but something isn't right.

I grip his door. "I can't find Dana."

"I was talking to her about fifteen minutes ago. She was looking for you." Svetlana says.

"Did you see the direction she went?" I ask and try to keep my voice respectful.

"Yeah, towards the gates."

I walk away and start towards the gates. I stop at them and look left and right up the street, but a few random people walk around. The car park across the road is nearly empty. Something on the ground catches my eye.

"Everything alright?" Shay asks.

I walk across the road. "I'm not sure." I don't stop until I'm in front of the object. Shay and Emma are behind me as I bend down and pick up the lipstick. I open it, and it's the same red as what Dana had painted on her lips.

"This is Dana's."

"It's lipstick. It could be anyone's," Shay says.

I rise and find Liam walking toward me through the gates.

I run my finger across the small imprint. Turning it over, I hold it up to Shay. "It's from my home; it has our crest."

Shay's looking around, and I do the same. I spot three cameras.

"I'll check that one." Shay points at the camera over a coal station.

"I'll get the other two."

Liam joins me. I hold up the lipstick. "Dana is missing."

He doesn't ask me how I know. Or why I have come to that conclusion. "You lost my daughter?"

"If you hadn't decided to have a go at me in the bathroom, I would have been protecting her." I bark.

We should have seen this coming. The funeral had the least amount of security. We didn't think anyone would be low enough to attack at a funeral.

I walk to a group of buildings. One of them has a camera that's pointed out over the car park. "You can go back; I'll find her."

A hand grips my shoulder, and I turn to Liam. "I'll find my daughter."

I allow Liam to take the lead as we climb the steps up to a large black door. He rings the bell, and the door buzzes, allowing us entry.

A small reception desk sits along the wall. A woman looks up and smiles. Behind her is an image of a blown-up set of white teeth. "Welcome to Navan Dental," circles the image.

"I need to see the security camera tapes." Liam steps up to the counter, and the woman's smile melts off her face. "I'm sorry, sir, I don't think I can."

I lean across the counter, but I can't get a clear view. Walking around, she rises and tries to stop me.

"You can't be back here."

I ignore her and find the recorder on a shelf near the floor. I press eject, and nothing comes out. I look up at her.

"The cameras are just for show."

Wasting our fucking time.

Liam's already out the front door, and I follow him back onto the street. Shay is jogging up towards us, Emma right behind him.

"Did you find anything?" I ask.

He looks at Liam, and I see the hate burning Shay up. "I did. It was Lucian."

"Lucian took Dana?" I question and frown. Why would he do something as stupid as that.?

Liam removes his phone and makes a call. This made no sense. Why would Lucian do this to Liam, knowing all the people were here and the cameras? Shay appears as troubled as I feel.

Liam takes his phone away from his face and puts it calmly in his pocket, not saying anything.

"He's not answering?" I ask since he isn't handing over the information.

"He won't hurt her. He wouldn't dare." Liam stares across the road, and I follow his line of sight. Svetlana is walking toward us. "Say nothing of this. I'm going to bury my brother."

Liam walks away, and I grip his forearm. He doesn't face me. "Like fuck you are. He took her. He took your daughter." I want to scream at him to do something. He had the most power here.

The bastard shrugs me off and presses a kiss to his wife's cheek. "Sorry to keep you waiting. I had a matter to take care of."

Svetlana takes a quick look at us. "Is Dana not with you?"

I'm staring at the back of Liam's head, even as Svetlana addresses me.

"She's with Richard or Jack, I'm sure." Liam answers and steers her away from us.

"He's going to do nothing." I turn to Shay, searching for answers.

Shay reaches for his breast pocket but seems to reconsider. "He didn't force her into the limo. It looked like they were talking, and she got in willingly. The only thing is she slipped the lipstick out of her pocket and dropped it when he wasn't looking."

I felt a swell of pride at her being so clever. I'd find her. "Lucian Sheehan taking Liam's daughter. Do the math for me, Shay, because I'm coming up empty."

"Maybe Liam really fucked up this time." Shay offers. "I'm going to get Emma home, and then I'll come back."

"I can take a taxi," Emma says.

Shay protests, but I think it's a fine fucking idea.

"I said I'm taking you home." It irritates me to waste time, but if it were Dana, I'd want to get her home safely, too.

When Shay leaves, I walk back to my car and get my phone. I ring Lucian, but he doesn't answer me. He had been angry with me this morning. Did he see how I looked at Dana? But to start a war with Liam isn't something Lucian would do. He isn't stupid.

I'm toying with ringing Skinner. I don't want anything from him, but he helped me with Aoibhe. I make the call, and he answers.

"I'm assuming you are ringing to finally thank me."

Cockiness turns his question into a sneer.

"I need your help."

His laugh is sharp. "Let's hear it then, Cillian."

"Dana O'Reagan was taken by Lucian Sheehan. I want her back."

Silence.

"Are you there?" I tighten my hold on the steering wheel.

"You are creating bad habits, Cillian."

"I don't know why I even came to you." I'm ready to hang up.

"Because you know I can help you."

I glance in the rearview mirror. "And are you going to help me?"

"You seem to think I owe you something."

Fuck it.

"Yeah, you do. My whole fucking childhood. You knew he beat me. He beat me because I wasn't his. I have no fucking idea why I was never told who you are. Why did I have to live under his roof?."

And not yours are the silent words I don't say.

"Because I wanted it that way. No one suspected you were my son; therefore, my enemies had nothing to hold over my head."

I laugh. "You selfish bastard."

"This selfish bastard is the only one who can help you."

I can't respond because of the anger that courses through my veins.

"When was she last seen and where?"

I exhale loudly away from the phone and try to compose myself. "The fair green car park across from St. Mary's church. It was no more than twenty minutes ago. Lucian is driving a black limo."

"I hear Navan is full of them today with an O'Reagan funeral."

"Can you find her?" I didn't want to chitchat.

"I'll be in touch."

I hang up and try Lucian again, but I don't get an answer.

Staying here isn't going to find Dana. I send a text to Shay to tell him I'm going home. I need to check on Aoibhe and make sure she's safe. I've left an army of men at my home, where my mother is staying as well. I ring Frank to make sure they are okay.

"Yes, Aoibhe is resting, and your mother is with Jo in the gardens."

"Can you see them?" I ask.

"No, sir, but I can check."

"Do and ring me back."

Most likely, I would be home by the time he checked on my mother.

Marrying Dana wouldn't have prevented Lucian from taking her. I didn't see him as a risk. I didn't think he would do something like this. I ring him again and throw the phone on the passenger floor when he doesn't answer.

What the fuck had Liam done? This has got to be because of Liam. Worry worms its way through my mind when I think of our angry exchange only hours ago. But if he wanted to get back at me, it would have been my family, not Dana. He knows who she is.

I arrive home just as Frank rings me, confirming my mother is in the garden, and she is fine.

I don't check on my sister, but send Frank to do that instead. After all she had suffered, facing her isn't something I am strong enough for right now. She keeps reassuring me she is fine, but she still has a young face but old eyes that hold too much weight. They saw too much. She suffered too much, and that is something I'll have to live with.

I enter the bar and pour myself a whiskey. As I look over at the couch, all I can picture is Dana bent over as I fucked her. Each time I asked her to marry me, she said no, and it turned me on.

I down the drink as my phone rings at the same time that Frankie enters the room.

"Aoibhe is sleeping."

I'm distracted as Lucian's name flashes up on my screen.

"Thank you, Frank." I turn my back, dismissing him, and answer the phone. I don't speak. I wait for Lucian to start.

"You're angry."

"You could say that." I tighten my hold on the glass. "I swear to God I will let this go if you just hand her back. It's over."

"Like you got your sister back?"

I fire the glass against the wall. "You listen to me, you hurt her, and I'll fucking hunt you down...."

Lucian starts laughing, and my anger dissolves. A new kind of rage takes over.

"Every O'Reagan, I'm sure, will hunt me until Liam stops them. So you are just part of the pack until your owner tells you to heel."

"Liam won't rest, Lucian. You took his daughter. You took Dana. From me." My voice rises. "I want her back."

"I can't do that, Cillian."

I slam my fist on the bar, wishing it was Lucian's face. "Why?"

"I no longer have her."

Ice forms in my veins, and the air turns sour in my mouth.

"Where is she?"

"I have no idea. I'm not lying."

"I'm coming for you," I promise, and I'm ready to hang up.

"No, you won't," Lucian says, and he sounds so fucking sure.

"Liam started all this. This is a debt he has to pay. He will stand down."

I'm ready to launch the phone at the wall, but I need answers. "What debt and to whom?"

"The Russians will take her as a settlement for what you did. You really damaged their operation, and to keep the peace and stop a war, they accepted Dana."

My chest tightens, and all I see is red. She's with the same men that had Aoibhe.

"You said this was Liam's doing?"

"Liam was the one who placed your sister in their hands the first time. It was to keep Davy loyal to him. Liam always likes having something over everyone."

I move back, and the stool behind me rattles as I bang into it before it hits the ground. I let the phone hang away from my ear.

Liam put my sister in their hands.

I bring the phone back to my ear, and a calmness I have never felt in my life takes over. "Dana O'Reagan is in the hands of the Russians right now?" I ask.

"Yes, and I have no idea where they took her. I'm sorry, my friend, but Liam needs to answer for this."

The door opens, and Shay steps in. He takes out his pack of cigarettes and lights one up.

I hang up on Lucian.

"Liam handed Aoibhe over to the Russians. This is retaliation for what we did."

Shay's brows drag down. "I always knew he was a cunt, but this...." Shay closes the door behind him. "That's below the belt."

"He did it to keep my father in line." I reach behind me and pull over a second stool. I need to sit down. "The Russians have Dana."

Shay doesn't respond.

"You know what this means?"

Shay nods. "We only have a small window of time to find her."

"They will not heel to Liam. We don't have the strength of the RA as they played their part openly in this."

Regret at not just taking my sister with me weighs heavily on my shoulders. If I had taken just her, Dana would be here, too.

The reality just keeps sinking in until the self-hate is consuming me.

"We will get her back." Shay grips my shoulder before walking behind the bar and pouring himself a drink. He glances over at the smashed glass on the floor before taking down another for me and filling it up.

"How?" My mind just won't work through all the scenarios.

"I don't know. But we will get her back."

I have to believe the fierceness in Shay's words. It's what I cling to here and now, so I don't charge out of my home and track down Lucian.

CHAPTER TWENTY-SEVEN

DANA

"WE PAY FOR OUR father's sins. That is a saying that really is relevant right now."

I grip the seat. Lucian's blue eyes drill right through me. "What are my father's sins?" And why am I paying? That's the real question I want to ask. I got into the limo because if I didn't, Lucian said my father would be shot.

I didn't exactly have a choice. But as I took a final look at the churchyard, my mind frantically searching for Cillian, I had gripped the lipstick and made a last-second decision to leave something. I could only hope he found it, but the lipstick might have no significance to him.

"I'm not the villain here, Dana, so you can stop looking at me like that."

"I'm sorry, Lucian, but I'm only here because you threatened my father's life," I say the words.

Lucian shakes his head. "I didn't threaten your father's life. It's already under threat. In fact, you could say I'm helping save his life. Your father has upset some very powerful people, and I am trying to make peace with them."

"Okay. So what's that got to do with me?" I ask.

Is that sadness or guilt I see in Lucian's steel-blue eyes? The click of the door behind me alerts me, but it's too late. A hand covers my mouth, and the world tilts as darkness seeps in and Lucian's face and my surroundings dissolve to nothingness.

The cold wakes me up. Awareness of my surroundings and my nakedness seems to seep in slowly, like a dripping tap. It's slow and painful. I pull my arms over my breasts. The rattle of chains has me rising too quickly. The length of the chain is restricting, and I'm yanked back to the concrete ground. My fingers touch the heavy steel chains.

My bare skin is cold to the touch as my fingers run along my legs. A half sob falls from my lips. What is this?

My head snaps up. "Hello?" Goosebumps erupt violently, tightening my skin across my body. The darkness around me crowds closer, and I focus on the ground.

This isn't real. Closing my eyes, I think of Lucian. My heart slams painfully in my chest, telling me this is very much real. I'm here—in this place.

"Help!" I scream and forget momentarily about my chains as I stand up, only to be dragged back down. The ground meets me fast and hard; the force vibrates through my body. "Help!"

My fingers dig into the floor. This can't be real. Please, please, God. Don't let this be real. Another sob falls from my lips as the cold continues to soak into me as if I were a sponge absorbing water. "Help!!!!!"

A man appears in front of me, and he kneels down close enough. I hadn't heard him approach. I'm still screaming, and I cut the sound off. My brain short circuits. "Help." I croak.

He nods. "Of course I will help." His accent is heavy.

I sob with relief and reach towards him, dragging the chains with me. "Get these off me."

He doesn't move, and I think I already know he isn't going to help me. I crawl closer to him, wanting warmth, wanting this to end.

"I will help you once you help me."

I stop moving and look into his blue eyes. "How?"

"Your father's operations. We want to know everything."

"He's mafia. He will kill you for this," I say.

The man laughs and runs a large hand across his beard before traveling up to the top of his head, where his hair is tied away from his face. He runs his fingers to the ends of his hair. "Your father's operations? What do you know?"

Nothing. I know nothing. Isn't that exactly what will get me killed?

"He is the king of the mafia." I try to hunch down so not all my flesh is on display, but the movement rattles the chains.

The man smiles and waves a hand across my body. "Do not worry about me seeing your naked body. I'm the one who stripped you bare. I have seen it all."

I start to move back as far as the chains will allow. "I know nothing." I break down. "Please, just let me go. I won't tell anyone."

The man rises and nods. He takes a pack of sweets from his pocket. Unwraps one and places it in his mouth. He holds out the pack, offering me one, and I shake my head. As he places the pack back in his pocket, I search the darkened space for someone else. Someone had to help me.

"He will kill you for this." Strength raises my voice, or maybe it's fear.

Either way, it didn't matter. His foot connects with my stomach, and my body burns with pain, unlike anything I have ever felt. My organs must be crushed, my bones smashed, I can't breathe, and I have no time to react as his foot drives into my stomach again.

This becomes my new reality. I'm asked questions that I can't answer, and I'm beaten each time. Mentally I'm ready to give in, but my body doesn't comply. Each time I wake up and each time, I relive it all again. Each slap, each punch until my body finally gives in, and I collapse.

Ice cold water hits my face. The sting wakes me up while sending sharp pain across my naked body. Everything inside me trembles as I become more alert. My wet hair weighs my head down. I focus on my fingers that shake in small pools of water that surround me.

My naked flesh is screaming for warmth. Large feet appear in front of me, my shoulders hunch closer to my ears as a second bucket of water is splashed across my frame. A short, broken scream is dragged from my lips before the sound of my chattering teeth takes over. The chains on my wrists rattle as I manage to raise my head through the pain and dizziness.

"Are you ready to talk?" The large Russian man drops the steel bucket. The sound bounces around the wide space. The empty shed has been my cage for days now. I keep waiting for someone to come and find me, someone like Cillian. His name has me wincing, and I push the image of his face away. His memory is too painful.

A roar rolls from me. My fingers rebel and try to wriggle under the weight of the boot that is slowly crushing them. I continue to scream in pain even as the Russian steps away—air stalls in my lungs as I stare at my hand, not daring to move a finger. The pain intensifies, and I'm burning up inside. Bile claws up my throat as I rock my body like I can extract the pain from my broken fingers.

"Just tell us about your father, and all this goes away."

My breaths are shallow and fast as I continue to stare at my crushed fingers. My vision blinks in and out.

The Russian's footsteps come closer, and I quickly look up at him. I swallow the dryness in my mouth; I swallow the scream; I swallow the pain. "I never knew...." I sob when I see the disbelief in the man's blue eyes. "I swear." I cry out as he kneels down with a smile that sends waves of fear coursing through me.

"You are naked, beaten, and chained to the floor. He will not expect this level of loyalty."

His large hand touches my face, and I shrivel away from him, sending fresh pain into my fingers. "You have been strong." The man's smile remains.

I sob. The truth is, if I knew anything, I would have given up the information the moment they chained me to the floor. The moment they stripped me of my dignity. The moment they put their hands on me. The moment they took me. But I didn't know anything about my father's dealings.

"I swear, I don't know."

His smile leaves his face, and he rises on a long exhale.

I try to brace myself, but it doesn't matter; nothing could prepare me for the pain. His foot connects with my naked torso that's already covered in bruises. Something snaps inside me, and I'm lifted off the concrete floor before I slam back down onto the ground. The chains restrict me; the heavy metal burns my wrists; the pain becomes forgotten as a large hand tightens around my hair and yanks my head back. I'm staring up into his face, begging him to stop this. I already know the answer before he hits me hard across the face. My head swings back, my mouth fills with blood, and I hit the concrete floor again, the small pools of water splashing up across my damaged flesh.

I can't see through the pain and fear. I curl up and cry, waiting for the next kick or hit, but his footsteps move away from me, and I start to cry some more. My body trembles as I lie there on the cold floor.

I try to tell myself that I will be fine, but the truth is, I'm hurting. The pain is so deep, and I'm close to giving in to the demands of my body. My body wants me to let go. It would be so easy to just let go and slip away from all the pain.

Another sob sends ripples across the small pool of water that I lie in. Seeing my dark tendrils bring me back, back to a moment when I was sailing through the air, my hair whipping in my face. I was so young. Maybe ten, but I was with my best friend, Maeve, as she pushed me on my swing in my backyard. The day was hot, my mother was smiling, and I felt happy.

I'd laugh if I had anything in me. I'd laugh that Maeve's secret led me to this dark place.

My body shakes, and my tears stop and all there is, is pain. So much pain.

I return to the memory of that day on the swing. I had been free, just like Maeve always appeared. She had such freedom in her life, that my parents never allowed me to have. I always felt suffocated, so I spent most of my teens traveling, trying to escape their smothering tendencies. They allowed me to travel, but something deep in the back of my mind told me I was never truly free or alone. I had shaken it off as paranoia at the time, but now I see that my father had men watch over me my whole life.

I can't stop the sob that rocks my body, sending fresh waves of pain down my side. Coldness seeps deeper into my bones, and I don't believe the cold will ever leave me. I don't think any form of heat could banish this level of coldness or pain. Time moves in shadows across the floor. My fingers reach out to the last stream of light like I can hold it hostage here with me, but like everything else, the light disappears, and I'm plunged deep into the shadows and the fear of what will happen next.

I don't sleep, but I'm not fully alert either. The tremors and agony keep me in a half-awake state, that is, until the door opens. I look up, unable to move as the Russian man enters the room again. The bucket in his hand swings, and I close my eyes and brace myself, but no water hits me. I look back up and notice something lumpy under his arm. He takes the material out from under his arm, and a blanket is spread across my body. I cry with relief.

It's a trick. My mind whispers, and I hush the pessimism inside my mind.

The large Russian man kneels and brushes long strands of hair off my face. His finger grazes a cut, and my body curls in on itself.

"You are resilient." He sounds impressed. "But that has no value here." His smile drips off his face, and unease skitters across my skin.

"If I knew anything, I would tell you." My chains rattle, and the blanket slips as I try to rise. His fingers press against my lips.

"Shhh. It will be okay."

My vision blurs, and I know it won't be okay. I'm going to die.

My heart takes on a new beat. The pounding jumps to the point that I think my heart is ready to come out of my chest; the sensation feels like my heart is in my throat, choking me, cutting off the air from my lungs, and without the Russian lifting a finger, I can't breathe.

I crane my neck back and gasp in quick short breaths that do nothing to fill my lungs; they aren't enough. The blanket slips completely from my battered body as I continue to gasp. I'm staring into blue eyes that laugh at me, but I can't look away. My body is shutting down, and I'm dying.

Loving life has me clinging to the man before me. I sway on my knees, and I know I won't recover if I hit the ground.

"His eyes are blue. His hair is brown." I keep repeating this as tears cascade down my face. Another wave of dizziness hits me, and my body trembles violently.

I have no regrets. I wouldn't have lived my life any other way.

With this knowledge, I want to scream because I don't want this to be my end.

Not like this.

Not like this.

My last thought is Cillian asking me to marry him; through my hysteria and my impending death, I give him an answer.

"Yes." Pain forces tears down my face. If I could go back, I'd say yes. So maybe I have regrets. "Yes," I whisper again. The Russian man grabs my face.

"Yes, you will talk?" His question is far away, but I close my eyes, and I feel life leaving me, so I tell Cillian one more time.

"Yes. "Yes, I will marry you.

CHAPTER TWENTY-EIGHT

DANA

S HAY LIGHTS UP A cigarette.

"I thought you quit." I don't look up from behind my desk. I've been trying to reach out to every contact I have or that my father had.

"It's been a week," Shay informs me as he sits down at my desk.

I glance at him. I don't need the fucking reminder. It's been a week since Dana disappeared and since Lucian handed her over to the Russians.

"I'm well aware of the time passing, Shay. Any word on Liam?" I ask.

"He goes into Cabra Castle daily, but no one sees him leave."

That's because he uses the underground tunnels. I stop going through files, looking for names. My father kept, or I should say, Davy, kept a list of everyone he worked for, the job he did for them, and how much he was paid. I've considered using some of this information as a form of blackmail to make them help me.

"You need to resign yourself to the fact that she most likely is dead."

My focus is back on Shay. "She's not dead."

"How do you know, Cillian? Think about it. She's Liam's daughter."

I get up from the desk, not wanting to hear this, but Shay continues.

"They won't place her in a whorehouse. They will kill her."

"She's alive," I repeat.

"What would you do if you had her?"

I turn to find Shay standing.

Get as much information out of her and kill her, is my silent answer.

"She's alive," I say, but my words don't hold the conviction they held moments ago. "How could he let this happen?" I still can't wrap my head around Liam just going underground when his daughter is in the hands of the Russians.

"There is still no word on the street. No one even seems to be aware that she is missing." Shay continues.

"What about Jack and Richard?"

Shay shakes his head. "Everyone is quiet. I think they are all coming to the conclusion that she might be dead."

I laugh. It's filled to the brim with anger and pent-up frustration at all the dead ends I was hitting. "No retaliation?"

Shay crushes his cigarette on a plate that had held a sandwich. "Not with the Russians. This is the one time that Liam will have to bow out." Shay looks up at me. "Unless he wants a war, and I think Liam knows he won't win."

The phone on my desk rings and I'm still staring at Shay, hating the truths he's brought here with him today.

"If she is alive, Cillian, she might as well be dead with what they will do." Shay zips up his jacket. "I hope she's dead. For her sake."

I march away and pick up the phone. "We have a man called Skinner on the phone," Jo speaks softly. I've been waiting for this call.

"Put him through."

The line changes. Shay hasn't left as Skinner speaks. "I got a meeting set up for you."

"With who?"

"The Handler of the Russian mob."

"The Handler?" I've heard of him. But like most Russian mobs, they were very secretive, so I have no idea who the actual handler is. "How do you know he's the real deal?"

Shay comes back to the desk.

"I had to pull more strings than I can hold. This is costing me big. He's the Handler."

Hope flickers to life in my chest. "When can I meet him?"

"Today. In a local café. I'll forward you the address."

"Thank you."

Skinner snorts. "Don't thank me yet; they might kill you on site."

"Thanks, anyway."

Skinner hangs up, and I look at Shay. "I have a meeting today with the Handler."

"What are you going to do? Just ask him where Dana is?" Shay doesn't look happy with my meeting the Handler. "We will find another way."

"Two seconds ago, you said she was dead."

"She is. But you will be joining her if you meet him."

I didn't care. I wanted Dana back. "There is no other way."

"You haven't tried." Shay steps closer to the desk.

"If Liam O'Reagan won't go against them, tell me who will? Lucian handed her over to them in fear, Shay. So the RA is out. There is no one else. This is my only shot."

Shay runs his hand across his beard. "So, what is your plan?"

I sit down in my chair. My phone dings and I open the message—the address to the café.

"I'm going to offer them Liam." I look up from the phone. Before Shay starts asking questions, I speak. "I don't know how I'll do it, but I am going to promise them Liam O'Reagan for his daughter."

Shay leans in on the desk. "Cillian, if you make this promise to the Russians, you will have to deliver."

I nod. "I will."

Shay still doesn't look away. "I'm not sure about this."

"Me neither, but I'm going to meet the Handler. If something happens...." I trail off as I stand to get my wallet, phone, and keys out of the desk drawer. "Take care of my family."

Shay nods and takes out another cigarette. "Emma won't be happy that you are smoking." I try to lighten the mood.

Shay doesn't light the cigarette. "Try to stay fucking alive."

I close the drawer and walk around the desk to Shay. "I'll try." I grip his shoulder. He's my best friend.

"I'll follow you, stake out the café."

I'm already shaking my head. "Let me do this. I need you alive."

"Fuck sake, Cillian." Shay rubs his beard again.

"She's alive," I say one final time before I leave the office. Shay walks with me to the door, and we separate outside. I have a feeling he will follow me, and something doesn't make me stop him. I want him alive, but believing he was watching my back gives me added confidence as I make my way to the café.

This is the first and only lead I will have on Dana. I need to make each second count.

I'm checking my rear-view mirror every second, checking to see if I'm being followed. I don't notice anything, not even Shay, but he would be smart enough not to drive up my ass. I enter the small village of Monalty. The café's windows are small, and the blinds restrict me from seeing in. I pull up to a small petrol station across from the cafe and try to see if I can spot any movement inside the café.

After a few minutes, I take out my phone and check the time. I'm five minutes early. I get out and walk towards the café. The gun in the band of my trousers gives me a sense of security that isn't real. This could be a setup, and I was walking right into it. But I've been left with no choice.

A lone server fills salt and pepper shakers. Three booths and six tables fill the small café. The tables on the main floor are all empty. I walk past the first empty booth; in the second one, a man sits.

"Sit down, Cillian."

I don't ask if he's the Handler. No one else is expecting me. I sit across from him. He doesn't look away from the menu in his hand.

"You know people in high places."

"Yeah, I must," I answer, and I'm still edgy as I look around the café.

"If I wanted you dead, you would be dead."

I look back at the Handler to find him watching me. He's slightly older than I am, but not by more than a few years.

"I want Dana O'Reagan back." I cut to the chase.

He nods. "That we can do." He looks away and waves the waiter over. "Can I get pancakes with maple syrup and coffee?" He hands her the menu.

When she looks at me, I wave her off. "I'm fine."

"Tell me what you need me to do."

"I like you. Very forthcoming. Not something I come across." He smiles, but it's not friendly.

"Name a price," I say.

The Handler smiles as he pushes the salt and pepper in front of me. "You think money can fix all problems?"

"Everything has a price."

"So, what is Dana's?"

He pushes the salt toward me until it tips over. "Are you superstitious?"

"No." I take a glance around the café again but redirect my attention back to the Handler.

"I am. If you spill salt and don't throw it over your right shoulder, you get seven years of bad luck."

I nod. Like I give an actual fuck.

The Handler picks up a pinch of salt and throws it over his shoulder. Once he's done, he looks at me expectantly. His eyes dance to the salt, and he wants me to do the same.

I entertain the fucker and reach across the table. My fingers graze the salt before a knife pins my hand to the table. Pain lances through my hand and travels up my arm. I'm fighting not to scream.

"How many of our men did you kill at the site?"

I try to wriggle my hand, the pain bending me over. The removal of the knife is worse than the stab, and I can't stop the cry. The Handler grabs my wrist, keeping my hand in place.

"I'll tell you. You killed thirty-two of our men."

Drool runs onto my chin. "Liam O'Reagan gave the order. He told me to wipe you out."

The Handler grabs salt, and I know what he is going to do before he does it. I scream as he rubs salt into my hand, and I manage to drag my hand back.

I hold it in my lap, and the Handler picks up a napkin and wipes salt and my blood off the table. The waitress arrives with his pancakes, and I keep my hand hidden under the table.

"Thank you." He smiles at her, but the waitress gives me a sketchy look.

He starts to eat, and I'm fighting not to pass out. I need to get the salt out of my wound.

"So we have established that I don't want money. That we do indeed have Dana and that you killed thirty-two of our men. And we know you didn't act alone."

"No, I had help." I'm trying to breathe through the pain.

"Anything else you need?" The waitress reappears.

"Could I get a glass of water?" I ask.

She nods, and I refocus on the Handler, who sips from his coffee. "Tell me who helped you?"

"If I do, will you give me Dana back?"

"It depends, Cillian." He smiles and pours more maple syrup on his pancakes.

The waitress arrives back with the water and leaves. With my good hand, I unroll the knife and fork from the napkin and dip the piece of tissue into the water. Bringing up my wounded hand, I tab the hole with the napkin. The pain erupts, and I fight not to pass out as I clean the salt out. I'm thinking if I hand over Shay, I could get Dana back. "How did you know I had help?" I ask.

"Too many bodies for one man, no matter how highly trained you are. We just don't know who you were working with. You left no survivors."

Shay has been my friend since childhood. Handing him over would be signing his death sentence.

"A Jaguar helped me," I confess as I get most of the salt out and take a break.

"Interesting. We have enemies in lots of places."

"You took my sister; my father is a Jaguar. They wanted revenge."

The Handler holds up his knife. "Correction. Liam handed us your sister."

"So, is that enough?" I know it isn't.

He smiles. "No. You haven't given me a name."

"Robert."

Robert had tried to take Dana from me, so if I got her back with his life, I'd fucking take it.

The Handler pulls a small square notepad and pen from his jacket pocket and slides it across the table to me.

"Write down his name and full address."

I do as he asks. I'm not one to sell out my own, but Robert betrayed me first. I push the notepad back to the Handler. His plate is empty, and he pushes the plate aside. He looks at the notepad and places it in his pocket.

"Now, can I have Dana?" I ask.

"I feel like you are wasting my time with these petty thugs."

"Then tell me what you want?"

"I think it is only fitting if you give us thirty-two men for the thirty-two you killed."

I'm sure there are plenty of runners and low-ranking men. "Done."

He nods. "Too easy."

I want to reach across and punch him in the fucking face.

I lay out my cards. Sick of this game. "I will give you Liam O'Reagan." I make the only top offer I can.

The Handler raises both eyebrows. "That is an offer." He thinks about it. "If you cut off the snake's head, more will grow in its place."

I nod. "I know. But I'm a king. I'm next in line. This ends. There will be no revenge for Liam."

"I am aware of his sons."

"Who wants him dead too," I say as I cradle my hand in my lap again. The pain keeps me alert and upright.

"Liam has done a lot of damage to us." The Handler sits back, considering my offer.

Time slips away as I wait for his answer.

"Robert will die for the killings. I still want thirty-two men, and yes, Liam O'Reagan."

That's a lot of people who will die for Dana.

"I want her first, and then I'll deliver. You have my word."

"The sentiment and your dedication to this girl are remarkable, but no. You deliver first."

He's ready to leave. "How do I know you will keep to your end?"

He takes out his wallet and throws a few notes on the table. "You won't."

"I need more than that." I bark.

He bends down. "Be grateful I'm even entertaining you and that you get to walk away with your life."

The Handler straightens. "I'll be in touch." The moment he leaves, I get up. The room tilts and sweat coats the back of my neck, but I make it to the bathroom. I turn on the tap and push my damaged hand under it. I growl in pain as I make sure all the salt is out of the wound. Taking off my tie, I wrap my hand and leave the café.

There is no sign of the Handler. The minute I get into the car, I ring Shay.

He answers on the first ring.

"I've made the deal. I'm getting Dana back."

CHAPTER TWENTY-NINE

CILLIAN

"WHAT'S HAPPENED?" MY MOTHER meets me in the foyer. I push my damaged hand into my trouser pockets, but it's too late.

"Cillian." She reaches for me, and I extract it.

"It's a flesh wound."

My mother holds out her hand, and I place mine in hers. She's seen enough wounds over the years. She doesn't cry or fret but examines my hand. "That is more than a flesh wound. I'll ring Doctor Alex."

I agree, and my mother gives me one last look before leaving to ring the doctor. I go to the bar and pour myself a brandy. I drink it down and hope it will take the edge of the shakes that are rattling my hands. I refill the glass and drink down another, all the while I'm trying to think of how I can pull this off.

"Doctor Alex will be here soon. Shay is here too." My mother tightens her robe around her frame.

"Thanks, Mother. Go get some rest. You can send Shay in."

She nods but doesn't leave. "Is Aoibhe okay?" I ask and walk out from behind the bar.

My mother holds up her hands. "Yes. She's fine, Cillian. I'm worried about you."

"Don't be. It's a flesh wound." I remind her.

She tilts her head while dropping her hands. "It's not just your hand."

The door behind my mother creaks open, and Shay steps in. He leans in and kisses my mother on the cheek. "You're getting younger looking." He says with a smile.

"And you are getting more handsome by the day." My mother touches his face, but the gesture is nurturing. "How are your mother and father?"

"They are doing great. Keeping quiet. How is Aoibhe?"

I return to the bar and pour myself a brandy. Shay glances at me, and I pour him one, too.

"She's good. It will take time, but I have my daughter back."

My mother looks at me. "I'll leave you to it. The doctor will be here soon." My mother turns to Shay. "Tell my son to take care of himself."

Shay smiles. "I will."

She leaves, not believing Shay.

He approaches the bar, and I slide him a drink. He picks up the brandy while glancing at my hand. "Didn't go well?" He asks and downs the brandy.

I drink mine too and put the lid back on the bottle. "I'm getting Dana back, but he wants Liam and the person who helped me at the site along with thirty-two men."

Shay twirls his glass. He nods. "You gave them my name." He doesn't sound pissed.

"No. I gave Robert's name."

Shay nods again. "Makes sense. He was a cunt."

"I have to hand over Liam first. So the question is, how do I pull this off?"

Shay grins. "How do we pull this off? Killing Liam has been on the top of my list for a long time. So I'm in."

"I think we should stick to the truth." I sit down and keep my damaged hand still. It's burning like a fucking bitch. "We know where Dana is. They are handing her over. The one condition is that Liam is the only one who can collect her."

"He will bring an army with him. Then what?" Shay says.

The door opens, and Doctor Alex arrives. "Come in," I say when he pauses.

I hold my hand out on the bar, and he immediately starts to work on my wound. Talking isn't possible. I'm just trying not to pass out from the pain.

Shay walks away and sits on the couch. He lights up a cigarette, and I focus on each exhale he makes. I use it to keep myself from pulling my hand back.

The doctor finishes. "Take two of these a day." He hands me a small bottle of brown pills.

"Thanks."

"I'll just check on Aoibhe before I go."

"I'd appreciate that," I tell him.

Doctor Alex packs his bag and leaves. I pop two pills in my mouth and wash them down with brandy.

"We tell him it's only us; he can't bring anyone else."

"Richard and Jack won't stay away," Shay speaks from the couch.

"Let them come."

Shay glances at me over his shoulder. "I could lead them away, and you take the kill shot."

Shay doesn't sound happy, and I know why. "Why don't I lead them away, and you take the kill shot?"

Shay gets up. "No. He won't trust me. He might trust you."

"Okay, we go now."

Shay walks to me and throws his cigarette into the glass. He swirls the small amount of brandy around the bottom, and the amber stops burning. "Cillian. Wait until tomorrow. It's late, and we need to allow some of this to sink in."

"We don't have time."

Shay grabs my shoulder. "They won't kill her if they get Liam. We have time."

"We need a location," I say.

"I can sort that out. We have plenty of abandoned buildings in the area. The only problem is convincing Liam that he is the only one who can save her. He gets clipped on sight. There is no sign of Dana, and Richard and Jack will believe it was a setup by the Russians. We say we fired back, but they got away. A lone shooter."

"I think we should go now," I say again.

"If we do, it gives Liam time to check the area. We need to get him on the run. So he can't check the location."

"It's an in and out job," Shay says.

He's right. This could work. This has to work.

"Okay, tomorrow it is."

Shay holds out his hand, and I grip it. "He killed my brother." Shay reminds me.

"He put my sister in the Russian's hands." I squeeze his hand. "He deserves to die."

"He does," Shay concurs.

"Stay the night. Pick any room you want."

Shay releases my hand and strips off his jacket. "I think this room will do fine." He walks around the bar and takes down a fresh glass.

"I'm going to get some sleep."

"Tomorrow is D day." Shay sings behind me as I leave him with a bottle of brandy.

***

I check the time. It's three in the morning when my phone lights up with a message from a number that isn't programmed into my phone.

It's an address and instructions. Dana will be at this location. Once she is removed, the collector will arrive for Liam within a six-hour window.

I'm re-reading it. I dial the number and get no ring tone, only a recorded message. "This number is not in service."

What made them change the plan? I was getting Dana first before Liam. That is all that mattered.

I delete the message after memorizing the address and get dressed. Shay is asleep on the couch.

"They changed the plan," I say as I shake him awake.

Shay's eyes crack open, and he sits up. "They gave me a location where Dana is. Once we have her, The Collector will come for Liam. We have a six-hour window."

"Did you ring Liam?"

Every cell in my body is burning up. "No." I take out my phone and know this is it. Liam answers the phone.

"Hello, Cillian." He doesn't sound like he has been sleeping.

"I got a message from the Handler. They have Dana. I have a location."

"Do you?" Liam questions. "The Handler?" He asks after a moment.

"Yes. I had a meeting with him yesterday."

"What did my daughter cost?"

I glance at Shay. "He wanted the person responsible for the killing at the site and thirty-two men as well."

"So you want me to supply the thirty-two men?"

"Yes. I do."

"That can be arranged. Are you telling me you gave up Shay?"

I spin away from Shay. "We have to make the drop at the location. I get Dana, and we leave Shay behind."

The silence stretches out.

"I love Dana. I'm going to marry her." I keep my eyes closed as I think of every time I asked her to marry me. "I asked her, and she said no. But I know she will say yes, so I'm willing to give Shay up to get her back."

More silence.

"How do we know this location is safe?"

"We don't. We keep it small. You, me, and Shay, of course. I'm sure the building is being watched."

"Richard and Jack will accompany us."

"No. That's too many." I start, knowing that I need to object to something.

"I'm not going in there without my sons."

I draw out the silence. "Fine, but they can't know about Shay. If they do, they will stop us."

"Agreed," Liam says.

"We move out in one hour. I'll forward the address."

Liam hangs up, and I don't turn to Shay, but first send the address to Liam.

"Now I'm fucking worried," Shay says.

I slap him on the shoulder. "Let's go."

He grabs his jacket, and we leave the bar. I stop by the armory, and we both load up and strap bullet-proof vests on. "I'll get Dana out. You take the shot." I say to Shay.

"Let's do this."

***

The building is smaller than I thought, and it's surrounded by fields. A sniper could be hiding in those fields. That's good for us; no one will be waiting to clip us. It's bad for Shay and me when we kill Liam.

He's in his suit, and he hasn't even drawn his gun. But he isn't stupid either. He stays behind his sons, who move toward the front door with guns at the ready. I fall beside Richard on the left while Shay moves to the right. He's behind Liam. Jack looks at us all and nods before he kicks the door in. We move fast. The inside is pitch black, and we move along like we are in combat—guns at the ready and right behind each other.

Jack circles his fist in the air. I make out the gesture, and we split up. He goes to the room on the left, and Richard takes the stairs. I don't look back. I keep walking and open a door that leads into an empty kitchen. I step back out just as Liam passes me. Shay follows him, and I move behind them. We needed to make this happen now. Liam veers to the left, and Shay is right on his heels. I look back to make sure the boys are still busy. Jack emerges from the first room and points at the stairs. I nod and disappear into the room where Shay and Liam are.

I'm looking at Shay, who's getting ready to take the shot when Liam falls to his knees. I didn't hear a gun being fired.

"Dana," Liam is saying her name, and that's when I see a bundle in his arms. I'm beside him, forgetting everything else.

I reach her and find a pulse. It's a flicker, but she's alive. "Dana," I'm reaching for her. Liam releases Dana without warning, and she hits the ground as he spins and fires a shot.

It happens so quickly as I turn, and Shay hits the ground.

No. No. No.

Liam scoops Dana up as Richard and Jack race into the room. "He ran out back. We need to move now." Liam barks the order while cradling Dana to his chest. I step closer to Shay, and my blood becomes frozen in my veins. A pool of red liquid forms under Shay.

"We need to leave now," Liam repeats.

"Is he dead?" Richard asks.

"Yes." Liam steps over Shay, and I know if I linger, Liam will know I lied, and he will shoot me, too. I step over Shay and try to look at him for signs of life, but I don't see any.

"Richard, stay with Cillian. I'm sure he's in shock." Liam barks. The fucker.

I can't stop anything; Richard gets into my car. Dana is taken by Liam, and Jack drives them away from the location. We leave the site. We leave Shay. I check my phone. It's five in the morning. I had six hours before they came back and found Shay and not Liam.

CHAPTER THIRTY

CILLIAN

"**Y**OU DIDN'T SEE THE shooter?"

I glance at Richard. "No."

"They got out of the house fast." Richard continues, and I focus on driving at a normal speed.

"Where am I dropping you off?" I ask.

"My house. But, there is no rush."

There is for fucking me. I need to go back. I can't leave Shay's body there. I turn up the radio to block out my thoughts. I can't show any cracks.

"You seem shaky." Richard turns down the radio.

I don't face him. "I am. Dana .... She means so much to me." The truth of seeing her bruised and damaged starts to seep out. I'm picturing my sister all over again. "And Shay..." I let that truth die.

Richard stops asking questions. Maybe he accepts my explanation. I arrive at his home and pull up at the gates.

"Come in for a drink. It will take the edge off."

I shake my head. "No. I need to see Dana."

Richard doesn't get the fuck out of my car.

"Are you sure about that drink?" He asks again.

"I'm sure."

Richard finally gets out, and I try to keep calm and not tear away from the gate. Instead, I drive at a reasonable speed until I'm out of sight. Then I break every speed limit on these roads. I take my phone out of my pocket. The bullet-proof vest restricts the movements, and I finally get the device out after a few tries.

Shay's phone rings, and I picture it ringing away in his pocket, as he lies dead on the floor. I hang up and ring again. I keep ringing until I arrive back at the abandoned house. I withdraw my gun and scan the area before entering the house. I don't move as slowly through the hallway, but I'm still keeping all my senses on high alert. I step into the room where Shay had lain bleeding. Slowly lowering my gun, I stare at the pool of blood, but Shay isn't here.

Had they collected him?

Fuck!

I retrace my steps keeping my gaze on the doorframes, the floor, even the walls looking for breadcrumbs, and I find some at the front door—three drops of blood. He left. I step out of the house and take another look around the dark field.

"Shay!" I start to move into the long grass. "Shay!" I don't keep the noise down. I have nothing more to lose right now.

"I'm over here."

I'm grinning and sprinting towards his voice. I stop when I reach him. "How bad is it?"

"Not as fucking bad as they want it to be." A shine of sweat glistens on his face. This isn't good.

"Let me see." I take out my phone and turn on the light so I can see properly.

"Where did you buy the vests?" He asks, peeling his off. He is hissing with pain. "Cheap shit. The bullet shattered when it hit the vest and hit my side."

I bring the light closer; then, I slowly pull up his top. His side is covered in blood. "Yeah, it's a nick," I lie, but he would survive.

Shay pulls down his top.

"Let's get you to a doctor." I reach for him, and he lets me help him off the ground. "I'm going to be honest; you really scared me back there."

"You fucking scared me, too. For a moment, I thought you and Liam just might be working together."

"My father isn't stupid."

I stop walking, with Shay's arm still wrapped around my shoulder. I reach for my gun.

"Don't even think about it." Richard has his gun pointed on me.

"You think when my father asks me to stay with you, it was just for the drive? He doesn't trust you."

Shay pushes my arm off him. "I trust him, Richard."

Richard doesn't drop the gun; he keeps it pointed at me. "Who shot you?"

"Your father." Shay steps closer to Richard. "I'm bleeding pretty fucking badly." Shay keeps walking, and Richard lowers his gun.

"I made a deal with the Handler. To get Dana back, I had to leave your father here. That was the trade."

Richard's jaw tightens.

Shay stops at Richard. "He killed Frankie. I always told you he would die. And I know he killed Finn. We both do."

Richard puts the gun away. "I could have helped you."

Shay nods. "I know you would have, Richard. But, no matter what, he's your father. I would have told you after the job was done."

An understanding passes between Richard and Shay. The only reason I'm not shooting Richard is because Shay seems to really respect him.

"We have…" I check my watch. "Five hours and twenty minutes to deliver Liam here. Or…"

"Or what?" Richard asks.

"They will take us out one by one." Shay fills in the blanks.

"Can you get a hold of the Handler again, ask him for more time?" Shay asks me. The notion of asking for more time seems ridiculous.

"No. Skinner had to pull in every favor for that one meeting. It won't be possible."

We reach my car, and I help Shay in.

Richard is leaning in, speaking to Shay. "What do you need me to do?"

"Find out where he is now. Tell him Cillian checked out and that he went home. That I'm dead."

Richard nods. "He's at the hospital with Dana. You can't go near there." Richard's jaw tightens.

"We won't. I know Dana has been through enough," I say. Richard looks at me over the hood of the car.

His attention returns to Shay. "Get yourself patched up. I'll find out and ring you."

I get into the car as Richard taps the roof and closes Shay's door.

"Do you trust him?" I ask as I start the engine.

"Yes." Shay's voice is strained.

I take off the t-shirt that's over the vest and hand it to Shay. "Put that on the wound."

He takes it and hisses again as he pushes the t-shirt against the wound.

I start to drive. We pass Richard as he gets into his car that he had parked further down the road. "He's sneaky."

"He's clever." Shay corrects. "You would have done the same thing."

None of that matters.

"How was Dana? Was me getting shot worth it?" Shay asks with humor in his voice.

"She's alive. But I have no idea the depth of the damage." I pull my mind away from Dana and look at Shay. "You getting shot was a bonus."

He half laughs. "You are some cunt."

He's rummaging in the pocket of his jacket. "Gotta find my cigarettes."

I reach across as the phone rings. Shay curses as I pick up my phone and abandon helping him get his cigarettes.

"He went back to the castle." Richard's voice carries a growl. "He left Jack with Dana at the hospital."

I want to ask why he didn't stay, but it's obvious. He would be on high alert after making a trade with the Russians.

"We are heading to the castle now."

"You won't get in. He tripled the security there. It's a fortress."

"I'll find a way," I tell Richard.

He doesn't hang up, and neither do I. "I'll find a way," I repeat. "When I get there safely, I'll need you to give him a reason to leave."

Shay hisses as he manages to get his cigarettes out of his pocket. His hand trembles as he lights up one.

"Like what reason could I give him?"

"What would make him leave?" I ask.

"Just let me know when you are there," Richard says before hanging up.

"You got a plan?" Shay asks the moment I'm off the phone.

"I'm not sure, but you are going to have to take one for the team and ride in the trunk."

"Just let me finish my cigarette first. It could be my last."

I sneer. "You can't kill a bad thing that easily."

Shay finishes his cigarette as we come closer to Cabra Castle. We stop, and it takes a bit of time getting him into the trunk. I remove the clean jacket that I keep stored in the trunk. "You'd better stay alive," I warn as I close the trunk on him.

I climb into the car and pull on the clean jacket. I take a look in the mirror to make sure I look like I'm ready for a day's work. I check my gun and keep it down at the side of my leg as I pull back out onto the road. The castle sign appears, and I take a right into the castle. A man at the gate, that's new. I pull up and roll down the window.

He bends his head. "Name?"

"Cillian O'Hara."

He checks his list, shakes his head. "You're not on the list."

"I'm here at Liam's request. Now open the fucking gate." I stare at the gate like I'm just waiting for it to open.

"I'll have to ring Mr. O'Reagan."

"Ah, Cillian." A second man in the booth waves at me using two fingers.

I can't remember the man's name, but I've seen him around the castle. "Well, how are things?" I ask.

"Dermot, you can let him through." The security swings back to me. "Things are good, but busy as usual."

Dermot doesn't open the fucking gate, burning my time away. "I think we should ring Mr. O'Reagan.

"Don't be such a tit. Cillian is good."

Dermot starts to open the gates.

I salute the other security man with two fingers. He smiles and does the same back, like we are part of some secret society.

I drive down the pass to the castle. There is a lot of security and a few cars. He must not be accepting guests. I drive around back slowly and stop when I see Liam's Bentley. There are no cameras back here, I know, because that's the way that Liam wanted it.

I get out and take my gun with me. When I open the trunk, Shay covers his eyes.

"You look like shit," I tell him as I ring Richard.

Shay sits up but doesn't get out.

"We're in."

"Okay," Richard responds and hangs up.

I get Shay out of the trunk. "You have a gun?"

He nods and takes it out of his pocket.

"We are nearly there," I say.

I close the trunk, and we make our way to the steps that lead down to a gate. I pull the heavy black metal gate, and the screech is loud as we enter the underground recesses of the castle. I've memorized every turn; Shay and I walk to the main cavern, and we wait. I can only hope that Richard did as we asked and didn't double-cross us.

I look at Shay, who leans against the wall. I want him to reassure me that Richard wouldn't betray us. I hear footsteps, and they are moving fast.

They slow down and come to a stop. I wait, and nothing happens. So I step out from behind a pillar to find Liam standing still.

"I thought maybe you could give me that history lesson now."

He's holding his gun, and I'm holding mine.

"My daughter isn't dead?" he asks, his voice steady.

"Is that what Richard told you?" I ask and step closer.

We both raise our guns at the same time.

"I'm the one you promised to hand over to the Russians?" Liam says.

I nod. "It saved your daughter's life."

"Do you think Dana will ever forgive you if you kill me?"

"Yes, when she finds out the man you really are. You handed my sister over to the Russians."

Liam doesn't waver or show signs of surprise or guilt. "I did. It was a means to an end."

He acts like I'm not a fucking threat. "I have a gun in my fucking hand. Show some remorse."

"Why?"

"Drop the gun." Shay presses his gun to Liam's temple, and Liam drops the gun, but the grin that drags his lips up says he's impressed. "A ghost," he says.

Shay slams the gun into the back of Liam's head, and he lands heavily on the ground.

"No, Liam. I'm your worst fucking nightmare."

Liam looks up at Shay. "I shot you."

"I was wearing a vest," Shay responds. "You know how the RA punishes traitors?" Shay asks.

Liam doesn't get to answer as Shay fires his gun into his left kneecap before firing into the right one. It's an odd sound to hear Liam screaming in pain as blood flows from his blown-off knees.

"That's for Aoibhe," Shay says.

I'm still holding my gun, and I can't lower it.

Liam's still screaming when he looks up at Shay. "You're a dead man," he warns.

Shay steps closer and pushes his gun to Liam's forehead. "Nah, Liam. You are, and this is for Frankie." The gunshot bounces loudly around the space as Liam falls backward, his brains staining the floor behind him.

Shay's shoulders shake. "For Frankie," he says before he stumbles to the side.

"Don't die on me now, Shay. We are nearly there." I put my gun away and reach him, and he's not looking so good. "You can't die, or all this is for nothing."

He nods. "I can die peacefully now. Give me a cigarette."

I wrap his arm around my shoulder and hoist him off the ground. He cries out.

"What about Emma?"

That makes Shay start to walk as I half carry him out of the tunnel and toward the castle.

"What are you doing?" Shay groans.

"Getting you help," I say as we walk around to the front of the castle.

"Finish the job," Shay growls. He looks fucking gray.

"I will," I promise as I round the corner and see a security man.

"Ring an ambulance. He's injured."

The security man takes out his walkie-talkie. "What happened?"

"He took a fall out back. Hit some rocks. Ring it in, or you'll be fucking sued." I bark, and he does. I lower Shay to the ground.

"I'll finish it," I promise him, and jog away.

"Hey, where are you going?" The security man calls after me.

"Any chance of a smoke?" I hear Shay ask him as I round the corner to the back of the castle.

It takes me a long time to get Liam's dead body up out of the caverns and into the trunk of the car. I hear the ambulance, but there will be no Gardai called. Not on Liam O'Reagan's property.

My phone rings, and I take it out of my pocket. " Yes."

"Is it done?" Richard asks.

"Yeah, it's done. Is Dana, okay?"

"She's been asking for you."

I smile at that. "I'll be with her in a few hours." All I had to do was get Liam's body to the house.

"We will be waiting for you." Is that respect I hear in Richard's voice?

"Shay should be arriving there soon. He was taken by ambulance.
"

"I'll keep an eye out."

I hang up and drive around to the front of the castle. Dawn is close to breaking and if anyone were to look into the car, they would see me covered in blood.

The ambulance is gone, and I drive down to the gates. The same security is there, and Dermot glares at me, but he finally opens the gates, and I'm free.

EPILOGUE

DANA

I T'S BEEN FOUR MONTHS to the day. Jo is here with me, and honestly, it's not how I pictured the morning of my wedding. Having a big wedding without my father didn't seem right, not so soon after he gave himself up to save me.

Jo sporadically places small braids in my hair before placing fresh white flowers like a crown around my head. When she is done, I get up from the stool. I spent most of the morning staring at myself in the mirror. The long fitted white lace dress is simple, but as I rise, I feel like the princess that Cillian insists I am.

"One flower leftover." Jo hands me the last white flower that still has its stem. I bring it up to my nose and inhale.

For you, Father. After everything, he gave his life to save me. I don't want to think about that moment when they told me or the screams of my mother.

"It's time," Jo says.

I smile at her. I move to leave the room but return to the vanity set. "Just one second." I run my finger along the lipsticks and find number 68 replaced. I take it out and cover my lips in deep red lipstick. I stare at the lipstick case in my hand. It saved my life. If I hadn't dropped the lipstick, I wonder if Cillian would have found me. The dark memories haunt me. "You are beautiful." Jo has stepped up beside me.

I put the lid on the lipstick and push it into my bra. "It's senti-mental," I say as Jo's eyes widen.

She composes herself and nods. "I'm ready." I nod.

The descent in the lift has me battling with memories. Memories of waking up in the hospital and the first thing I said to Cillian was Yes. Yes, I would marry him.

The happiness of him finding me, and the peace I felt, dissolved as the news of my father was delivered to me.

He gave his life to allow me to live mine.

My throat burns as the elevator dings when we reach the ground floor. I follow Jo and feel sheepish as each head turns towards me. The foyer and outdoor area are full of security men.

We reach the back door, and Jo stops. "This is where we part. You look beautiful."

I lean in and place a kiss on her cheek. "Thank you, Jo. Thank you for helping me."

"My pleasure."

My mother wouldn't have been ready for this. But Cillian said we could have a big wedding when I felt strong enough. I open the backdoor and inhale before exhaling as I smile at Shay.

"I should have known you would be here." He grins and holds out his arm that I take.

"You need a witness. You look stunning, love."

"You clean up well, too, Shay." He's wearing a suit, but it's not even his clothes, it's him. There is something softer, lighter about Shay.

"So, where is my wedding taking place?" I ask, but we walk past a vehicle and stop at a field. Shay whistles and a horse starts to gallop closer to us.

"I am not getting up on that thing." I protest.

"Emma trained me. I know what I'm doing." Shay reassures me as he opens the gate. The horse slows down beside him, and he fluidly mounts and holds out his hand to me. "He's waiting for you."

My abdomen tenses before erupting with excitement. I take Shay's hand, and he easily pulls me up in front of him on the horse. I'm still holding the white flower for my father as we gallop toward the forest.

Streaks of sun break through the trees, casting pockets of light. It's eerie but magical too. The horse slows under us, and Shay brings the horse to a complete halt. He gets off first before helping me down. He holds out his arm again as we walk toward the forest. The branches bend and dip, forming a canopy above our heads as we enter what feels like an enormous dome. I'm not entirely sure if this is man-made or just nature at its finest.

My heart pitter-patters as Cillian's large form comes into view. A priest stands in front of him, dressed in his white vestment and black robe. The priest smiles at me, and it's then that Cillian turns to me. My fingers tighten on the flower as he raises both eyebrows, his shoulders rise, and a slow smile lights up his eyes. I reach him, and Shay releases me.

"I'm a lucky guy." He bends his head, ready to kiss me, but the priest clears his throat.

"Shall we begin?"

"Can I just have one minute?" I ask, holding up a hand.

Cillian's jaw tenses, and I reach up and touch his face. "Don't worry."

I turn away and walk to a large tree. I kiss the flower and fight not to cry. "For you, Father. I hope you are here watching me. I love you." I place the flower at the base of the tree and walk back to Cillian.

His face is strained, but he takes my hand, and we face the priest where we make our vows to love each other until death do we part.

"I now declare you husband and wife. You may kiss the bride."

Cillian takes my face in his hands, and I've never seen him more handsome. He's happy. Our lips touch, and my soul sighs.

I know with Cillian I have found my happily ever after.

***

Mafia Secrets Book Five in the "Young Irish Rebels Series" can be pre-ordered HERE

ACKNOWLEDGEMENTS

I'm very lucky to have such amazing readers and Beta Readers. I want to thank the following people who worked with me on this book.

Developmental Editor: Amanda Cuff

Editor: Sherry Schafer

Proofreader: Michele Rolfe

Blurb was written by: Tami Thomason

Beta Readers

Amanda Sheridan

Lucy Korth

Tami Thomason

About The Author

When Vi Carter isn't writing contemporary & dark romance books, that feature the mafia, are filled with suspense, and take you on a fast paced ride, you can find her reading her favorite authors, baking, taking photos or watching Netflix.

Married with three children, Vi divides her time between motherhood and all the other hats she wears as an Author.

She has declared herself a coffee & chocolate addict! Do not judge.

Website: www.authorvicarter.com